THE
MURDEROUS
MISSES
OF
CONCORD

THE
MURDEROUS
MISSES
OF
CONCORD

A CONCORD MYSTERY

ELIZABETH DUNNE

First edition

ISBN: 978-1-68512-553-0

Cover art by Level Best Designs

This book was professionally typeset on Reedsy.
Find out more at reedsy.com

For Mum, Dad and Aunt Betty

Contents

Miss Collier Departs

I t was a glorious morning in November when Miss Emily Collier departed this world. One of those days that stirs the blue lakes and skies into a grand and sublime celebration of color. One of those perfect days before the onset of a bone-rattling winter, but as it darkened over Concord, it also promised endings.

Miss Evie Briers discovered what happened at ten o'clock when she went to Rosebud Cottage to consult Miss Collier about the Concord Festival Committee row over dried apricots. There was no answer to her tap at the garden door, but since it was already off the latch, she called and went in, expecting to find Miss Collier in the kitchen. She found her, instead, slumped in her purple armchair in the sitting room, where the previous afternoon, Miss Collier had celebrated her forty-second birthday.

"Oh dear," Evie said and gasped as she touched Miss Collier's cold hand. Her heart crammed into her throat, and she searched for the free armchair, falling into it.

"Poor Miss Collier. Oh, dear." She looked down and saw Hierophant, Miss Collier's snow-white stray cat and companion of many years, lying forlorn and forgotten under his mistress's chair.

"What a terrible shock you've had," Evie said, leaning over and stroking his soft fur. She ignored her immediate fears and glanced lovingly at the feline. "What an awful thing; you must be so hungry." Evie stood with difficulty and went into the kitchen, wondering if a bowl of milk and some bread would coax the poor animal out, but he just stared from under his eyes, rubbing tiny paws together. "Maybe you'd rather stay with your mistress. I'll bring you something later. After…"

Evie hurried home to Kame Bluff to fetch her brother, Captain Everett Briers, Justice of the Peace for Concord district, who was always called upon when somebody died and knew precisely what to do.

* * *

Louisa May Alcott disliked the word "Miss," mainly when applied to her by a man of marriageable age, engaged as he was in selling her pigs. The sun had begun to work its morning alchemy in Concord, burnishing the blue surface of North Bridge River sparkling silver, turning the leaves of larch and willow into an iridescent opal, and transforming every rooftop to pure gold. The sky was scattered with white clouds as if the playful breeze had flung the cotton harvest to the heavens, tattered and torn. The air was frosty and laced with the fresh scent of heather. It was the sort of day Louisa loved, apart from the impending chilly winter, which made her nose run and her joints ache.

"As you wish, Miss," Edward Lounsey said, taking his hat off.

"It's not as I wish, Edward; it's how I choose," Louisa replied. Louisa wasn't thinking of the beautiful morning but surveying her pigs. Or rather Edward's prize Berkshire pigs that stood nuzzling into the grass by their feet, and for which he was demanding a small fortune.

"They're good boys most of the time," Edward said. Louisa regarded him and then said dryly, "I will try to remember that when I'm serving them with my homemade applesauce."

Edward took his cap off, scratched long nails in his black hair, and smiled at such an honest response, for Louisa had made it quite clear she wanted the best-tasting animals for her pigsty. Only the best breed would do, and if she was to sustain herself and her family on Castle Farm, it included getting stuck in farm life. One couldn't exist on lettuce and rosemary tea or thrive on potatoes alone. And since her health wasn't the best, she needed to take better care of herself.

Louisa regretted leaving Hillside, but with the success of *Little Women*, she'd paid her dues and wrote with passion in the solitude of Castle Farm. Her mother and father agreed to the move after much discussion, and they all accepted Louisa's desire for freedom and that their needs could be met at the farm. It was substantial, and her family could live with her in harmony and within the surroundings she'd created. And she never abandoned her plain living and high-thinking upbringing, which made life much more straightforward. She discovered virtue was short in areas of Concord and over-supplied in others, perhaps even absent in Edward Lounsey.

"Let's go to my office and settle up," Louisa said, gesturing towards the peeling and in constant need of repair house she now called home. Edward seemed to find the idea of a spinster running a farm with an office highly amusing. He swept up the tiniest pig, gave it a passionate kiss goodbye, and followed Louisa through the smooth, short meadow to the stone entrance to Castle Farm. Louisa waited patiently for him to stoop down, pick a dandelion and blow it childishly into the wind. She found him decidedly irritating, but Edward was nothing if not a capable farmer who loved his work, and his dedication to quality breeding could only be admired.

In her home's cold, narrow corridor, a large vase spilled over with winter clematis, and the scent filled the hallway with splendor so easily achieved by nature's beauty. Her family agreed to her independence and never interfered with her dealings. Edward stopped to inspect some pencil sketches, leaning closer to examine them and search for a signature.

"They're mine," Louisa said, standing in the doorway of her office.

"Very accomplished," Edward said. *For a woman*, Louisa instantly thought but decided to hold her tongue. It wasn't productive to be too outspoken with a man such as Edward Lounsey. Or most of Concord, for that matter.

"I take it your resounding success with pigs isn't your only talent?" Louisa asked, removing the key from her pocket and turning it carefully in the heavy oak door.

"Not now," Edward said. "Not with Miss Collier's bees to look after." They

3

entered her office, and Louisa took her place on the hard chair behind her partner's desk. She invited Edward to sit, and he did so, with a little hop towards her.

"Why is Miss Collier parting ways with her bees? Is she ill?"

Edward looked at her strangely. "Miss Collier is dead, Miss Alcott. Found this morning by Miss Evie Briers."

"Well, the first order of business," Louisa said, "is to forget this entire Miss-this and Miss-that business." Louisa had no objection to the term for other women, especially those for whom it was a prerequisite for respect. A delicate matter in Concord.

"How did the woman die?" Louisa asked.

"I'm sure Captain Briers is making those inquiries," he said, not using her name or daring to repeat *Miss*. "He's Justice of the Peace around here."

"I'm aware of that, Edward. Miss Collier was here last week, and she seemed perfectly fit to me."

Louisa stood from behind her desk, and two minutes later, they were settled in the kitchen with a plate of her rosemary scones in front of them and a China pot snuggled cozily under a crocheted hood.

"Maybe it was her heart," Edward said. "A weak heart strikes at the best of us."

Louisa poured the hot coffee and uncapped her heart-shaped sugar bowl, plunging some into Edward's coffee without asking.

"The nefarious hand of unknown forces strikes the good and great down," Louisa said.

Edward swallowed and took his tobacco out. "You don't mind, I take it?"

"Not at all. There will be much smoking to be done at Miss Collier's funeral."

"What was her visit about, Miss...Louisa. If I might ask?"

"A social call, Edward. Nothing more."

Edward let the silence deepen, but something was troubling him. Louisa watched his calloused fingers run around the rim of the saucer and decided to put him out of his misery. Not entirely, though. No village gossip would come from her mouth. She was very determined about that. She had her family under the same roof to consider and their reputation and respect were something she valued. And small communities were peculiar beasts, the veneer of privacy was easily tarnished. The odd scenario whereby every individual is aware of burning secrets, but not one dares disclose them.

"Why do *you* ask, Edward?"

"There was some unpleasantness," Edward said.

"Oh, please do me the great favor of letting me in on the secret, Edward?"

"Rosebud Cottage," he said with a fierceness that caused her to shrink back. "Miss Collier wasn't going to sell it." His temper was roused, it was clear to Louisa, but she held her composure and stared into his slate-grey eyes.

"Well, now, Edward," Louisa said. "Rosebud Cottage was Miss Collier's to sell or not to sell, surely." She gave him an encouraging look.

"Not when she'd *promised* to sell," Edward said.

"And this upsets you so much because?" Louisa asked.

Edward drew himself back into the chair and put his hat on. He was ready to go, not in any urgent manner but one that suggested he'd lost the run of himself and now desired to make a quick escape without seeming rude.

"There's only one way onto my farm, and that's over Rosebud Cottage land. Miss Collier said she'd sell it so I could have the right of way. Heard it around Concord; she was thinking of leaving it to the bees." He said his piece with his eyes directed at the table. "Now, who knows what'll happen."

"Mr. Joseph Miller will know, I'm sure," Louisa said, pouring a hot drop for Edward. "He's Concord's lawyer, so I assume he knows all about those matters which will take their natural course."

Edward glanced upwards and then gave her an unpleasant, forced smile.

"And the new owner, of course," Louisa said, at the risk of being bellowed out of it. "Who is the new owner, Mr. Lounsey?"

Mr. Edward Lounsey didn't seem to have any answer to her question.

Louisa sat back in her seat, took her watch out, turned it the right way around, and frowned. Beyond the fresh morning air lay the afternoon and a dark one. "It is getting on, Edward. I must get back to my work."

When Edward received payment in silence for the animals and politely took his leave, Louisa allowed herself a few moments of silent contemplation. She'd succeeded in refusing to add to this already mysterious situation. If nothing else, she and Miss Collier shared a lot in common. Including the unshakable belief in the sweetness of self-denial coupled with the odd or occasional treat. Or the confidence in being everything one wants to be in the face of undeniable adversity. She was unwilling to describe the circumstances of this even to herself and certainly not to the trusted family under which she shared a roof. What is unsaid often remains unsaid because the listener has such a connection, such an understanding of the teller's words, that one needs nothing but silence to fill in the gaps.

* * *

The news of Miss Collier's unexpected death swept swiftly through Concord.

Up the hill at Hangman's Cottage, Louisa and her family's closest neighbors, June Birch, learned of Miss Collier's death from the baker's boy when he delivered the usual order of three loaves and six currant buns—three for each of the two Misses Birch. The boy had stopped at Rosebud Cottage on his way towards the main street and heard the news from Evie Briers when he knocked on the door. June Birch immediately went to tell her sister, April Birch, whowas playing the piano in the sitting room.

"Oh, my word," April said, flinging the end of her blue fringed scarf over her shoulder. "Who will I find to lead Miss Collier's solo in *Comfort, Comfort, Ye My People*?"

"I'm sure I've no idea," June said in a shrill, nasal voice. "Miranda James, perhaps, although she starts well, the rest is usually painfully flat. Miss Collier reached it so angelically. She will be so missed." She took out her pressed cotton handkerchief emblazoned with a scarlet "J" and dabbed the corners of her eyes. "Oh, yes, she will be sorely missed." Her voice trembled but never failed her. June gave dramatic readings at parties, plays, and funerals and had schooled herself in the art of seamless expression of grief. Many relied upon June's clear delivery, especially if the recipients were fully aware, for example, of a particular individual, they mourned was less than wholesome. June, impressed with a suspension of disbelief most welcome on such occasions when honest appraisal is not appropriate, and a rather inaccurate memory of a person is essential to maintain decorum.

"Oddly, Miss Nash didn't mention any illness," April said, referring to the teacher at Concord School. "Wasn't she at that ridiculous birthday party yesterday?"

"I believe so," June said and folded her handkerchief away.

"See what we're missing by avoiding such social events, June?" April said. "*You* really ought to be more social. For both of our benefits."

"I must go and arrange my black ensemble. I shall want it for the funeral," June said.

* * *

Within the half-hour, Mr. Miller, Concord's most fervent transcendentalist and town lawyer, had placed a worn copy of Miss Collier's favorite songbook on the wall of *Long House* to mark her passing. He sat in a hardback chair beside it after fixing a dried yellow rose from his summer collection on the page where *"Annie Lisle"* lay open.

By now, the news of the death had reached the farms around Old North Bridge, where men picked the stubborn remains of a runner bean crop. A visible shiver ran through Concord's community as they got on with the daily life of selling shoes or hardware and delivering post to the remotest silent parts of Concord, spreading the word of an untimely passing, even those with no knowledge of Miss Emily Collier received it with stunned regret.

"What a terrible pity about Miss Collier," Miss Sylvia Murdock, Concord's school headmistress, said to Miss Jean Nash, the teacher of the infants' class. The two stood in the doorway, watching their exuberant charges rush around the yard following lunch.

"It is the end of an era," Miss Murdock said, in a tone that suggested sarcasm rather than any commiserating sentiment. "We will be lost without her."

Miss Nash, who had lately been distracted by something approaching irrational fear, folded her arms across her crisp cotton-frilled blouse and glanced at the younger woman. "It is sad and so very sudden. Dried limes or apricots at the Festival? We really must decide now. Miss Collier can't." Her attention was directed to the yard, and she raised her voice, "John, don't push Jo. It's not nice."

Miss Murdock gave her teacher a startled look.

"The Concord Festival Committee will surely decide such matters, Miss Nash. I imagine the school fund and its depleting resources should be utmost on your mind."

"It is my understanding, Miss Murdock, that although the leak from the school roof appears over my desk and not yours, the Concord Festival will very much go towards replenishing our reserves," Miss Nash replied in a reproving tone.

Miss Murdock knew there was no point in arguing the matter. Miss Nash's memory could not be relied upon, or at times, Miss Murdock wasn't sure if Miss Nash somewhat made up events with little or no consideration they might be verifiable or not. They might be completely false, although to hear Miss Nash, one would never know. The listener, in this case, rarely rebelled. And if Miss Murdock corrected her, it led to almost certain unpleasantness. Only the day before, she misplaced her map of Concord's physical features before it was found in the confectionary cupboard in the small kitchen near the school's herb garden. The daily woman had been blamed until the truth was revealed by a five-year-old witness who'd seen Miss Nash stow it away following a long and somewhat fervent lesson on kettle holes. The incident caused ill will and suspicion, with the cleaning woman taking umbrage and refusing to clean the lavatory until her name was publicly cleared.

"I think you mentioned that you intended to call in on Miss Collier yesterday before the party," Miss Murdock said, tactfully returning to the subject. "Do you remember if she was ill?"

"I didn't see her," Miss Nash said with a short sniff. "It was late, and that awful Evie Briers was fussing over the cakes for Miss Collier's birthday party. I wouldn't mind, but I'd baked some oat squares she'd forced me to consider above more appropriate candidates."

Miss Murdock's eyes widened, and she watched one of the children hopscotch across the yard, which was now illuminated by a sudden flash of sunshine.

"A rather Puritan choice for a birthday party, Miss Nash. I doubt one can be forced to bake, but I'll grant you the benefit of the doubt as regards oat squares."

"She was quite adamant, Miss Murdock. She required twenty-two and put her order in while I stood in the hardware store last week. Most inappropriate of her, I should say. I will not swear to it, but I imagined she had some designs I've yet to figure out."

"I would not encourage such a rumor, Miss Nash," Miss Murdock said. "Nonetheless, she will be missed dreadfully."

Almost everyone shared Miss Murdock's view in the post office by late afternoon, but for one notable exception.

* * *

"I simply won't believe it," Mrs. Lucy Miller, the plump, red-faced post-mistress, said and came from behind the counter. "Miss Collier wasn't that old. Never a day's ill health. Only the other morning, she was in here after a brisk swim up at Fry's Creek. I'll tell you, Fry's Creek isn't for the faint of heart on a November morning."

Miss Maisie Taylor, who had stepped into the post office to buy a stamp for her letter to her sister out west, replied with a melodramatic sigh. "Lucy, a woman of her age, plunging into the Creek would disappear like a ghost. Now, if I told you I jumped off North Bridge, you'd believe me. Right?"

"If you'd taken that smirk off beforehand, I might."

Miss Taylor gave Lucy her best scowl, which by all accounts outdid the competition in Concord comprehensively. Miss Taylor continued with a frown on her face, "All I want to know is where Concord's best honey is going to come from now, sweet old Miss Collier's fallen off her perch."

There was a subdued silence, a rarity in Concord's busy post office, and

Lucy removed herself back behind the counter, lowering it with a slam. Whether Miss Collier was "old" or not remained a controversial matter, certainly open for sensible debate or discussion. Miss Taylor had earned the title of "elegant" by universal agreement in Concord. A definition of this was not easily come by, however, as elegant did not include polite or liked.

As silence hung in the air, Captain Everett Briers walked into the post office with an officious air about him. Unlike his sister, Evie, he was as handsome a man as one could find in Concord, with no shortage of attention from the women in the town. Tall but not overly so, his lean, muscular frame filled his uniform, and he had a square jaw, expressive brown eyes, and shiny brown hair touched blond with the sun. Lucy blushed, a pity for a married woman and leaned provocatively to one side. Miss Taylor let out an agitated sigh as she still hadn't paid for her stamp.

"Afternoon, Captain," Lucy said in her stilted tone. "What might we do for you today?"

"I need to send a telegram, Mrs. Miller."

"Is it important?" Lucy said.

Miss Taylor stood beside the Captain and gave him a quick smile.

"Telegrams are usually important," Miss Taylor said, "otherwise the Captain might just as easily send a letter."

"It's important and *private*," the Captain said, uncapping his green fountain pen and writing five words, two of which caused Lucy's eyebrows to rise sharply.

"I see," Lucy said, swiftly taking the piece of paper from under the prying eyes of Miss Taylor. "There'll be no delay, Captain," she said. "I'll ensure it gets off right away."

Miss Chandler Cries

L ouisa had trouble sleeping even though a tight frost had run up her window, and her layers of fine wool covers were light but cozy. And then she heard it—a meowing—soft and insistent, not demanding. She turned on her side to hear better with her good ear. The ear infection she'd caught last Autumn muffled everything, and now it ached occasionally when the bad weather set in, gnawing painfully when it got chilly like now. She lay perfectly still and heard it again, this time louder that the cat, and she was confident it was a cat, must know she was there. She pushed herself upwards, each creaking bone sending a slice of pain up her back until she was upright and able to lay her feet flat on the floor and feel out her slippers. She lit a candle and went down the stairs, listening to the sounds of old boards expanding and other strange noises. She still had to get used to the house, and no matter how hard she tried, it was a foreign place in which she felt awkward or reached for things in areas she knew they weren't. She heard her father's gentle snores from the room off the large landing and tread gently.

She leaned upwards and glanced out the frosty glass to see Hierophant looking morose and forlorn up at her. His tiny paws reached out as if looking for a hug. Louise undid the latch, and he squeezed in through a few inches to the resonant warmth of the kitchen and stood where he'd now intended to remain, searching for food. He'd chosen his new home, and Louisa couldn't but smile even though it was very late, probably after midnight, and she had an early start in the morning.

"So, this is where you want to stay," she said, leaning downward with some difficulty to stroke the soft fur. "You're very welcome." Now and then, Louisa could hear mice in the attic or the walls. She wasn't sure how they managed to exist so easily within the house, but now she had a very agile mouse catcher who'd relish the task of ridding Castle Farm of the pesky vermin. She didn't mind the company either, or now that winter had arrived, it would be such a treat to have him by her feet as she wrote by the fire.

She laid out the milk and bread, which he ate quickly and then promptly fell asleep on the tiles by the hearth, still warm from the fire.

Her mind drifted to Miss Emily Collier. Louisa refused the birthday invite, despite her family urging her to attend. Louisa preferred to write and considered this preferential to an overt display of civil manners, as she'd long realized pleasing herself was more important than pleasing others. She thought back on her conversation with Edward Lounsey. What was the man really trying to say during their discussion? She'd been flippant. But what if now, considering the nuances of the talk they'd had, something sinister had befallen Miss Collier? He drove at a dispute over Miss Collier's refusal to sell her land. A deal that would have given him an obvious advantage. And land and property caused such heartache.

As Hierophant purred gently, she considered if her writer's brain had invented such an interpretation. After all, this was her natural proclivity. A fiction formed in her mind, one involving a perfectly fit middle-aged woman found dead. Of course, she had no facts. At this stage, it was just a tragedy. But wouldn't that be precisely what a *killer* would hope? To hide behind the pure idea of Miss Collier's demise was simply life's cruel nature.

She decided that Edward Lounsey implied Miss Emily Collier might have been murdered.

* * *

That evening, the moon floated like a globe over the dark North Bridge Woods, where bright slivers of light showered down, and noisy nocturnal animals skittered. Mr. Miller, who came leaping down Market Street, his arms held up and out like a human wishbone, stopped suddenly like a March hare in fear of a predator. His face was still flushed, his hair was stuck to his scalp, and he sniffed the air, which was rich with heavy scents, peat, decayed leaves, and moist earth. Mrs. Miller's cooking.

Lately, his hearing was heightened with his work being solitary and refined, so it meant he enjoyed the walk through the woods, bringing him back to nature. The memory of his wife's cooking, however, would remain, even if his olfactory senses failed him. He could only take so much of farm life that the better inhabitants of Concord felt he should taste, but as he'd said on many occasions, God, if there was one, wouldn't want us all to be farmers. He'd written seven wills earlier, settled two disputes, and adjudicated what he liked to call "delicate matters" where people paid for silence and confidentiality.

How different to a damned pastor was he anyway? Then there was the delicate and delicious Miss Taylor, who'd swept in at noon like a slow-moving tornado with an intriguing tale. After both were seated respectively in their appointed areas and after he'd regained consciousness from temporarily losing his senses, the story made him frown. Something about flowers, bees, and a wild lily basket woven so tight it could only belong to Miss Collier. He lifted his silver hip flask to his mouth and took the remaining drop clean out, just about kicking himself because he could not remember the point of Miss Taylor's story. With those ankles and green eyes and those sharp, witty retorts that made his manly blood boil, there was no remembering the details of her story, which seemed irrelevant. He was lost in some unforgiving reverie.

His dream burst in the shape of his wife, Mrs. Miller, who appeared from the shadows, round, and suet soft, dressed like a pink feather bed tied in the middle. She pounded an object with unforgiving and merciless thumps, rounding fiercely on the outline of her husband.

"Mr. Miller," she said in a startled tone. "What are you doing prowling in the dark?"

"Working, dear," Mr. Miller replied.

She crossed herself violently and stood away before hurling a burnt pot into the shrubs a small distance away. Mr. Miller stared at her and then at the brown slime dripping down the green leaves.

"Spoiled," she said politely, as though it was his fault. "Utterly ruined."

"I wish you wouldn't cross yourself like some demented heretic," Mr. Miller said. He swayed gently to the cracked door saddle and took the sides one careful step at a time, placing a well-meaning and protective arm about his wife that she shrugged away.

When Mrs. Miller was angry, the kitchen turned into this blustery, wet, and wild place with things hurling about and muttered breath rising and falling like a madwoman on the make. There was no escape, not in the bright parlor that smelled of crushed peaches or in the hallway where a man might stand and wonder what had become of himself in a well-polished mirror. When the tempest subsided, Mrs. Miller was to be found stitching harmoniously, carefully applying blue stars onto a white baby's blanket draped over her knee.

"There's a storm coming," she said. "We'll need to lock the windows upstairs tonight." That was Autumn's end, the signal that if one slept in the upper rooms, one might die of frostbite before morning.

Mr. Miller loosened his shirt from his neck, thinking she might be joking about the storm, some of which he'd already witnessed and dismissed as seasonal disharmony. His blood was hot. But of course, there was talk about Miss Collier, and he knew his wife was bursting with the information she plainly wanted to rid herself of to her nearest and dearest.

"Captain Briers sent a telegram today," she said, pulling the blanket up to the light and shaking it in a vain attempt to whet his curiosity.

Mr. Miller grumbled soberly, with no excuse to imbibe company or not, and plunging deeper into melancholy over the odd glances he'd received for his monument to the sweetest voice in Concord.

"Not a single person stopped by Miss Collier's songbook," he said.

"To hell with her songbook," she said.

Mr. Miller looked sharply at her.

"You heard me. And To hell with June and April Birch and awful Miss Maisie Taylor."

"What on earth has got into you, Lucy?"

Mr. Miller rubbed his head, gripped by crippling sobriety that was getting direr, and he did not want to have this conversation but was assured of it since he said I do, or "I did" all those years ago.

"I'm bound to secrecy," Mrs. Miller said. Which she was. The post office provided a lucrative career to a married woman and put the Millers in the running for wealthiest in Concord. Nothing could jeopardize it.

"You can't have two of these words in the same sentence. If they are, you're inviting disaster."

"I'm in no mood for childish games," Mr. Miller said, reaching for yesterday's newspaper and trying to keep the pain off his face. "There's enough of that in Concord."

"Yes, there is. And if you only knew what Captain Briers wrote and to whom he sent it, you'd turn right back to the Almighty."

"But you're *not* going to tell me, Lucy, because Captain Briers, like every other citizen, sends telegrams he considers private. Now, I don't come home performing my private business like it's some cheap public play in Market Street." He shook the paper out, hoping to provide a convenient barrier to further discussion, but Lucy, being all the while careful in what she might say, couldn't resist another go.

"You think you know people," she said, absently putting her blanket to one side and staring into the distance as if contemplating a great mystery.

"And then Miss Collier dies in odd circumstances."

Mr. Miller sighed and eyed the drinks cabinet. "Hardly her fault if she died in odd circumstances."

He let the silence settle, not for effect but for the peace of it. These days, he'd to listen carefully for signs of quiet outside his office, where it just didn't seem fair to him that the only peace he ever got was neck deep in someone else's problems.

"Perhaps if I told you," Mrs. Miller began, "your assurance as to the confidential nature of our discussion would be taken for granted."

"Why would my assurances be needed," Mr. Miller said.

"In case you were called upon," she said, with an edge of pride, she pushed into the word "called," as though Mr. Miller was indeed a pastor or a doctor with some divine vocation that elevated him above the general populace.

"Why would I be called upon?" Mr. Miller persisted. "If Captain Briers has the matter in hand, things are surely taken care of."

"What if Captain Briers is compromised in the performance of his duties? It wouldn't do for you to be in the dark about it, now, would it?"

"And how would Captain Briers be compromised by the death of a middle-aged spinster with a cat named Hierophant?"

"Well," she said, picking up her stitching and hoisting it in the air. "There's no call to be rude or cruel. You'll be thanking me for introducing the subject in such a cunning manner under such terrible circumstances."

"Remind me again," Mr. Miller said, "of your opinion on Miss Collier's Rosebud Cottage lifestyle. *Heathen*, and I think that's what you called it."

"Unfortunate choice of words," she said, her face getting redder.

"So now Miss Collier is both odd *and* unfortunate," Mr. Miller said. He rattled his paper furiously and pretended something caught his eye in the corner, which, of course, it finally did, and it was a date, which was wrong but not obvious to any other Concord resident. He grimaced and moved his dry tongue around his mouth in concentration, wondering how such an error could be made. It wasn't as if the *Concord Sentinel* was overcome with journalistic fervor or burdened with exciting stories. No, this was something done by an entirely stupid typesetter or entirely on purpose by the editor. "When is the Concord Festival?" he asked.

"I'm surprised that it interests you more than my telegram," she said from the dark corner where she'd miraculously poured herself a crystal thimble of sherry and was wafting herself in the alcoholic afterglow.

"Well, do you know or not?"

"With Miss Collier's death, the Festival might be put off."

"But when was it supposed to be?"

She searched in the pocket of the burgundy loveseat beside her and pulled out a diary, the pages loose, tied together with a string. "Now, let me see. It was the 9th, but moved to the 11th. Why?"

Mr. Miller looked ahead, lost in thought. "No, why. Just wondering."

"Well, as I said, with the tragedy of Miss Collier's passing, there'll likely be no Festival."

"Don't be so dramatic, Lucy."

His wife turned over the blanket in greater despair, huffing like a giant puffer fish and pouring more sherry, then rising and standing directly ahead of Mr. Miller. A swift swoop later, she'd grabbed the paper out of his hands.

"Do not under any circumstance complain to me when the true nature of Miss Collier's demise is made public."

* * *

Miss Evie Briers stood in Kame Bluff's yellow parlor wearing a practical and composed demeanor. Everybody expected it to be so, and now was not the time to let anyone think things were any different. The neat curls under her hairnet broke free with oppressive sweat on her lined forehead, and she wiped it away only for it to come back. She was ready to act, to do something, but she wasn't sure what. None of Concord was the slightest bit suspicious, except for Lucy Miller, but now a growing noxious murmur from Market Street to North Bridge suggested something wicked befell Miss Collier. As the notion of what this something might be ranged from evil to mysterious goings on, the image of Miss Collier's lifeless body sat in her mind like stale bread. It didn't look any different, but you still couldn't make sense of it. In the dwindling light, she ran her hands over the right-angled shelves of dried herbs, apricots, limes, and oatcakes. Under a cream muslin cover, the spots of grease spread, turning it see-through, and she lowered her nose to sniff the oat squares. Nothing strange, but Evie didn't imagine herself a detective. No, she was far too practical.

On the bleached veranda with its box hedges, ordered and fertile still with the rising frost in the air, she threw the oat squares across the flat still-green lawn, watching them break into tiny pieces. From the way one or two of Concord's residents carried on about Miss Collier's passing, you'd swear a mix between the Virgin Mary and God himself had died, leaving space for the eternal Misses of Concord to step into her place. That was the only good thing about death in Concord. It made space for newcomers and brought on some new fondness for those who have departed. Evie rarely gave into these thoughts in public, even thinking them twisted her usually placid features into something demonic and wild that might kill a small animal.

She hid the muslin—or instead stuffed it—into a small hole beneath the wide-planked steps of the house that led to the garden. She saw Scout, her brother Captain Briers' luscious black-coated Labrador demolishing the shards of oats, licking his chops, and wandering off in the darkness. Evie stood with her hand over her mouth, peering into the foggy air that hung around the edges of the woods, hoping to see him bound back out, but silence descended. Nothing stirred.

"Scout?" she whispered, not expecting him to come back. He liked to run wild in Hunter's Field on the other side of the woods, round and round in circles until he'd collapse in a dizzy heap panting. Usually, Captain Briers gave up chasing him, and Evie couldn't be bothered. She waved her hand into the darkness as if the animal could have it his own way and stomped wearily up the steps to the hall. Upstairs, the Captain, her brother, was poring over maps, reading books, and balling up expensive paper to throw away. *Evie, get me more paper. Evie, do this, do that, and Evie, where's my coffee and soft rolls?* Their rhythms were discordant, just like the current flowing under the genteel veneer of Concord, and he was no different.

Love struck Captain Briers with his secret trysts, he'd cover up with Puritan virtue and refuse to talk about it because it was plainly obvious even in a small town like Concord everyone knew the other's business.

Justice of the Peace was the kind of title he so richly deserved. When their father was around, life was more problematic. He'd question every detail of a carcass found in a field. Get to the bottom of the tiniest amount of money missing from the till. Everett Briers was different, relaxed, obliging. Nothing like their predecessor father, obsessed with the outward view of matters and determined in his pursuits like a bloodhound.

Just as Evie was about to climb the stairs to bed, a soft knock on the front door made her stand still.

Who'd be calling this hour of the night? An outline through the mottled glass of the headscarf and gloved hands crushed to the side of the head, distorting the face.

"Miss Taylor," Evie said in an imperious tone. "What brings you here at this late hour?" Miss Maisie Taylor walked past Evie and right into the breakfast room, where she sat in the shadows.

"Is there something I can do for you, Miss Taylor?" Evie's voice was a mix of constrained anger and a tinge of fear. "There are some things I need to discuss with you, Evie," Miss Taylor said. "You might want to sit down."

Nobody enjoys being asked to sit in their own home, but Evie had an inkling about Miss Taylor's visit, and there was no getting out of it.

"Those oat squares, Miss Briers," Miss Taylor began, opening the subject with obvious tack. "What became of them?"

"I disposed of them, Miss Taylor. Even in this weather, nothing keeps."

"I see," Miss Taylor said. "What if the Captain wishes to inspect them?"

"For what purpose?"

"An investigation, perhaps."

"Into what, may I ask?"

"Miss Collier's death, of course," she stated.

"You don't think I'd have anything to do with that now, do you, Miss Taylor?" Evie said, a nervous smile stretching across her weary face. "Your imagination would be better spent on the Concord Festival."

Miss Taylor leaned forward and spoke with a calm, exacting voice that chilled Evie. "I may be forgetful, Miss Briers, but I am not blind."

* * *

One light burned at the Chandler's Clamshell Farm, low and running out of oil in a turned-down lamp. Young Miss Mary Chandler lay across her bed wearing a thin nightdress barely concealing her youthful curves, and a hell-bound moth crashed the light, buzzing free, searching for freedom. She fidgeted at her swollen eyes, sore and red from crying, but the minute they stopped, and she thought it was over, they'd roll again with such velocity it took all her strength to stifle her sobs so as not to wake the whole household. Clutched in her damp hand was the telegram received only two hours earlier, read and re-read, hoping the words would change. She took it up one last time and held it to the lamp, and her tears had finally stopped. It would never change. The words just sat there like ominous warnings loaded with sorrow.

"What is the matter, Mary?" Agnes Chandler said. Mary didn't hear her mother open the door, and she stared past the light to see her standing there with a pewter candlestick and one thin candle spluttering in the cold air. She glanced at Mary's hand and came over to her bedside. "Show me the telegram, Mary. Is it for your father?"

"No, it's for me," Mary said. "It's nobody's business but my own." She glared at Agnes with such a grown-up look it frightened her. Agnes reached out to take it, but Mary snapped it away and was now standing on the other side of the bed. "I said it's mine."

"Mary," Agnes said in a tiny voice. "Please don't act this way with me. I'm your mother." Mary stretched out her arm and let the paper drop into the oil lamp, where it withered and charred in seconds, lost forever.

Agnes Chandler put the candle down and pulled her grey shawl around her shoulders. "Tell me what was in the telegram."

* * *

Miss Evie Briers walked to the center of her lawn, feeling it crunch and crack beneath her feet, and stopped beside the stone fountain of the girl with a sad face. Captain Briers loved it; however, to Evie, it was symbolic of fading hope, and she wanted to be rid of it. She'd almost forgotten why she was out there and remembered it was to see if her brother was back. There was no sign of Scout, and Evie felt worried. Her brother rose at five and put on his thick coat and boots to go in search of him in the woods. Scout was known to frequent the bakery, hoping for some fresh bread or buns to be thrown his way, but nobody saw him. A tingle of fear and worry bit at her, and she pulled her shawl around her shoulders, breathing the dark, crisp November air into her. She had a bad feeling that something wicked might happen, and as it gathered strength, she saw her brother in the distance making his way through the final part of the woods onto the path.

In his arms, the large glossy head flopping was Scout, and Evie's eyes narrowed onto them. Captain Briers was silently crying, not huge sobs or wailing but gentle tears.

There was no mistaking the fact Scout, the faithful dog, was dead.

The Captain Confesses

Miss Sylvia Murdock stood by the doorway to the school, ushering in the stragglers. In her world, there was simply no room for bad manners, tardiness, or slovenliness. Today, however, as the last of the children—including the late ones—bustled down the shiny, polished corridor, her mind was not on her work.

She was so careful of the school records; she let no one within a breath's reach of them. The daily woman always asked for special permission to dust the corners and polish the surfaces in the cabinet. Miss Murdock would move them herself and ensure the task was carried out under supervision. There were days Miss Murdock needed to work on them and refused any interruption in case their private contents were accidentally read.

Miss Murdock clapped her hands sharply together, bringing her charges back to the present. There was an inspection due that day, and not a soul was let in on the secret time, so order must be maintained at all costs.

"Children, please, no noise," she announced in her most authoritative voice. "There is to be perfect behavior for the remainder of the day." Out of the window, beyond the tumbling ivy, a figure in black made its way to the gate.

"Children, please," Miss Murdock said sharply. Miss Nash replaced the bell on its stand, wiping a soft cloth over the brass to remove any finger smudges, when Miss Murdock came rushing down the hallway towards the entrance.

"Are they here already?" she asked Miss Nash.

"Is who here, Miss Murdock?" She snatched the cloth from Miss Nash's hand and replaced it beside the bell.

"Could you kindly see the inspector in?"

"It is not the inspector, Miss Murdock."

"Well, who is it, Miss Nash?"

"Miss Alcott. From Castle Farm."

Miss Murdock's stern face lost some hardness on the mention of the name. Miss Alcott's timing was certainly inconvenient, and she was quite sure it was not a social visit. She hated hordes of unwelcome visitors tramping all over the place, but as she'd always invited members of the civil community in to see how well the school was run, it was inevitable.

"Very well, see her *straight* to my office at once."

On her way down the corridor, Miss Murdock stopped by a wooden framed mirror hanging beside the kitchen to check her hair that always went awry when she got herself excited and looked into her own anxious brown eyes. She was becoming too old for this vocation and couldn't bring herself to figure out how Miss Nash, now almost sixty, stood it so long.

By the soft knock, Miss Murdock knew Miss Nash had disobeyed her orders and allowed Miss Alcott to wander unaccompanied about the corridors with most likely some vague directions that would eventually bring her to the head office. When she entered, Miss Murdock poised herself over a roll call, ensuring that Miss Alcott would be under no illusion of how busy she was. Louisa's presence was severe, the coal black hair, pouty lips, and somewhat incongruous pink sash about her stark, stiff, dark dress. Her appearance was at once tidy but somehow chaotic and unenticing.

"Good morning, Miss Alcott," Miss Murdock said, placing her pen down and rising slowly as if engrossed in the examination of a document before her and wished not to be disturbed, but would be polite, nonetheless. "I trust you are well."

"I apologize for the intrusion, Miss Murdock, but I need to speak with you about a matter that cannot wait."

"And what might that be?"

"Miss Emily Collier."

"A dreadful loss," Miss Murdock said, wringing her hands and reaching for the cross pendant around her neck.

"Truly a terrible thing to happen to her," she then said.

"Oh," Louisa said, "Did something terrible happen to Miss Collier?"

Miss Murdock took a sharp intake of breath and circled around Louisa to close the door.

"A death under such circumstances is always terrible."

"Quite agreed. And I must say she'll be missed at the Concord Festival. "

"She sang the opening every year. She loved the sound of her own voice," Miss Murdock said.

Miss Murdock tried to keep the contempt from her voice, but the meaning registered on her visitor's face. "I see. And what else did Miss Collier contribute to the Festival?"

"She raised money. For municipal projects."

"Like the school roof?"

Miss Murdock smiled tightly. "Like the school roof."

"I believe Miss Collier withdrew her support for the Festival only last week," Louisa said.

"Where did you… the committee had difficulty agreeing on decorations. Miss Collier was extravagant in all she did. She was not confined by simple pleasures."

Before Louisa could continue, Miss Murdock was already explaining. "Limes and apricots, dried figs, that sort of thing are what people of simple tastes place on wreaths. Items found in nature's beauty are not alien to it. Miss Collier's tastes ran to silk and frills. Very inappropriate for a mid-winter celebration. Concord Festival celebrates nature's abundance in the face of man's mental and worldly impoverishment. In the face of nature's brutal superiority."

"But she had no other role in the Festival," Louisa continued, unaffected by Miss Murdock's speech.

"Not initially. She tried to impose forbidden vices on us. A mysterious love for conjuring acts and special powers."

Louisa let the silence grow since Miss Murdock was in a quiet rage, the kind that simmers and boils and is not extinguished even by death itself.

Her anger seemed to outlive the moment of Miss Collier's death and grow ever more powerful and public.

"Are you telling me, Miss Murdock, that Miss Collier was fond of the black arts?"

Miss Murdock's eyes widened, and once again, she clasped the cross around her neck.

"I meant no such thing, Miss Alcott. If you're asking me if Miss Collier is a witch, then decidedly, no. There was no such evidence, and I merely suggested she saw the Festival as a spectacle and something to celebrate in high fashion when most citizens of Concord would disapprove of such things."

"I was under the impression Miss Collier's role as Festival benefactor was very much cherished," Louisa said. Miss Murdock's lips tightened.

"When she provided funds and kept her wild ideas to herself, it was very much cherished."

Louisa put her arms on the chair, ready to foist herself upwards, and noticed the unashamed relief in Miss Murdock's face. "One more thing, Miss Murdock."

"Whatever I can help with."

"Miss Collier's birthday party, were you there?"

"Yes, I was there, Miss Alcott."

"Was there anything strange about the party, anything you may remember?"

"No, Miss Alcott, there wasn't," she said. Louisa got up to leave, this time taking the appropriate angles to allow her with as little pain as possible to remove herself.

"Except for one thing," Miss Murdock said suddenly. "Miss Taylor *wasn't* there."

"Is that of significance, Miss Murdock?"

"Well, she organized the whole thing."

"I see," Louisa said.

"What is the reason for your questioning? A new book, Miss Alcott?"

"Nothing of the sort, Miss Murdock. Just expressing some interest in an acquaintance."

"Even so, I assure you I would make a very dull character," she said.

As soon as Louisa left, Miss Murdock dismissed the idea she'd said anything out of line. You shouldn't speak ill of the dead, but what could they do about it?

What could Miss Collier do about it? Miss Murdock herself was a humanist. Cherished the flaws that make us unique. She'd not intended to paint Miss Collier in a bad light in front of all people but Louisa May Alcott, but she was sure of all people, Louisa would understand. Her mind drifted to the school records, and it occurred to her that Louisa wouldn't know about what she'd discovered earlier. She wondered if Miss Nash knew anything about it.

That morning, she'd glanced at the rosewood cabinet with its rectangular glass front, immediately noticing the disarray. With the inspectors calling, they might very well demand to view them as part of their assessment, and any irregularity would not sit right with her. Miss Murdock stored them perfectly straight, lining up the pages—even the worn and torn ones—so they looked as neat as possible. She took the keys from her pocket, counted them, and wondered who had been able to gain access when she had the keys. True, they were not in her possession all of the time, but during school hours, they never left her side. It didn't make any sense. None at all.

* * *

Night fell on Concord like a sweeping black blanket with tiny silver specks across the sky. An uneven line of daylight stretched over the horizon, the dark so soft and quiet it swooped over before your eyes. It was deadly darkness, Captain Everett Briers always thought. Like water and ink mixing. As a child, he'd remember those days following July like nature decided it was time to press the night in quickly. He swore he could tell the day, just as August began when that smell of cinnamon and spice and Christmas wormed its way into the air. Everything had a purpose, unlike the tranquil laziness that spread over the land during the summer months.

It wasn't late when he put on his heavy wool coat over his suit, but the shadows of dusk crowded into the room, and downstairs, he saw the silvery grey light of the rising moon, bright and impertinent, wedged between two trees as though cradled in its branches.

"Are you going out at this hour?" It was his sister Evie. She was hunched down, slowly brushing the sooty fireplace that sat low in the hearth. When he didn't answer, she stood up, the small brush dangling in her hand. "Will I save you supper?"

Captain Briers glanced upwards at her as though he hadn't heard what she'd said. "Scout was poisoned."

"Oh dear," Evie said.

He seemed relieved to divulge the information if a little shy about putting Scout's demise over the investigation into Miss Collier's death.

"Vet. Parsons knew from the moment he looked at him. Poor animal, " he said. He seemed so upset, so out of sorts, that Evie wasn't sure whether to say anything. "How could that happen, Everett?" Evie said.

"Foxes, perhaps. The vet believes he ate something he shouldn't have."

Evie said nothing. Then: "You're not going to do anything silly, are you, Everett?"

"Lest you call burying him silly?"

"No, of course. Scout must be buried, " Evie said.

There was a time you'd hear the thud-thud-thud of Scout's tail, nose in the air, head moving backward and forwards as Evie walked across the kitchen with a chicken or beef stew. His snout would follow the trail of steaming hot food to the slow cooking range, where Evie did her magic. Not that he wasn't a good guard dog he was so alert, just she'd miss his furious attention to her sticky buns when someone knocked on the door, and he didn't know whether to run and investigate or stay put. Her brother loved that dog and would miss him terribly. And the awful thought slowly dawned on her that she might be responsible for his untimely departure.

* * *

As Louisa lifted her hand to knock on Miss Taylor's door, she thought it inappropriate to visit her so late at night. It was dark when she'd cracked a few eggs and made her favorite omelet. Pitch black by the time she'd resolved to make her visit. There was nothing to be done but get on with it.

Miss Taylor lived in Field House on Market Street, every bit as elegant as her. With its mullioned windows and hand-beaded wooden front door, it was as fine a property as one could come across in Concord. A grand townhouse, one could say.

"Pardon the intrusion, Miss Taylor," Louisa said when she appeared. Miss Taylor didn't seem to mind intrusions of the mild and educated kind and was still dressed in her daily finery.

"Miss Alcott, it's always a pleasure," she said. She ushered her through, and Louisa felt the waft of cold air coming from a recently closed door through the kitchen. Four frosted glass lamps gave out so little light, but Miss Taylor was known for her intimate and soft preferences, much to the consternation of the locals. There was something odd about a woman who disliked bright lights.

"Did I interrupt you in something?" Louisa asked. Two cups still leached steam on the round table by the window.

"Let me get you a cup of coffee," Miss Taylor said, covering the awkward question up, and Louisa took her hat off and slumped into one of the flowery sofas by the wall. She always accepted any kindness that allowed her to conceal the fact that sinking into a chair was most unladylike.

"You have a visitor at this hour of the night?" Louisa asked through the noisy clashing of China in the parlor, trying to get Miss Taylor to admit it. Someone had been there, and she wasn't in the best of moods with a stiff neck for the question to remain unanswered. She could be a tricky one, Miss Taylor, and it didn't help she ignored her question so wholly it was bordering rude.

"Black," Miss Taylor said, placing it beside her. "I remember from the Concord Festival last year."

Louisa eyed her and then gratefully downed the hot, warm coffee into which she'd put a spoon of Miss Collier's honey. Clearly, this wasn't going to be easy.

"I'm afraid I'm on official business, Miss Taylor."

"That can't be helped."

"No, it can't. Miss Collier...."

"Poor Miss Collier. She was so full of life the last time I saw her. Now, there were rumors she'd climb up North Bridge and fling herself off like some strange wanton siren in search of a dip, but I think she was just plain called too early. None of us know the day or the hour, do we, Miss Alcott?"

"No, Miss Taylor, we don't," Louisa said. "But we know you organized Miss Collier's birthday party the evening before she was found."

"By Evie, of course. The poor dear, I hope she's okay?"

"Yes, Miss Taylor, but I was wondering why you organized it." Miss Taylor lifted her cold coffee, the one Louisa noticed she hadn't touched. On the other hand, the mystery visitor drank half, so either Miss Taylor was doing all the talking or simply didn't want to drink it.

"Miss Collier loved parties," Miss Taylor said and smiled. "Concord is full of people who think you're dead by the time you get married, Miss Alcott. Celebrations are limited to church ceremonies or babies being born and fasting and whining over death. Now, with Miss Collier, she knew how to enjoy herself. That's the closest thing to a sin, Miss Alcott, when you're an unclaimed treasure like Miss Collier."

"I beg your pardon?" Louisa said.

Miss Taylor tried hard to blush, but Louisa saw a twinkle of deception in her eyes, even if she figured she wouldn't notice. "Unmarried and unclaimed. She liked to shock the citizens of Concord, Miss Alcott, and it was something she was very good at."

Louisa considered this statement and realized she didn't know Miss Collier as well as she thought. Realizing she'd missed the party, it appeared to be for certain ladies only, she finished her coffee.

"How did you find Miss Collier the evening of the party?"

"She seemed well. But I wouldn't know. I didn't stay that long."

"Why?"

"I had more important things to do than sit around with Concord's spinsters eating cake, Miss Alcott." She said it like she knew she'd understand.

After some moments, she leaned forward with an air of confidentiality. "Is there something about Miss Collier's death that is troubling?"

Louisa rose awkwardly, refusing a vague offer for help from Miss Taylor, and walked to the window. "Yes, Miss Taylor, there is. I believe, though I am not certain, Miss Collier may have been poisoned."

"But who on earth would want to poison Miss Collier?" She put her cup back on the table and looked at the ground like she was searching for something, perhaps even the answer.

"Well, now, Miss Taylor, there is an official investigation, but Captain Briers sees to such matters."

"Aren't you supposed to warn a potential suspect, Miss Alcott?"

"Are you a potential suspect, Miss Taylor?" Louisa asked.

"Of course not," she said, managing a stern look. "I told you I left the party shortly after it started."

"But as I understand, you organized it?"

"It was one of those events which nobody wants to organize but will see to it they attend. And what's more, they enjoy themselves. Do you understand now?"

"Where did you go?"

"Why, may I ask, is that important?"

"Because the poison that left Miss Collier slumped in her chair—if indeed she was poisoned—must be of a kind that was administered at the party."

"That is quite an allegation, Miss Alcott. Well, then, you do certainly have a problem."

"In what sense, Miss Taylor?"

"I've just explained that to you. Most of the Concord ladies were there."

After some coaxing, she revealed she was not feeling well the day of the party. Miss Taylor did not have a stomach but an "abdomen" or, as she sometimes preferred, "anxious cavity." Suffering pains and worry over such personal matters that she simply refused to discuss them without, as she informed Miss Alcott, bringing phantoms of agony upon herself.

"Did you see Dr. Jennings?" Louisa asked.

"It wasn't that serious, and I didn't require the services of Dr. Jennings, whom I might add is a shadow of a man compared to his predecessor."

Miss Taylor had apparently returned to Field House on the night of the birthday party and indulged in warm cocoa fortified with honey. She went to bed early and did not feel the griping symptoms until the following morning. However, as indicated most strenuously to Louisa, she had not eaten a single thing at the party, and it all began much earlier. In fact, she had been unable to eat anything substantial for the previous few days.

"Might I ask on what authority you're questioning me?" Miss Taylor asked. "I'm sure the Captain will begin *his* investigation."

"I'm sure Miss Taylor, you'd appreciate my coming here first?"

"I suppose," she said, lifting her elegant face haughtily, "the Captain might be a little preoccupied at the moment." She sipped from her cup and then gave Louisa a sly look.

"Meaning, Miss Taylor?"

"Why he's in love, Miss Alcott. One cannot disguise the blossom of lust, can one now?" With widened eyes, she gave her a grin. "Even you must be able to see that."

Louisa, at that moment, needed to decide if Miss Taylor was leading her astray, or plainly lying. Such was the need of the murderer—or potential murderer—to deflect attention. She'd read this in books, of course, and nothing subtle would counter the insufferable attraction and manipulative capability of a woman like Miss Taylor. And, of course, Louisa had to apply logic to the situation rather than fanciful speculation.

"And you needn't think he's fallen for just anyone in Concord either," Miss Taylor said, enjoying its effect on her coffee companion. "You're likely to be disappointed."

* * *

Hangman's Cottage was ablaze with light, and the tinkle of piano—tortured—stopping and starting drifted through the cold air.

"Oh, for heaven's sake, April, it's getting late," June Birch said. She was standing in the doorway to the more flamboyant Miss Birch's boudoir, holding a black dress in one hand, a stitching needle in the other. She'd interviewed all available daily women after the last one left—citing April Birch as "impossible"—and found not a single one capable of putting up with her sister. Now, the mundane awfulness of everyday life thrust June into action. There simply wasn't enough time in the day to attend to April's needs and her own.

April's artistic temperament meant she was unavailable for ordinary tasks like cleaning and mending, which interfered with her creative drive and stifled her imagination. June glanced at the grandfather clock with a border of flowers and the moon phases turning inside a blue pearl circle at the top, but it didn't deter April.

"What is it, little bird?"

"I said it's late, April," June said, her characteristic tight lips white and persistent. "I must fix my dress, and I cannot concentrate with the racket."

April was very modern. She smoked a pipe and shoved her enormous frame in the high-back chair she used to compose her most outstanding work, allowing the grey plumes to spew out like a tiny steam engine racing through the countryside.

"You really are an awful old virgin, little bird. My best work arrives on a swiftly flying muse late at night."

"Then be so kind as to confine your muse to paper," June said.

"Really, June, your commitment to Miss Collier's funeral is admirable," April said, and then under her breath, "anyone would think you'd killed her."

"How dare you," June said, in her voice reserved for outrage and indignation. "How dare you insinuate such a thing?"

"Come now," April said, smiling. "You can't hide the fact you're somewhat relieved?"

"How could I possibly be relieved?"

April turned to her cut glass sherry decanter and slowly poured herself a dram. It assisted—or rather was imperative—to her flow of internal thought and put a stop to June's hysteria. One never interrupts a person pouring as it's such a precise task, particularly if you've been engaged in it all evening.

"You must be happy Captain Briers' little plan is scuppered," April said.

"I'm sure I know nothing of Captain Briers' plans."

"Everybody knows Captain Briers' plans, little bird. And you will get to wear your best black, delivering a highly emotional farewell to Miss Collier from Concord's altar. Captain Briers will see you in a new light," she said with bright eyes and a generous gulp of sherry.

"You are truly offensive, April," June said. "To insult Miss Collier's memory like this."

April laughed, a long one, so conceited it shook her enormous frame from top to bottom like a quivering jelly.

"Really, little bird, you should put your creative talent to better use. I almost believed your shock and horror. It will come across Concord's congregation like an eruption of lava, hot and sticky. I can see the teary eyes on those hardened farmers now."

June was about to speak but didn't. Her sister's insensitivity moved well beyond the boundaries of civility.

"You're inebriated. Like some crazy, demented railway worker," June said finally, lifting her head up. "I had nothing but respect for Miss Collier."

"Save your performance for the good folk of Concord June."

As June turned on her heels to furiously go about mending her funereal dressage, both heard a knock on the door.

"Now, who could that be," April said, filling her glass again. "I love a person flouting convention; they get my attention every time." Rather than greet the caller, she fanned her flabby radicals in her sister's direction. "Go see who it is, little bird. Invite them in."

Louisa wasn't expecting to be admitted and was surprised to see the pale moon face of June Birch a few inches before her. June was dressed in a red and turquoise bathrobe, as far as Louisa could make out, and her black hair was pulled tight into a shiny, perfect bun. Louisa wasn't welcome, she imagined, but she would not sleep just now, and while out and about, it seemed reasonable to call on the ladies of Hangman's Cottage, who were her closest neighbors.

"I'm sorry for the intrusion, Miss Birch, but I was hoping to speak with you."

June's face darkened, and she glanced over her shoulder. "It is very late, Miss Alcott."

"Who is it?" April roared from behind, her voice sharp and insistent. "Come in, whoever you are, and ignore the little bird."

June still didn't move until Louisa saw a shadow looming in the background and was admitted, greeted by the tall and forbidding April Birch most enthusiastically as though invited for a late breakfast and more than welcome. She said it several times on the way in, much to June's horror.

April seated herself on an oversized sofa, built for two but from which she surveyed her guests in comfort and upon which she refused to allow anyone to sit.

"We have not seen you, Miss Alcott, in such a long time," April began, waving June away for drinks. "Brandy, little bird. The *good* one."

"Indeed, I haven't been well."

April clutched her chest. "Oh, how terrible. A good brandy will sort it out."

"I'm sure you don't wish to waste your brandy on me, Miss Birch," Louisa said.

April waved the idea away and revived her pipe with several furious puffs. "Really, Miss Alcott, a good brandy is never wasted. Consumed in moderation, it will lift the soul and feed the imagination. You're not one of these pesky prohibitionists? I may say it's so easy to be like that these days. My sources are truly legal."

"Oh, how is that, Miss Birch?"

"Mr. Miller is fond of good brandy. I have him to blame entirely for my addiction. Thank God he's a transcendentalist." June Birch struggled with a tray containing two cut glass tumblers—April despised genteel glasses—and the open brandy.

"Are you a prohibitionist, Miss Alcott?" June asked.

"Yes, of course," Louisa said proudly. "I founded several temperance gatherings, should you require some relief."

"Well then, if you don't mind, I will say goodnight before my sister finds

34

another chore for me. I can at least be satisfied that someone here in this house might be sensible."

After a short silence, April cleared her throat and poured the brandy. "Don't mind the little bird. She's rude when she's hungry or tired. Always has been like that, and she's too old to change now."

"I was hoping to speak with her," Louisa said. "I'm here to discuss Miss Collier."

"Angelic voice," April said. "She could be trusted with such complicated scores. I'll miss her terribly."

"So, every single person tells me. Were you at the party for Miss Collier?"

"Me? Oh dear, no. I'm not a cake and coffee woman, Miss Alcott. As you can see, I might well tolerate the cake, but I wouldn't sit around with the mischievous Concord women drinking coffee." She gave a hearty laugh but stopped as Louisa remained stone-faced.

"And why is that, Miss Birch?"

"It's nothing personal, but I dislike ladies congregating in such numbers. Like wolves gathering in the woods, breeding danger."

"What kind of danger, Miss Birch?"

April put her glass down with a little sniff of frustration. "They are a nasty lot, the Misses of Concord. June and I avoid any social occasions that bring them together in public or private places. And there's a rumor."

"Rumor of what, Miss Birch?"

"That Miss Taylor is married. To whom or to what is another matter, but knowing Miss Taylor, he's bound to be rich. Her preference was always loot over love."

Louisa thought about that. Not only was Miss Taylor missing from the party, but she also had a mystery guest about whom she was unwilling to reveal the identity. And now, April Birch was almost suggesting that Miss Taylor wasn't welcome at the birthday party because she was married.

"I may look judgmental, Miss Alcott, but I assure you I'm not. Miss Collier was in the choir, but she was not a friend of mine, if you understand. An acquaintance at best, if you will."

"Who were Miss Collier's close friends?"

"Well, that is a bit of a different problem. If I had to single out one, it would be Miss Jean Nash from the school. Evie Briers spent some time at Rosebud Cottage, usually in the mornings, but I suspected long ago she was cleaning or doing menial chores for Miss Collier."

"But surely she and the Captain are well-maintained?"

April smiled and took another unladylike gulp of brandy. "Captain Briers keeps a close eye on the purse, Miss Alcott. He's stingy as they come. You'd swear he was saving up to buy Concord, and you might consider questioning him."

Louisa was taken aback. "Captain Briers is investigating the circumstances of Miss Collier's death." *Or he was supposed to be,* Louisa thought, but very little evidence of such occurred to her.

"So, what do you think, Miss Alcott? I'd much rather be questioned by you than the Captain. Do you think one of the nasty Misses knocked her off?" April said.

"I would rather not say, Miss Birch."

"Oh, come now. A gentle ripple of a rumor is circulating that Miss Collier might have been poisoned. Can you believe it?"

"Who would spread such a rumor?" Louisa asked.

"Well, Mrs. Miller, of course. Quite possibly the worst gossip monger in Concord and, without a doubt, a loose tongue. I travel to Fairgreen to send my telegrams, even if I'm ordering paper or stationery. The most boring of communications I send from Fairgreen. It is far enough away from Mrs. Miller's inquisitive ears and eyes. I simply don't trust her to keep her mouth shut about my business."

Louisa felt tiredness invading her bones, leaving her with a sense of growing dislocation from the conversation. The room was stifling hot, and the fire was a blasting base of red-hot embers. But she was determined to speak further with Miss Birch, who seemed to be an intelligent and insightful woman.

"Have you any idea why someone would want Miss Collier dead?"

April let out a long, brandy-soaked sigh. "Really, Miss Alcott, Miss Collier was very wealthy, for starters. She was also very vocal about the projects she supported or didn't, as the case may be. I've heard it was poison, and if that is the situation, then surely, we have a murderer not affected by the moment's passion. Money is so grubby a reason. Perhaps she did withdraw her support for a project or offended some disgruntled inhabitant. She was rather good at causing dissent."

Louisa considered this and did not object when Miss Birch filled her own glass up yet again.

"How could a thing like that arouse such hatred, though?" April said.

Louisa stayed silent.

"It's not as if Concord is poor, and there must be another motive," April said.

"Did Mrs. Miller indicate how she knew Miss Collier had been poisoned?"

"Captain Briers sent a telegram the day after she was found. Mrs. Miller didn't say exactly what was in it, but there were other interesting pieces of information she alluded to but refused to divulge."

"And who did he send it to?"

"That Miss Alcott, I'm afraid I don't know. Mrs. Miller likes her position of power in Concord as a postmistress, and she wouldn't fall too foul of her duty."

* * *

Louisa bid goodnight to April Birch and walked the short distance to Castle Farm. Of all the inhabitants of Concord, she was lucky to count the Misses Birch as her closest neighbors, even if they were a little odd. Now, the ideas of what Miss Collier could have done to bring about her misfortune became more apparent. Money makes people mad. She was aware of that. Having spent much of her childhood in poverty, Louisa knew only too well the power it had over any number of lives. To be without, it was felt sorely by herself and her family that perhaps Miss Collier promised something she made up her mind later not to deliver upon. That could cause grief of a kind destined to produce evil. To play the bountiful lady was one thing; to pull the resources out of spite or anger was another.

And was it so, Louisa wondered. Her own success came late, not after threatened penury, which led her to the most undignified of positions before writing provided her with a manner to express her passion and, of course, led to money. Perhaps not wealth dreamed of by most, but she felt its power. And she was not ashamed. She needed to make sense of the world around her, and writing provided that uncompromising passion like an antidote to the curse of poverty.

When she reached Castle Farm, she noticed a dark figure standing close to her window, leaning in as if to see if someone was home. A shiver of fear ran through her. It had to be a man judging by the coat and the height. She held her head high, and when she reached the gate, she called out, and the man turned around. It was Captain Briers.

"It is very late, Captain Briers, to call to a lady's home," Louisa said, taking her keys out and unlocking the large wooden front door, her hands shaking from fear. She had to push it open with her shoulder, and Captain Briers helped her. He stood at the stone entrance.

"I hope I didn't frighten you," he said.

"Of course not, Captain. I'm made of rigid material and not prone to frighten easily."

"May I speak with you?"

"At this hour?"

"I would rather, yes, it's important."

Louisa invited Captain Briers into her living room which was intensely cold because of her absence, and her family were long asleep upstairs. There was no point in lighting a fire this time of night, so she made coffee, and they settled themselves in the kitchen, where the hearth's vestige of heat provided a more comfortable environment.

"I understand you're questioning Concord residents about Miss Collier's death," the Captain said, taking his coffee in both hands. They were raw, red, and sore-looking with minor scrapes and bruising as though he'd been fighting with a thorny bush.

"And you're here to tell me to quit and keep my nose out of it."

Captain Briers couldn't help but smile, for indeed, that appeared to be his mission.

"I wouldn't quite put it like that, Miss Alcott, but since you have, I guess that's pretty much it."

"You're aware most of Concord knows about your telegram, Captain."

He put his cup down, a f tremble in his fingers as he did. Louisa wasn't sure why the Captain would be nervous, but he'd the look of a man deeply upset about something. It was how he moved and showed up on her doorstep so late. He needed to be occupied, and she'd felt the same way. He clearly needed to satisfy himself concerning a matter she knew nothing of.

"Mrs. Miller has been spoken to," he said.

"What was in the telegram, Captain?"

"That is confidential information, Miss Alcott."

"Well, Captain, it seems you wrote it without thinking. You sent it in a state of emotional upheaval, and that is no way to conduct your business." He smirked. It wasn't malicious, but Louisa was sure there was a hint of anger lying buried. A note of unhappiness lurking.

After he remained silent, Louisa continued, "Which one of Concord's Misses has your attention, Captain?" Now his eyes illuminated, so much Louisa knew she'd touched a nerve.

"You might watch what you're saying, Miss Alcott," he said in a low voice. It wasn't harsh, just sad.

"My guess is Miss Mary Chandler," Louisa said. "It was poor judgment to act in such a state of confusion. If you wish to continue your investigation, I strongly suggest you tell me what was in the telegram."

Louisa poured more coffee, and the Captain didn't object. He stole some glances at her and finally clenched his hands open and closed, raising them to his face.

"*Emily poisoned, we cannot marry,*" he said. "Now, are you satisfied, Miss Alcott?"

"Most certainly not, Captain," she said. It was, of course, very satisfying.

"Why does Miss Collier's death prevent you from marrying?"

"Mary's family don't support our desires to be married, and I don't have the means to buy a marital home."

"Because of Evie?"

"Kame Bluff was our parents' house. I cannot throw her out."

"What was Miss Collier going to do?"

"Miss Collier supported our intentions and agreed to help me out with the wedding and new home. It was very generous of her."

"Were you and Mary engaged?" Louisa asked. "Why did Miss Collier refuse you the money?"

Captain Briers got out of his seat and wandered to the sink, looking out over the silvery moonlit landscape. He braced himself against the stone tiles and spread his hands out in frustration. "She seemed to change her mind before her death."

"Why?"

"I don't know Miss Alcott. She visited Kame Bluff a week ago and asked me to go to Rosebud Cottage on what would have been the day after her birthday, saying there was something she wanted to discuss."

"I see," Louisa said. And she really did.

"Can I have your word that you won't disclose this to anyone?" Captain Briers asked.

"I worry the gist of your predicament is already common knowledge, Captain. This is a dire situation. You must excuse yourself immediately from the investigation."

He lowered his head like he knew she was right. "You cannot possibly be involved, Captain, and it isn't right," Louisa said.

"What should I do, Miss Alcott?"

"I believe, Captain, we should go to the higher Justices and discuss the matter. I would not wish your career to be in jeopardy, but this is a fundamental issue and must be brought to their attention."

"It was a very foolish thing to have done," the Captain said. "Madness."

"Rash, Captain," Louisa said. "We have all been guilty of sudden moves which hardly benefit ourselves or others."

"Mrs. Miller should have held her tongue."

"Yes, she should have. But you should have known better, Captain. You are in a position of power and importance, and such an office demands integrity and actions beyond question."

Mary Chandler Confides

The morning after the Captain's visit, the sun rose in gold waves over Concord, turning everything a bright shiny brass. You would be forgiven for thinking it was a spring morning, but for the sun's position. Low and determined, spilling rather than rising quickly as if awakened from a lingering slumber and unwilling to burst into life. Louisa slept late and woke with a start. She closed her eyes momentarily, avoiding the day a little longer than necessary, and immediately thought of Dandy and Doodle. Her pigs.

She'd fed them early the previous day, a mixture of potato peelings, carrots, and oats which they'd reveled in. They must be hungry, she thought and set out about stirring herself out of bed, away from the coziness and pushing full thrust into the day. She was surprised and delighted to find Hierophant curled into a tight ball at the end of the bed. A slow, steady, rhythmic breathing mass of fur. As if he sensed his new mistress was awake, he opened his eyes, stirred, blinked, and sniffed. Following an enormous yawn, he stretched his full length, digging his tiny paws into the coverlet with such satisfying precision it encouraged Louisa to do the same. Despite the later hour she'd risen, there was much to think about.

She regretted her decision to accompany the Captain to his superiors, feeling she had suffered a defect of reasoning. No doubt, Mr. Jeremy Founts, with whom she was regrettably familiar, would wonder about her involvement, which seemed to have just happened out of nowhere. She was curious by nature but felt confident the Captain had seen the errors of his ways and submitted to remedy the mistake. He was still, after all, the Justice of the District and fully competent to continue his investigation.

Danny and Doodle were making a terrible fuss when she finally made it out to the back of Castle Farm. They nudged each other out of the way to reach her with a force of will, amusing in animals, hardly in humans, and she began to wonder about the nature of desire. This ill-fated attachment of Captain Briers to Miss Chandler begged many questions, none the least around the very substance of what constitutes a love affair. She'd been corresponding with a man for some time but not involved. There was no other word for the arrangement but "correspondence." Undoubtedly, the Captain and Mary Chandler were suited to one another as quickly as any other couple. What could be the impediment which kept them apart? Knee-high in mud and with an oddly satisfying smattering of sweat across her brow, she unloaded the last basket of scraps into the pigsty. "That should do you," she said.

Hierophant had stretched himself out in the only foot of sunshine that penetrated the backyard, and a biting, inhospitable wind blew up between the two outhouses. During the summer, the fresh gusts were pleasant, but now Louisa gripped her shawl tight around her and grimaced into the blustery onslaught.

She then noticed a slight figure in a lavender cloak waiting at the door to Castle Farm. Louisa met Mary Chandler at the Concord Festival the previous year and found her, at best, morose and, at worst, unpredictably belligerent. By the wisps of blonde hair and youthful, slim figure, Louisa was sure it was her, and although she'd only been at work for a short time she wasn't looking forward to a dose of Miss Chandler. She upset her stomach in a most disagreeable manner.

"Good day, Miss Alcott," Mary said and bowed. "I hope you are keeping well." Louisa, quite out of breath and in need of a solid reviving coffee, simply nodded and waved the young Miss Chandler inside. She couldn't help but notice the provocative ensemble of low-cut summer dress bounded by frills barely sustaining Miss Chandler's bosom and white stockings embellished with tiny silk flowers of the barest pink most unsuitable for a farm visit. Louisa idly wondered if she'd a good pair of work boots, she could provide for Miss Chandler to wear and continue wearing. But Louisa was spent and intensely given over to the thoughts that crowded her head.

"Well, Miss Chandler, to what do I owe the pleasure?"

"Miss Birch suggested I come to see you," she said, flipping her velvet hat off and tucking it under her arm. She glanced around inquisitively, as Louisa rarely invited anyone to Castle Farm, and noticed the slight pucker of Miss Chandler's nose suggestive of distaste.

"I'm about to make some coffee. Will you have some?" Louisa asked.

"A sherry might be nice. Miss April always recommends a lady to drink sherry on a visit to restore her for the return trip."

"Does she now?" Louisa said, taking up the large metal pot for coffee and filling it with water.

"Oh yes, she's very particular about it."

Mary sat, without invitation, on Louisa's armchair, the one she liked to read poetry in. It wasn't an enormous imposition, but she felt the need to coax her out of it and into the front room, where she lit a fire, all the while watching the vain Miss Chandler, fuss over a tiny piece of Hierophant's stray hair on the seat.

"I'm sure you're aware Captain Briers and I are engaged to be married," Miss Chandler said. "I trust you understand the situation."

"What situation is that, Miss Chandler?"

"Well, this awful tragedy with Miss Collier has put him off," she said. Now a line of welled-up tears appeared, and Miss Chandler reached into her lace bag to pull out a handkerchief to dab dramatically at her face.

"He must be steered back on course by a woman fully aware of how awful it is to be abandoned by a man," Miss Chandler continued.

Louisa could barely hide her irritation or confusion, but it was, after all, a pleasant, cold day outside, andshe reminded herself this was Concord. That Miss Chandler was young and in dire need of urgent guidance and had her pick of several women in Concord from whom to choose for this enlightenment. Louisa didn't reply, instead stepped as sprightly as she could manage into the kitchen, where she poured the coffee and set out—with some annoyance—her best blue filigree edged China for the visiting princess.

There was no cure for an affected woman, none that Louisa had been able to determine, and this was just another example to be endured.

"Where did you get the impression I can assist you with Captain Briers?" Louisa asked.

Miss Chandler straightened her skirt, admired her calf-skin mauve gloves, and turned to the kitchen, where Louisa appeared with a tray. "I'm afraid I don't have anything fancy," Louisa said.

"That's quite all right, Miss Alcott. To answer your question, I understand you and Captain Briers are asking questions about Miss Collier's death."

"That is correct. At least for the moment, Captain Briers is official in his capacity whereas…"

"Whereas you are one of the wiser Misses of Concord." She smiled with such force Louisa felt inclined to wipe it off her face.

"I am not one of the Misses of Concord," Louisa said. "I detest the term."

"I was paying you a compliment, Miss Alcott."

"Miss Chandler, what are you doing here?"

Mary swept herself to the middle of the room as if on stage and about to recite a soliloquy. With a majestic, irritating swing of her arms, she turned. "The curse of the Concord Misses is what I'm talking about. I'm here to avoid being one."

"There's no such thing as curses, Miss Chandler." Louisa could tell Miss Chandler would rather be Mrs. Briers, although, with this performance, Louisa was positive the girl—for that's what she was—was no more suited to marriage than a pig was to wear a crown. There was something absurd about the idea. She was permissive and insolent, with a view of the world that was dangerously naive.

"Tell me, Miss Chandler, why do you think Captain Briers is not pursuing your engagement?" Louisa asked.

"Because he's scared of Concord," she said.

"If you don't mind my saying, that makes no sense," Louisa said. "Captain Briers is a sensible, respectable man, and there must be a reason."

There was a considerable silence into which Miss Chandler's admirable display crashed and collapsed like a theatre prop. Louisa listened while spurious claim after another gushed from Mary's mouth.

"She supported it. Miss Collier was willing to do anything to help us out, and now something terrible has happened."

"Why did she change her mind?"

"Can I tell you something?"

"Yes, of course."

"You can't tell Captain Briers."

Louisa looked into Miss Chandler's eyes and now saw a child's face. A very tiresome, worried, and disappointed child.

She wrung her fingers for all they were worth, unknotting them and wrapping the string of her lace bag around the tips until they almost went blue.

"What is it, Mary?"

"I went to see Miss Collier. *After* the party."

"I see."

"She was very unpleasant. Decided the money for our wedding wasn't available, and I've never seen or heard her so awful."

"Miss Collier was most likely poisoned, Miss Chandler," Louisa said. "You see how difficult it could make things knowing you were possibly the last person to see her alive."

"You are not suggesting I murdered Miss Collier?"

"Murder, Miss Chandler," Louisa said, "is about motivation and opportunity."

Miss Chandler stood up, indignant, with a horrified, pained expression on her pale face. "I would not have come here if I'd known you'd accuse me of murder."

"I am not accusing you," Louisa said. "Tell me about the telegram." The sudden change of subject brought Miss Chandler back to her seat. Her composure returned, her bearing demure and bashful. She'd been put in her place without knowing it, and Louisa took out her stitching basket where she'd left a piece of cloth on which she practiced her woeful quilting. Without looking at Mary, she asked again. "The telegram, Miss Chandler."

Mary Chandler had the intelligence to appreciate the Captain's fatal mistake and flaw in sending such a silly message under Lucy Miller's nose, but not the wisdom to snare her mouth shut.

"I knew our secret would be discovered."

"Who else knew you were to be married?"

"My mother and father, of course. Miss Taylor." Louisa looked up, but Mary was deep in thought about who else in Concord knew of her plans. "April and June Birch."

"Did any support your engagement? That is, apart from Miss Collier?"

"Mother and father are against it. April Birch said I'd outgrow Captain Briers very quickly. I was too flighty for him, and he'd resent me." She shook her head from side to side, for this was clearly apart from the etiquette training that garnered her honest seal of approval. Louisa couldn't but agree with Miss Birch, for different reasons, but clearly, Mary Chandler was in the throes of foolish passion and lust, determined to use all her wiles to attain her goal. Louisa watched for traces of hysteria since, although she'd never profit from Miss Collier's death, it might please her to do away with her just in case. Or have the rush of satisfaction associated with meting out the ultimate penalty to a traitor. It wasn't a popular notion—women murdering—but Louisa was sure many an innocent man hung on the gallows or lay rotting in jail, permitting the actual perpetrator to roam free, accounting for her sex.

"How was Miss Collier when you left her?"

Mary hesitated and examined her hands in great detail. "Well, she was most assuredly alive."

"Don't worry, I'm just inquiring."

"Agitated."

"Agitated," Louisa repeated thoughtfully. "Was anyone else there?"

"No. We were alone."

"What was the real reason she gave for not supporting your marriage?"

"It was a mistake. I was too young, and she'd changed her mind."

"And that was it? Nothing else?"

"Nothing else," Mary said, and by now was crying, tears cascading down her face. "And Captain Briers is convinced for some reason we shouldn't be married. That all of this is some ominous sign or omen, and it's all for the best."

Not the words, Louisa thought, of a man in love. Or a rational man in the position of authority he occupied.

As if the meeting had been mildly successful, Mary dried her eyes expertly and turned to Louisa. "I should be leaving."

"If you think of anything more, Miss Chandler, about the evening of your nocturnal visit to Miss Collier, perhaps you could let me know."

"She had a visitor after me," Miss Chandler said, as though now this information might be of use—to her. "I glanced back but could not see who it was."

Louisa took this new fact with very little weight. Mary Chandler understood the gravity of her situation owing to her visit to Miss Collier and was not above providing some additional safety to her position by implicating an unknown individual.

"Can you describe what you saw?" The question predictably took Miss Chandler by surprise, who struggled to figure out if it was even a man or a woman.

"It was too dark," she replied upon being pressed by Louisa. "I was far too upset to pay attention."

Louisa put her stitching away, signaling that the meeting was ending. "Very well, Miss Chandler. But you must prepare yourself for more questions."

* * *

Mr. Jeremy Founts greeted Louisa and Captain Briers with rigid suspicion. Louisa was unimpressed by him as always, but he never ceased to shock her, and appeared to enjoy the effect his booming voice had on his visitors. He was dressed in blue tweed with a perfectly manicured beard that made him look older than his years and herded them briskly to two chairs set out in front of his desk.

"Sit," he commanded, then instructed a young man to fetch water and coffee. His office was cold and in the rafters of a former guild hall. Louisa congratulated herself for wearing suitable attire to avoid freezing to death and found thawed out in the spring. Without any concern for his visitors, apart from the light refreshment of warm—not hot—coffee, Mr. Founts took great care in recording the meeting by setting out his paper and pen in front of him.

"This is a matter of grave concern, Captain," he said once Captain Briers set out the main points behind the reason for their visit. Although there was no view from Mr. Founts' office, he rose and barreled across to the window and stood gazing out for some time.

"A miserable and odd situation."

"I am happy to continue with the investigation with the assistance of Miss Alcott," the Captain said.

Mr. Founts turned and looked over his glasses at Louisa.

"I hardly think that's appropriate," he said. "I must remove you or allow you to continue subject to certain conditions. Of course, I'd have to take over myself, which is inconvenient at the present moment."

"I assure you Miss Alcott is well-informed and capable of assisting me, and I have the utmost confidence in her judgment." Mr. Founts appeared to consider this, and Louisa tried her hardest not to fold her hands impatiently across her knees and project her disgust.

"My reservations are well founded, Captain."

"Would those reservations be greater considering the Captain's suitability?" Louisa said, cutting across the final breath of Mr. Founts' words. Mr. Founts appeared decidedly irritated by not only her presence but audacity.

"I'm not sure I understand what you mean, Miss Alcott."

"Well, if the Captain isn't able to fulfil his duties, those are the reservations that must occupy your mind. Not my suitability to assist the Captain."

"What are your precedents, Miss Alcott?"

Louisa outlined her roles as a seamstress, teacher, governess, domestic helper, and writer. "I've been a success at all of them, Mr. Founts, in particular as a writer."

"This is not silly fiction, Miss Alcott. These are not characters in some foolish novel. A woman has lost her life, and it seems *too* many women are involved as it is."

"A profoundly illogical statement, if I may say, Mr. Founts," Louisa said.

Louisa felt the Captain bristle and saw Mr. Founts' color rising above his stiff collar.

"Given the Captain's unfortunate entanglement in the matter, it would be entirely suitable for you to express your gratitude for my involvement. Instead, I found some obstruction," Louisa said.

Louisa hardly moved a muscle and stared at Mr. Founts without emotion.

"This will require careful consideration, Miss Alcott," he said in his lowest tones.

"Not too careful, Mr. Founts. As you say yourself, a woman has lost her life, and she requires burying at this point."

"Has this been arranged, Captain?" he said, barely acknowledging Louisa.

"No, Sir, it has not."

"Well, it must wait," Mr. Founts said.

"It cannot wait," Louisa interjected. "This crime is fresh, and so observing inhabitants of Concord after such a terrible act is but another part of the play, Mr. Founts. At least on the surface, Miss Collier was popular and liked in Concord."

"And murdered," Mr. Founts said.

"Yes, precisely. Murderers attend funerals. The perpetrator will be there, and the Captain and I intend to examine the event closely."

Such was the man's rudeness, he insisted they wait until he completed his notes on the matter, with Louisa and the Captain exchanging glances while Mr. Founts scratched his head and searched wildly for papers in the corner of his office.

Finally, he consulted a calendar which required spreading out on the table in front of them and inspection for a further unnecessary amount of time. He explained in tedious detail how he'd personally attend Miss Collier's funeral out of respect and professional curiosity.

"We must prepare ourselves for the possibility of another tragedy," Louisa said as they walked to the front entrance.

Mr. Founts, who appeared to find her considerably more agreeable, stopped and frowned. "On what basis do you make that assumption?"

"I'm not assuming anything. There can be consequences following such an act."

* * *

In the carriage back to Concord, the Captain was strangely quiet, watching the bare trees and slivers of early afternoon mist passing them by with the carriage window open full. On the approach to Market Street, he finally closed it and leaned back into the safety and anonymity of the leather seats. They didn't escape the beady eyes of Mr. Miller, who was standing outside his office, taking in the weak sunshine and fragrant scents of the early evening. He appeared to be wielding Miss Collier's poetry book and stood right out in front of the carriage, which came to a shuddering halt.

"I must have a word with you, Miss Alcott." He stared with unreserved suspicion at Captain Briers, not a helpful reaction in a murder investigation, Louisa thought. Captain Briers nodded in Louisa's direction, and she assured him out of earshot she would discuss the structure of their duties later, which would now include this urgent demand of Mr. Miller.

As previously indicated by Miss April Birch, Mr. Miller enjoyed his comforts. Nothing austere about the homely aspect of his principal place of business. It was intimate without being overly familiar and provided a most assuring level of privacy. Mr. Miller retained a reception area that resembled a small day room, complete with buttoned leather chairs, a low wooden table, and a footstool. A modest fire simmered in the fireplace, and a large decanter of what Louisa assumed was Bourbon seemed available to all visiting. Perhaps to steady frayed nerves or calm divisive situations, which appeared to Louisa astute and appropriate given Mr. Miller's line of work. Louisa helped herself to a tiny glass to assure Mr. Miller she was trustworthy, but did not drink any, and Mr. Miller appeared at his office door and invited her in.

He took his glasses off and laid them in front of him, rubbing his eyes furiously and helping himself to an alarming amount of sour mash. Bourbon

51

was the only ingredient which would help.

"Miss Alcott, my position in this community is one of trust," he began as if reciting a carefully rehearsed speech. "There's disquiet about Concord at the moment that can't be silenced."

He pulled open a drawer and took out a piece of crumpled paper.

"My wife received this today." He got up and wandered to the window, giving her time to read it and study the contents of cut-out letters from the *Concord Sentinel*. It simply read, *"YOU ARE NEXT."* Over dramatic, Louisa figured and certainly didn't require the time Mr. Miller loitered at the window.

"Your wife had a good relationship with Miss Collier?" Louisa asked.

Mr. Miller sat down again, allowing himself another dram before pursing his lips and clearing his throat.

"Acquaintances, Miss Alcott. There is no earthly reason my wife should be threatened."

"And yet, she appears to be. Have you told anyone about this?"

"Except for you, no one. Of course, she shouldn't have divulged the telegram Captain Briers sent to Mary Chandler, but it was hand-delivered. Any number of people could have seen it before it arrived at the Chandler home."

"Captain Briers has admitted his faulty judgment on this, Mr. Miller. We have seen his superiors, and I am to assist the investigation," Louisa said.

"There is a funeral to be had, Miss Alcott. There is a will to be read, and I assure you I am not relishing any of it."

"Why?"

"Miss Collier and several unmarried women in Concord hold a significant portion of the town's property through inheritance. Miss Collier was a very wealthy woman, Miss Alcott, and I believe her untimely demise is everything to do with that."

"Who benefits, Mr. Miller?"

Mr. Miller snorted with pride. "I will not disclose anything in light of recent events where such information isn't treated with the confidence it requires."

"You're not suggesting, Mr. Miller, I divulge confidences?"

"Hold the funeral, and the will can be read. I've nothing further to say on the matter." He glanced down at the paper in front of Louisa.

"If Mrs. Miller wishes to see me in private, it can be arranged," Louisa said.

"Mrs. Miller has nothing to add to this, Miss Alcott."

"It would be useful if she could provide that confirmation voluntarily, Mr. Miller."

Despite his modernity, Mr. Miller was just like any other husband in his determination to answer for his wife.

"Is there some reason she can't see me? Is she hysterical with fear and taken to her bed?" Louisa leaned forward and enjoyed Mr. Miller's poker-faced reaction.

"My wife is not hysterical."

"Thank goodness for that. I was hoping that would be the case. I'm free in the morning; tell your wife to come to see me."

"She is rather put out by the childishness of this anonymous note," Mr. Miller said, returning to the letter's subject. "I would have thought the author is fishing for a reaction."

"My feelings exactly, Mr. Miller." Unless, of course, Mrs. Miller was hiding something, she wished to add. Louisa rose with some difficulty and felt the irritation across the table. Mr. Miller was not accustomed to having his meetings cut short, as evidenced by his quick movements to the doorway, shielding Louisa's exit for one last moment of her time. "I take it Captain Briers has recovered from his infatuation?"

"Sufficiently so to carry out his duties with admirable professionalism."

"And you're satisfied he will carry out his duties?"

"Yes, of course, Mr. Miller."

"I'll see to it Mrs. Miller visits you in the morning."

Mrs. Miller Asks a Question

A ferocious storm ripped through Concord that night. Louisa was forced to walk the distance from Market Street out past North Bridge, where the river swelled with rain like a slow-moving snake from the mountains. The wind picked up, blowing her about as she made the final way to her door at Castle Farm. By the time Louisa reached it, the rain had lashed in straight, heavy rods about her, making it almost impossible to see anything. Although not given to cursing, she made an exception in Mr. Miller's case, who'd assured her he was too busy to arrange a carriage up to the farm, preferring she not wait in the building until his last client left.

Louisa's curiosity was aroused by his indifference to her plight in favor of seeing a mystery guest. Now, she realized with much discomfort, that being on the opposing side of the investigation with Captain Briers caused some suspicion amongst the residents. She could barely think with the rattling windowpanes and Hierophant's digging claws with each flash of lightning. Finally, it eased, and Louisa fell into a heavy sleep, waking to a frosty sunrise that melted on the window in tiny droplets. It wasn't freezing, but something had woken her. Hierophant was rolled into the covers, sound asleep. The wind had died to a rustle, and Louisa realized she'd been startled by a knock. At first, it was soft and insistent, but by the time she'd arisen out of the bed, it was an undignified banging.

"Miss Alcott," an urgent voice said.

As the hand lifted to assault the door with a further bang, Louisa pulled it open, finding Mrs. Miller standing blue-lipped and frazzled before her. She brushed past, foisting her arms upwards, removing her gloves, and looking around with about as much attention to detail as she could manage while searching out the most comfortable seat to position herself for this urgent meeting.

"I'm afraid you've caught me asleep," Louisa said. "Make yourself at home."

"I will, thank you," Mrs. Miller said with a curtness Louisa found unsettling. Louisa made coffee with all the hurry of a snail because Mrs. Miller demanded attention from the living room with a series of huffs and puffs and tongue clicking, so rude and so early in the morning. Louisa felt no need to be civil.

"Did you bring the anonymous letter?" Louisa said, finally depositing a tray of her chipped crockery to a table nearby with a crash. She poured, sugared, and milked the coffee, handing it to Mrs. Miller, who had the nerve to glare at her and her abandoned manners. She was dressed for a funeral—already—like she couldn't wait to get it all over with.

"My husband informed me he showed you last night."

"Is this inconvenient for you, Mrs. Miller? We can meet later if it suits your mood better."

"There is nothing wrong with my mood, Miss Alcott, apart from this scandalous and infantile communication. Honestly, I'm perplexed."

She turned the cup around to avoid the large crack above the owl effigy and glanced with distaste at the plain bread Louisa left to cut in squares beside it.

"In fact, I'm quite beyond annoyed at such behavior."

"I'm assisting Captain Briers with his endeavors, and it would help me greatly to know the circumstances of this correspondence," Louisa said.

"Correspondence implies friendship and reciprocation. This is nothing of the sort." She put her cup down and searched her bag, pulling out the offending paper.

"I defended Miss Collier against the slurs and accusations thrown at her for as long as I can remember. If I am next, then I sincerely hope you, Miss Alcott, will find the time to discover why before this lunatic has her way," Mrs. Miller continued.

Louisa put her hand out gently to pry the paper from Mrs. Miller's tight grasp.

'If being nice to someone is so offensive to this murderer, then I would like to know why they're still on the loose."

"You said, has *her* way, Mrs. Miller," Louisa said, glancing up from the paper. "You think whoever poisoned Miss Collier is a woman?"

Mrs. Miller rose from her seat as if the question was an invitation for her to walk out.

"Miss Alcott, it is quite obvious the perpetrator of this heinous act is one of the Misses of Concord. I have a husband, and it seems to offend almost all the unattached creatures in Concord, many of whom crawled out of their lonesome boudoirs to attend Miss Collier's celebration. I may have been a little negligent in mentioning the contents of Captain Brier's telegram, but the seriousness of it cannot be underestimated."

"So, you have no reason to believe you're next for some particular part you've played?"

"You have an insane lunatic on your hands, Miss Alcott. The sooner you find out why, the better. Although this," she said, grabbing the paper out of Louisa's hands, "indicates a state of mind so deranged it might be impossible."

"Did you notice anything at Miss Collier's celebration which caused you concern?"

"There was some frostiness between Miss Nash and Evie Briers," she said, her tone softening. "Miss Murdock talked conspiratorially with Miss Chandler while that flagrantly unbearable Miss Taylor showed up for a start to ensure we all saw her new winter coat and promptly left."

"How did Miss Taylor seem?"

Mrs. Miller pursed her lips and allowed a frown to spread gently across her infuriated features while thinking carefully.

"Like she always seems, Miss Alcott. As disconcerting as ever with a smug look on her face." She was now staring into the distance, and Louisa remained silent.

"She isn't an open person. It's as if she's hiding something or evading conversation." Mrs. Miller said.

"How do you mean?"

"When she heard Miss Collier was dead, she wondered where she'd get her honey from." Mrs. Miller smiled, despite herself. It was an interesting, if inappropriate, conundrum.

"And why is that hiding something?"

Mrs. Miller grimaced with impatience. "Really, Miss Alcott, you're not doing very well at this, are you? Miss Taylor employs a second meaning in everything she says, and I do not believe good morning from her mouth."

"She struck me from what little I've spoken to her as private."

"Conniving Miss Alcott. You are making a fundamental mistake about Miss Taylor. Her outings about town are always very public and loaded with some purpose, and the sister she writes to has yet to make an appearance."

"She may be unwell or living very far away," Louisa said.

"Or imaginary," Mrs. Miller said with a sly grin. "I don't wish to implicate Miss Taylor without any evidence, but I believe you must start with her."

"She claims she was unwell the night of Miss Collier's party, and you've said yourself she left almost immediately."

"I said she showed up for a start. I don't keep a roll call at social gatherings, do you, Miss Alcott? I suppose your problem is anyone could have done it."

Louisa considered this and offered to pour more coffee, which Mrs. Miller declined with an apologetic nod of her head.

"Are you aware of any unusual facts about Concord, Mrs. Miller? Or unusual communications similar to that sent by Captain Briers."

"There are unsubstantiated whisperings that Miss Taylor and Edward Lounsey are overly familiar with each other. Of course, Miss Taylor is allergic to females once a man is close by, all the better if he's rich. Edward doesn't exactly fit the description, but you are aware, of course, that Edward's farm relies on Miss Collier's farm for access to the main road. Well, are you?"

"Yes, he told me himself," Louisa said. Mrs. Miller's eyes widened. "I see, but I also assume you know Miss Collier had agreed to sell the farm to Edward. I do not wish to betray my husband's confidence, but Miss Taylor attended on occasion in respect of their meetings."

"What sort of meetings?" Louisa asked.

"Negotiations, Miss Alcott, were at an advanced stage. Miss Taylor showed her face at the final few, but something went wrong."

"I've said to Edward Lounsey already that it was really Miss Collier's decision to sell or not," Louisa said.

"Yes, but changing one's mind at the very last minute creates bad blood, Miss Alcott. And after that telegram business, my husband arrived back late. Drunk. It's not that unusual, but I'd an idea that Miss Taylor visited him."

"Oh, dear, you're not suggesting anything improper?"

Mrs. Miller recoiled back and pulled her handbag close as if to shield herself from what she alone must say. "Yes, Miss Alcott, I am suggesting it. A wife knows her own husband even if he doesn't."

"And this doesn't alarm you in any way?"

"My marriage to Mr. Miller is assured by other means, Miss Alcott. The allures of the Miss Taylors of this world are never far away, so I've prepared to be amicable in the face of such complications." She began putting her gloves back on and fixing her attire, brushing imaginary crumbs to the floor. "If she or Edward is not the murderer, Miss Alcott, some business involving them is sure to bring you closer to the culprit."

* * *

It was still early when Mrs. Lucy Miller made her way out of Castle Farm and into Concord, leaving Louisa with her chores undone, which didn't bother her in the slightest. A watery sun struggled up from the horizon, and by the time she'd made more coffee, it cast a yellow film over her pigsty, where she observed Danny and Doodle panting gently, turned upside down on their backs with pure joy. Which only served to remind her that April and June Birch were required to make themselves available for yet another discussion on Concord's Choral Society row. It occurred to Louisa that she must establish what each participant in Miss Collier's soiree was doing at any given moment.

She pulled an old diary off the bookshelf given to her by Thoreau on why men kill. Of course, women kill also, but it takes a particular type of woman to engage in murder. The nature of the crime, which she'd given much thought to but applied hardly any theoretical wonder, bore all the hallmarks of someone desperate to conceal their identity. Especially in a small community. The party—for which she was increasingly irritated she'd missed—seemed to present the only opportunity in a village where everyone was aware, at the very least, of some of the participants' movements and business.

Thoreau shed very little light on the murderous qualities of women. It maddened her, quite irrationally, that this should be the case in light of her desire to wring the neck of some residents she'd had the misfortune to cross. John, the baker, for instance. She'd lowered herself to an intolerable level for the sake of assisting his ignorant daughter to compose a letter of recommendation for a finishing school in Boston. Her advice—to show some spirit and toughen up made John remark that his daughter was going there to find a husband—preferably rich—not supervise railway chain gangs.

She looked into her bowl of beaten eggs, frothing white and bubbling up as though alive, and realized something very sinister. To conjure up the simplest anger and execute the distant plan from sheer hatred was so quickly done. Men would indeed attack in the heat of the moment and bring with them the misfortune of being discovered. Still, if she chose to, she could slip some poison into her mixture, leaving some leeway with the liquid so it still gazed upwards appetizingly, offering it with a smile to the unsuspecting victim. The revengeful ardor would subside, but with the plan in motion, her casual and pleasant mask would disguise the dreadful deed.

Louisa stared into the sticky eggs and realized it was the distance. The fearless motive to kill combined with the tremendous knowledge that regret would surely never come. If it did, they could suffer in silence and away from the heat of the crime itself. The murderer simply didn't even have to be there. And so, Miss Collier's murderer put the plan into motion so very early, or at least with some surreptitious manoeuvring, could administer the poison well before the first bite of a luscious piece of cake would ever be taken. And Miss Collier would bid her guests goodnight—possibly curse them a little—and take to her seat to rest herself. The feeling of illness must have gradually come over her until it completely engulfed her senses, perhaps disabling her sufficiently to avoid calling out. At which time it would be too late.

Stiff as a sheet on a winter clothesline, she'd be there, discovered eventually by a kindly neighbor about some other business, and the shock would reverberate, and the mystery deepen. The killer might have any combination of motives, swimming along many in a vast whirlpool of accusation.

Louisa retired to her bedroom and put on her best clothes for the approaching, deeply unnerving December. She had to concentrate on these instinctive pulses and listen to their desired outcomes as they flowed with logic and reason. Thoreau would disapprove, but however strict his theories were, a little more imagination was required when it came to this heinous, cold-blooded attack on a woman who so mildly irritated people it was difficult to imagine she would be callously done away with. Laid before her was the diary, its yellowing pages musty and thin with use. She found something she disagreed with: a slight provocation was not sufficient. Nor was it slightly aimed at a man's honor in some mysterious way. This was so personal an affront committed by Miss Collier—be it known to her or not—she would be unaware of the effect it had on the perpetrator. This indifference, not from a lack of empathy but ignorance, would drive the murderer insane with anger. Delivered with such determination, such a need to ensure Miss Collier's final moments would not only be spent alone, but thoroughly tortuous.

She slammed Thoreau's journal shut. It was of little use to her now, and a tiny victory swelled within her. A small amount of pride pushed itself upwards. She had formed her very own theory, and now, with just as much fervor, she would document her findings in a diary and take enormous pleasure lecturing the bewildered folk of Concord when she exposed the murderer.

Miss Birch Investigates a Robbery

With a measure of assistance from some nettle soup, Louisa felt adequately fortified to burden herself with a visit to Hangman's Cottage. She knocked twice—hearing raised voices inside and finally pushed the door open, standing in the hallway listening. This approach felt highly risky given the nature of the conversation she was about to overhear, but formed part of the instructions she allowed herself to follow from part two of Thoreau's theories. An innocent bystander must overhear and eavesdrop on snatches of deliberations, especially if one is bound to an investigation.

"Really, Miss Murdock, you can't hurl accusations around like this," April Birch said, an ominous tone to her voice. "Do you honestly believe I would disturb the school records, or June here would have the energy to steal the school roof money?"

There was a silence—not a particularly encouraging one—and Louisa maintained her distance, now almost afraid of what her intrusion might signal. A cork was pulled loudly from a bottle, and Louisa heard pouring.

"Miss Collier withdrew her financial support from the Choral Society, and you, with all those airs and graces, haven't a bean. Everyone knows it."

"Do they now?" June's shrill and weedy voice rose up. "It's a pity you're the only one with access to the school records now, isn't it, Miss Murdock? An even greater pity we don't need Miss Collier's paltry donations to the Society."

"That's not what I heard, Miss Birch," Miss Murdock announced. "If you must lounge about drenched in sherry all day, surely your remuneration won't last long."

There was a movement, and Louisa realized it was time to announce her presence before the matter spilled along a different path, bounding out of control and likely to distress the occupants.

Louisa cleared her throat and entered the room, lifting her hand a little weakly to indicate the door had been, in fact, left open. All three sat around a roaring fire, Miss April Birch's face high in color as though the gathering was already distressing to her. June Birch sat across their low-slung, baggy sofa with one foot tucked under her. She was attired in a silk dressing gown, her dark hair tied up directly on top of her head, a scowl of disapproval souring her face. There was silence.

"The door was open," Louisa said and innocently installed herself down the way from June Birch, who simply turned the other way.

"We're discussing a matter of theft, Miss Alcott," April said, fluttering her arms about and pouring a sherry. "Sherry?"

Miss Murdock stiffened and clasped her hands ever more tightly on her lap. "For heaven's sake, April," she said. "Can't you have a sober conversation?"

"This is my house, Miss Murdock, and you have come with nothing but shocking accusations."

"What theft?" Louisa asked, refusing Sherry.

"The school records have been tampered with, and the roof money pilfered from the same cabinet."

Louisa pretended she didn't really understand what Miss Murdock would be doing at the Birch's cottage, and she was inclined to agree with the earlier part of the conversation.

"Miss Murdock's fantasy is that I—or June—took the money destined for the school roof. Miss Collier did rescind her agreement to fund the Choral Society, but really, music sheets are not that expensive," April said.

"Sherry is expensive," Miss Murdock persisted. "And by the looks of this place, it's screaming for a little care and attention, which you seem incapable of providing."

"And what business is it of yours?" June retaliated, pulling her leg out from under her and standing up. "How are we supposed to have carried out this monstrous plan?"

Miss Murdock's mouth pursed, and she seemed ready to leave, so sure of the threat of exposure and the facts. "You were seen near the school very early, the day the money was stolen," Miss Murdock said, glancing in April's direction. "I was very distracted by the inspector's visit, and Miss Alcott herself was there."

"I was nowhere near the school," April Birch said. "It is preposterous to suggest that I would steal anything."

"Well then, where were you, April?" Louisa asked.

"I was here, Miss Alcott."

Miss Murdock sighed loudly and squeezed her hands into her gloves with an apathetic look on her face.

"We have been raising that money since last Christmas, Miss Alcott," Miss Murdock said, as though that added something to the mystery. "It's a substantial sum."

"Why not put the money in Concord Bank, Miss Murdock? It seems that plenty of people knew you kept it at the school?" Louisa said.

"Exactly, Miss Alcott," June said. "That is precisely my point. April was feeling depressed that day and never left the house for any reason. She couldn't have been at the school, and everyone in Concord knew the school roof funds were kept there. It's simply not fair of her to suggest such a heinous act."

"The records, Miss Murdock?"

"They were not stolen, Miss Alcott. They were rifled through.'

"What could someone possibly be looking for?"

"They might have disturbed them looking for the money, but the way they were jumbled about suggests something else," Miss Murdock said.

"Perhaps the burglary was intended to divert attention away."

Miss Murdock's face darkened with obvious impatience.

"This is a pointless and ridiculous conversation, Miss Alcott. It's quite clear to me that the person who disturbed the records, stole the money, and Miss Birch here was seen."

"By whom," Louisa said.

"I will have the person verify the sighting all in good time. I feel no reason whatsoever to continue this preposterous meeting. I bid you good day."

All three women waited until the front door shut, but Louisa took the liberty of checking to ensure Miss Murdock was gone. There was a significant silence, and June Birch rose and asked aggressively, "Would you have some coffee, Miss Alcott?"

"Yes, that's an excellent idea, Miss Birch," Louisa said. "I shouldn't wonder we could all do with some after that encounter." She glanced briefly at April Birch, who appeared highly worked up and distant at the same time, nervously twisting her beads about her neck.

"Why would Miss Murdock imply you were at the school April if you were not," Louisa asked finally. "It seems an unusual accusation, to say the least."

April moved forward in the chair, her attention entirely fixed on Louisa. "I have not the slightest idea what she's talking about, and it's quite clear to me June is not taken to wandering about Concord or sneaking about like a burglar either."

"She appeared adamant," Louisa said.

"Well, I'm telling you, it's simply not possible," June said, hauling a tray from the kitchen and giving April a poisonous stare. Louisa took this as some kind of signal, but it was difficult to unravel the meaning and put some interpretation on it. June proved surprisingly gentle about serving the coffee, even glancing at Louisa with a warm smile as she placed the cup beside her.

"I must ask," Louisa said, "about your finances. To what was Miss Murdock referring?"

"I can be of assistance here," April said with an insincere smile. June supervised her actions and movements and chose to fix her neutral stare on her sister with an intensity Louisa found unnerving.

"Miss Murdock is an unfortunate woman, Miss Alcott," April said. "She likes to imagine the wealthy, unattached women of Concord are as poor as she is. The truth is that Miss Collier and her ilk—us, for instance, are well accounted for. Miss Murdock masks her dissatisfaction with her position beneath the cloak of drudgery and vocation."

"She seems dedicated," Louisa said.

April laughed and then frowned into her coffee. "Dedication, Miss Alcott is the child of necessity in this instance. Miss Murdock has no choice but dedication to her children," she said. "None of which are her own," she added, taking a tortuous sip from her cup. "I would imagine also she's lovesick these, oh, twenty years for a certain Mr. Miller."

Louisa saw June flinch. "More coffee, Louisa?"

"Lovesick? For Mr. Miller?"

"Oh, quite. Of course, as we all know, love isn't enough, is it, Miss Alcott?"

"I'm sure I don't know."

"We all know good matches, particularly in marriage, are more complicated than love followed by an ostentatious wedding. In this case, Mr. Miller is a man of commerce and business given over to the facade of respectability with an undercurrent of mischief."

Louisa didn't need to consider this too deeply as it was pretty obvious to her that Mr. Miller was a man open to the possibility of marriage, which on the surface made perfect sense but allowed him a certain freedom. Mrs. Miller had all but conceded this fact during their meeting. There was enough of this sentiment coursing through Concord's veins to enable her to fully appreciate the tone, if not the ultimate meaning of April's words. Matters of the heart were a mystery to Louisa, who'd all but decided she was better off on her own. Perhaps she understood the implications so well it seemed hard to consider it from another perspective. The distraction wore off immediately.

"Yes, but why accuse you of stealing the school money?"

"If you want my honest opinion, Miss Alcott, Miss Murdock's main concern here is the records. I believe I know when Miss Murdock is suffering such astonishment, anything is possible to drop right from her mouth. I've seen it before."

"Really," Louisa said. "You must enlighten me."

"April," June said ominously.

"Be quiet, little bird," April said.

"You've seen this before?" Louisa said, steering April back to her subject.

"Last year at the Concord Festival, she lost her mind with Mrs. Miller."

"Married to the man she desired so long ago," Louisa said.

"Yes, but this was about something so trivial it is difficult to imagine anyone being so utterly ridiculous about it." Louisa continued to hold April's attention. She didn't like being kept waiting, but it seemed to be worth it.

"The children were about to sing the opening introduction as they always do with the Festival. We have to cooperate with Miss Murdock on this issue every year, and it seems only right, of course. Mrs. Miller was late and innocently forgot to close the door on her way in. Miss Murdock lost all reason."

"For not closing the door?"

"That's only part of it, Miss Alcott. Yes, she forgot the door, and since we were all facing up to the stage to see the children, it was only after some ferocious whispering that those at the back became aware of a row."

June poured more coffee, eyeing her sister warily. "Don't forget the other part, April."

"Well, it went on and on, Miss Murdock ignoring the parent's pleas for her to hush while the children concentrated on performing, and even June here, who directs the children up front, turned around."

"Is this true, June?" Louisa asked.

"Yes. I'm afraid it created quite a distraction for us. When I direct Miss Alcott, I do so with precision and passion, and the children can't be disturbed as they're so young."

"Afterwards," April said, cutting across June, "some donation envelopes were empty." She nodded in Louisa's direction as though this should mean something. "Ripped open with such force, it could only be an opportunistic robber with very little time."

"And you saw nothing?" Louisa asked.

"Well, how could I? The door was open. You're familiar with the town hall, Miss Alcott. It is bad manners to lock latecomers out if they're orderly and polite, and when the news came out of the theft, I see Miss Murdock's face enraged, holding Mrs. Miller by the arm."

"You can't think that Miss Murdock had anything to do with it?"

"I very much think she did. We may profess what we like in this life, Miss Alcott, but it does not make us practice it."

"What exactly do you mean, Miss Birch?"

"My meaning should be obvious, and Miss Murdock's demonstrations of outrage should be taken very lightly. If you place the blame on another individual, the dye is cast, and very little will budge any conclusions reached. I do not go about Concord accusing people in their own homes of crimes without the slightest evidence. But yet here you are, questioning myself and my sister about it. Surely, I've made my point about Miss Murdock?"

"Which, of course, means Miss Murdock is equally capable of being the perpetrator of such crimes she accuses others of," June said. "My sister, for once, is correct, Miss Alcott, and she has already planted the idea in your mind that we're impoverished."

"And heinous lying, pilferers," April added.

Just as April finished, a soft knock fell on the door, and they all turned around.

"Come in, Evie," April said. Evie Briers seemed lost in thought as she pushed the door open to find the three women seated and staring at her. Evie's face was ashen, and rather than walking in, she shuffled with some invisible weight, pressing her down like a mighty burden.

"I can come back later if this is a bad time," she said to June Birch.

"Not at all, Evie," April said. "Miss Alcott was just discussing the robbery in Concord School of the roof funds." The news startled Evie, who felt for a chair and succeeded in sitting down, her face draining further of color.

"I wouldn't think you've heard that news." June got up from her chair and brought Evie a cup of water, stroking the woman's arm with affection. Evie's hands trembled so much she could barely move. June seemed perfectly capable of putting Evie at ease, which in Louisa's eyes seemed to suggest Evie was in no fit state to be venturing out of Kame Bluff. There was something quietly hysterical about Evie Briers, and although not qualified to make such a diagnosis, she felt the need to, given the current circumstances.

After a few awkward moments, June got up abruptly and pulled Louisa by the arm into the parlor.

"I do apologize, Miss Alcott, but Evie is rather frail of late," she said. She'd lowered her voice to conspiratorial levels, her dark eyes flashing.

"What is she doing here?" Louisa asked. "She isn't in any humor to be wandering about."

"Well, the truth is she's helping us domestically," June said. "Frankly, neither myself nor April are very good."

"But surely Captain Briers can see she's not well?"

"She asked for the position," June said. "I suspect she needs the additional income."

Louisa said nothing to this as it was clear June Birch was sympathetic to her predicament. Why would a woman want to engage in such work when Captain Briers clearly had a duty to provide for her, mainly as older age approached? It didn't sit right with Louisa, but she felt there had to be another reason. A darker one, altogether more imperative than she'd first realized.

"I was saying to Evie you'd joined the Captain in the hunt for Miss Collier's killer," April said. Evie seemed upset and hunched over herself like she wanted to disappear.

"Isn't that right, Evie?"

"Do leave her be," June said. "She's tired, aren't you, Evie?"

"Scout is dead," Evie said in a tiny voice. "I killed him." In several stuttering sentences, Evie recounted the episode with the oat squares and Scout's disappearance. It was so disjointed that Louisa found it testing to follow what with the sobbing that ensued as she explained how Captain Briers had to bury the poor animal. Her heartache softened—and silenced—April Birch.

"Where did the oat squares come from, Evie?" Louisa asked, just to be sure. "Did you make them?"

"Miss Nash." This statement brought a fresh flow of tears, the onslaught progressing to an occasional quiet hiccup. It was genuinely undignified, Louisa thought. Miss Nash was not on Louisa's mind, and now it dawned on her the murder instrument might have been found. It was as she imagined it.

"Good Lord," April said, finally reaching for more sherry. "You must answer Miss Alcott's questions, Evie, should she have any." She fanned herself dramatically, puffing her cheeks in and out.

"Not now, please, April," June said. "She's said quite enough."

"You just tell her June she must answer any questions. Miss Alcott?" Louisa felt their eyes on her but reluctantly allowed herself some moments to consider Evie Briers' story.

"This isn't a good time," Louisa said.

"What?" April said, her voice shrieking it out again, this time accompanied by a wild waving of arms. "You must find out all there is to know about these oat squares," April said. "I'm thinking of never eating again after hearing this awful tale. Perhaps we should insist the Festival be canceled altogether lest one of us is injured by the communal punch."

"Be quiet," June said. "Haven't you said enough already?"

"I must ask you both about the Choral Society," Louisa said. April blew through her cheeks like a train coming to a halt.

"I believe we've already explained that Miss Collier's death puts us to some inconvenience, Miss Alcott, so murdering her in cold blood doesn't seem to have done us any good," April said, finally. "Neither were her meager donations of much use in the overall scheme. We are far from destitute and not nearly as interested in slaying an innocent woman as you might think."

June patted Evie Briers' shaking shoulders and said, "April is right, Miss Alcott. We simply can't have had anything to do with Miss Collier's death."

After this rather convincing display, Louisa needed some sleep. By the time the early afternoon sun tarnished into wintry gold, word had spread around Concord that Miss Collier would be laid to rest the following day.

Miss Collier's Sleepy Hollow

Louisa woke the day of Miss Collier's funeral with no expectation of a typical ceremony. Premonitions struck in the early morning when the moon was still high in the sky and cold permeated her bones. She'd been terrorized by the most awful dreams, wandering in pain down narrow, dark corridors with a single light evading her each time she reached it. The more she stumbled, the tighter the pain in her forehead became until she'd stirred awake, unable to lift her head from the pillow. Once, it was her pleasure to run in the forest or up the mountainous trails. Now, her body barely responded to her calls for action.

These horrors that afflicted her started with her illness, one which almost killed her, and there were times she wished it had. With this thought lingering, she closed her eyes and begged forgiveness of herself, if nothing else, for such a prayer could quickly be answered with such tragic consequences. The mysterious headaches she suffered would abate, if she thought differently about them instead of allowing them to fill her with weary regret. They seemed to accumulate at night, rapidly, while dissipating in the morning like burnt-off fog. The pleasure of this was matched only by the accompanying weariness and exhaustion she encountered, but this left her. Decent food and a boiling pot of coffee in front of a fire would satisfy most of her needs.

Louisa avoided Doctor Jennings as much as possible, and since her arrival, nothing was so awful she needed to seek his advice. He preferred not to mix his domestic affairs with that of his profession and, in keeping with the more modern trends, kept a surgery of two rooms on Market Street, in which, rumor had it, he spent most of his time avoiding his wife. Louisa arrived early, just as the headache which had persisted so long into the night vanished.

"You have no appointment?" he said, staring vacantly at a journal on the table. He took his glasses off and cleaned them, then rubbed his forehead as if inundated with patients. "My secretary is given over to the ridiculous grief engulfing the whole town at the moment."

"Ridiculous grief?" Louisa said, seating herself behind the partner's desk. She glanced at the open leather appointment book with its neat columns and red iterations.

"Well, I suspect, like most of Concord, she is keen to ensure she's dead." He smiled at his own joke. A rather handsome man he was, with clean blond cornflower hair and large blue eyes.

"Who is your secretary, Doctor?" Louisa asked, looking around the office. "Your wife?"

"My wife doesn't engage in menial work, Miss Alcott. She's a homemaker."

"I see," she said. "So, well, who is it then?"

"Is there something medical I can assist you with?"

"No, actually, I suddenly feel quite well,'" she said. "I am assisting Captain Briers in the matter of Miss Collier's death, which we are certain is unnatural." Doctor Jennings sniffed and removed his glasses again.

"Apparently, my talents as a humble doctor don't stretch to establishing a cause of death. I even get the odd cat or dog in here instead of humans." For which Louisa quite understood to mean the vet, James Parsons wasn't up to the task due to his adoration of whiskey, which competed with April Birch's fondness for sherry.

"Miss Nash is my secretary. She helps out when she's not at school. Administrative talent isn't widely available in Concord." Louisa allowed this to register slowly rather than giving the Doctor any cause for alarm. For sure, Miss Nash would be aware of ailments that afflicted the residents of Concord, if nothing else. Such private information could be helpful—to a murderer.

"Is Miss Taylor a patient?" Louisa asked. What was that? A blush? Indeed not, but there it was. A slight coloring on the Doctor's cheek.

"I cannot discuss patients with you, Miss Alcott. You know that."

"It's Louisa," she said. "I just wondered if you saw her the day of Miss Collier's party."

He opened his journal up and ran his finger down several columns. "Yes, Miss Taylor was here that day." And which meant Miss Taylor was lying.

"Why?"

"I cannot tell you that."

"Everyone, it seems, has heard about Miss Taylor's infamous digestion problems, but none have seen her actually suffering from it. I merely ask because everyone in Concord knows about my stiff limbs and incapacitating headaches," Louisa said.

"I can tell you she has had a child, and I can tell you she is a shameless woman."

"Shameless?"

"She lacks common decency and imagines every man is besotted by her. I don't like having her as a patient. An extraordinary and uncomfortable state of affairs."

"Was Miss Collier a patient?"

"Yes."

"Well, she is due for burial today. Surely, she won't object if I ask to see her details?"

He returned to his office and repeatedly sighed, with the door open as he retrieved Miss Collier's details. "I have given this to Captain Briers already, and he found nothing of use."

She was about to agree with Captain Briers when something caught her eye. "Why was she taking honey, peppermint, and baking soda?"

"She didn't like traditional remedies, so I told her to try those for a sore throat."

Louisa thought about this for a moment.

"Is there anything else that's not in her details that would be relevant?"

"Well, yes, there is actually. I wanted to treat painful skin flare-ups Miss Collier was having with oats."

"I see. Please continue."

"She said they didn't agree with her."

"Any particular reason?"

"Well, we know something about reactions to certain things but little about why it happens. Apparently, when oats are eaten by certain individuals, they can't breathe and take days to recover."

Louisa returned Miss Collier's details, unsure what use the information was. Perhaps it would become more apparent, and when she had time to fully consider it, the meaning would appear.

"One more thing, Doctor," Louisa said before inflicting her medical problems upon him. "Are you sure Miss Taylor had a child?"

He let out an exasperated sigh. "There are certain procedures and information I need to know. So, I am certain there is a child."

Doctor Jennings scratched his head and wondered out loud if Louisa was imagining her own ailments, which she disliked intensely since his presumptions tended towards diagnosis of a form of hysteria.

She reminded him there were doctors for brain disorders and the like, none of which related to her physical symptoms, which clarified her opinion of him as a patronizing man capable of being just about anybody's husband. She felt entitled to dismiss his diagnosis based on rational thought, which ironically hadn't seemed to cross his mind. It seemed to her that if a doctor kept you alive, his job was done. Living was the problem. Existing within the walls of pain, confined to a misery thrust upon you, seemed unfair to Louisa. Some sympathy or relief would have encouraged her opinion of him to more benign feelings but at that precise moment she despised him intensely.

* * *

After her walk home, she rested her head on a pillow on her couch, feeling the soothing heat of Hierophant against her leg, and thought about the information the day would bring. From the warmth of her seat beside the fire, she opened her eyes halfway and saw it was bright. Clean, light clouds of snow dust spread across the meadow like refined sugar, glistening under the low sun. Despite herself, she enjoyed a brisk, frosty funeral. The thought seemed so selfish and unrestrained, but with it came a certain warm feeling that spread slowly. The body put into the ground was an important passage for the dead and bereaved, leaving no room for uncertainty.

Most, however, were inclined towards the quiet and befitting, whereas Miss Collier's journey to the soil was not so straightforward. It was this part that conflicted with her rational self, the part that couldn't be resolved even if Miss Collier's murderer was discovered. No death was perfect in the same way as no life was perfect, and Louisa tried to remember this until it brought new feelings. A life lived and death endured. The deserved end was unattainable, and the unpleasant idea of how it manifests itself in a murdered soul was even more unsettling.

How many people died a peaceful death who'd lived terrible lives? How many people died a horrific death who'd led peaceful lives? Perhaps Miss Collier's murderer would have a peaceful death free from pain and illness, swift and uncompromising. Was this deserved? Or were the final moments of Miss Collier's untimely death less awful than what lay further down the natural course for her?

Louisa realized she was being selfish again as thoughts of her fate crowded her mind. She rose quickly, ignoring her joints, and pushed the back door open onto the cold, dark corner of Castle Farm. Under a patch of dreary sun, Danny and Doodle lay huddling against each other at first glance like one large fat animal. Their contentment with each other led her to reappraise her comments to Edward Lounsey about apple sauce. The happiness was reassuring, and it occurred to her they'd no idea capture, and at some stage, slaughter awaited them. The design and purpose were different but not entirely so. The control and pace of their fate were not exactly precise. They could escape, or perhaps Louisa was falling in love with them and pictured in her mind's eye Edward Lounsey kissing Danny before taking his final payment and leaving.

Was Danny and Doodle's fate so different from Miss Collier's? Once the decision was made to take her life, the design set in motion with the purpose, she hardly stood any chance. It was the decision that was the key to finding her murderer, Louisa thought, not any other part. The initial grievance flared and simmered, finally settling into cold, harsh determination, and this was what was required to follow the plan.

In her bedroom, she made notes as Hierophant demanded her attention from the doorway, where he sat purring insolently and behaving like a spoiled child.

"We will eat, my dear. I need a few more moments," Louisa said, realizing she was hungry. And she was, rather than thinking such things, saying it out loud to an empty room. She was sure Hierophant heard. Suddenly, he stopped and sat, his tail curved about her in satisfaction of being finally listened to, and the thought made Louisa momentarily happy again. She couldn't imagine being without him now and wondered if Miss Collier spoke to him so often and affectionately as she did. Judging by the animal's demeanor, it was apparent. Hierophant missed Miss Collier and was in the throes of conflict with his new benefactor. Dependent on Louisa for food and love, it was evident this was the way forward, the way to sustain himself. And she, too, must start thinking this way.

Louisa noticed the time and forced herself into action. She opened her kitchen window to allow the chill air to flow freely, and after a late breakfast of oats and sweet black coffee, she sought out her unique black among the common occurrence of it in her wardrobe. She realized she'd spent most of her life in self-imposed mourning, or at the very least, this is how it felt. It may be time to let go of such feelings, but despite being accustomed to them, it gave her personal satisfaction. It had become her signature, her defining uniform, and people expected her to appear and behave a certain way. This was her choice. Her health was not good, and despite all the air and beautiful benefits of Concord's open space, she could not help but think an early death awaited her. These foolish thoughts made her sad, but the great mystery of it made her or rather forced her to carry on as best she could.

And what better place to contemplate one's fate than at a funeral in which most likely a murderer would be present.

Communication of the hour was by mouth first and then in the *Concord Sentinel* window, midday. An odd time, Louisa thought, but then it was Concord, and perhaps the church had other arrangements to occupy itself with. She was first into the dank, damp chapel. Great swathes of pungent evergreen were tied to the benches with black ribbon, not even a winter berry to lighten the mood.

In the coffin was the body of Miss Collier, her features squarish and set; the lines that ran from the corners of her mouth to her jaw were deep plowed, and Louisa barely recognized her. Miss Collier had not been overtaken happily. Her fists appeared clenched as though she'd grab the sides of wood and haul herself out any minute to castigate or point the finger at her killer. Louisa brushed such thoughts from her mind, but peace was not a feeling from the corpse. An uneasy feeling filled her, and she was glad to see the Birch sisters arrive, April leading the way in a black feathered gown and turban adorned with a single pink butterfly.

"Louisa," she said urgently. Behind her, June appeared somber in black, with a red sash glaring and robust around her middle. Her face was deliberately white, her lips almost straight across her face. April swigged from a hip flask.

"We must be wary of them all. The place is teeming with suspects."

"I am aware of that, Miss Birch."

"For all manner of things. Not just for toppling poor Miss Collier off her perch. Just look at them." She fanned herself with an Ostrich feather despite the icy atmosphere of the chapel, batting away the disapproving glances of Miss Murdock. The latter glared at her for several menacing moments before marching resolutely away.

"We should take our places here to observe the whole performance."

She pushed June awkwardly into a pew, Louisa waiting until April moved her large frame sufficiently in to allow them all to be seated in comfort.

"Do move over, April," June said, settling her outfit.

"You should be closer to the top, little bird," April said, now pushing her out by the shoulder. "You need to give your best speech today for the choral society. See the looks on the faces of the Misses and report back to us.

Search for traces of guilt."

"I am here to mourn, April."

"Yes, yes, but also see their faces as you glance across the crowd, horrified by Miss Collier's demise. Terrified of her murderer."

Louisa gave April a withering look.

"Miss Chandler will be busy wondering if the Captain is still interested in her," April continued. Louisa couldn't argue with that point. A tense situation between Miss Chandler and Captain Briers could be very revealing, if not disruptive to the proceedings.

"You must bear your most sorrowful face and let your words express the emotions for all of us, little bird. Let Captain Briers see what he's missing."

"Don't be so melodramatic, April," June whispered. "I am sure Miss Alcott has decided we're suspects too."

"I cannot remove anyone from the inquiry," Louisa confirmed. She hoped the Birch ladies would calm down. Now they were not in their usual habitat, and they drew unwanted attention from the same task April set out at the start—the observance. The inhabitants of Concord arrived thickly now led by the loud huffing Mrs. Miller, red-faced and disturbed, Mr. Miller in his best attire with the look of a man hoping to set aside several hours, if not years of sobriety in favor of a dram to block his wife's ravings out. Louisa caught a powerful whiff of brandy as he took his wife's arm and led her to a spot midway down the chapel. He grimaced in a peculiarly gentlemanly way as they drifted past.

Miss Chandler and her mother arrived both in heavy black coats, Miss Chandler still wearing her mauve gloves, her hands completely covered in what was now approaching a cloak of suspicion. Underneath, she wore a peach dress with delicate cream daisies embroidered into the hem, and her mother encouraged her to cover up as eyes inspected her as she walked past. Mary shivered uncomfortably and allowed a weak smile to linger in the direction of Louisa and April.

"Peach," April thundered. "Miss Collier would appreciate that." She took her opera glasses out to inspect the pair from a distance.

"Miss Birch, could you please put away the glasses," Louisa said. "You are making a spectacle of yourself."

"Quite right, Louisa," she said and snapped them closed. "We ought to be observing quietly." With that, she took her pewter hip flask out and took a long gulp, ending with a satisfied sigh. "I wonder who is next?"

"I haven't figured it out yet."

"Surely you must have some idea?"

"What if it is me, Miss Birch?" Louisa asked.

April let out a loud laugh, causing several heads to turn around. "Really, Miss Alcott, this is no time for jest."

"It could be a very clever ruse, Miss Birch. My family are strangers after years of absence to Concord, after all. I could easily have murdered Miss Collier with an unknown motive."

"Yes, but you're respectable," April said with a sniff. "And anyone up to their elbows in pigs all day must be a gloriously honest person."

"Still, I don't imagine it could be that obvious," Louisa said.

Edward Lounsey arrived and took his cap off, cradling it in his large hands. He nodded at the Chandlers and Millers, taking his place further up. Careful not to look too closely in any particular direction but surreptitiously seek someone out. The chapel's darkness mixed with a scent of sulphur, a row of candles lit, their flames tracing up the walls. Louisa felt an anxious foreboding as the flames whipped from side to side as the cold air caught them and threw them about. Just like Concord. Some of its secrets, yet to illuminate themselves to her, left her wanting.

"Watch him," April said. "He knows more than he's saying."

"Who?"

"Edward Lounsey." April's opera spectacles were out again, this time with her attention on the arrival of Miss Taylor. "Another new coat, I see."

Miss Taylor paraded up the aisle past Edward Lounsey. Louisa could feel the intent stare on April's face without looking at her as Miss Taylor took her place almost to the front. A hum of whispers rose. The empty cavernous space of the altar with its brass bowls and bright red cloth seemed a world away from its audience.

"See," April said.

"See what?"

"They didn't even acknowledge each other."

"And what does that tell us, April?"

"They're involved, Louisa, that's what. Nothing surer."

Louisa couldn't fault April's deduction. Edward, intent on finding someone, cautiously ensured the surrounding Concord residents would not notice.

After a moment, Louisa felt a hand on her shoulder. "Miss Alcott, I must speak with you."

Captain Briers stood aside, and Louisa followed him to the open door, the light fading over the Sleepy Hollow graveyard. A gunpowder sky frowned down, a faint damp rain falling in tiny sparkling specs on Captain Briers' soft hair.

"The school has been burgled again," he said.

"That is strange," Louisa said. "Do we know when?"

"Only discovered."

"By whom?"

"Miss Murdock, this morning."

Louisa thought about this. It was of no assistance that the timing was appalling. Any one of the congregation already seated inside could idly pass the school at a convenient time to help themselves and conduct the mischief according to their leisure. The entire town of Concord simmered to cold the night before in preparation for the day's events. Not a soul could be heard up to Castle Farm. Even the animals were bedded on an excellent night's sleep before the impending cortege would make its way the following day.

Only the penny boys were out to ensure the main thoroughfare of Market Street would be clear and clean before the whole town came out to display their respects.

"What was Miss Murdock doing there this morning, Captain?"

A look of confusion came over his face, and he hunched his shoulders. "You can ask yourself."

Miss Murdock approached with a thunderous look on her face. Her agitation grew as she came closer, and Louisa detected an air of preparation around her. As though whatever she was about to divulge must outbid the previous outrage.

"Something must be done, Miss Alcott."

"What were you doing at the school, Miss Murdock?"

The question surprised her. "I have work to do which cannot always be done during school hours. Those in Concord believe the position of schoolmistress is a whimsy engaged in by those with nothing better to do. I will not tolerate such horrors."

She was about to take her leave. "The new incident, Miss Murdock. Are you going to enlighten the Captain and me?"

"Whoever committed this indecent act must pay dearly, Miss Alcott," Miss Murdock said.

Captain Briers attempted to hold her back, but Miss Murdock brushed his hand away.

"You must find this lunatic before we're all murdered." There was less upset in her voice than a resolve betraying some far fiercer act that must await their examination.

"We will have to leave this matter, Miss Alcott, until after the funeral."

"Well, is it safe to do so?"

"I've stationed a man up there with instructions not to let anyone in or out."

"It will have to do," Louisa said. "Where is the Justice, Mr. Founts?"

"His carriage went into a rut outside Concord."

Louisa laughed.

"I cannot see the humor, Miss Alcott," Captain Briers said. "His continued forbearance ensures we might put this matter to rest before he imposes a curfew."

"Captain, that isn't a bad idea. It appears to be the case our murderer is fond of the hours before midnight and just before dawn."

"There will be uproar if we confine the citizens to their homes, especially on a day such as this."

"Do stop speaking like a statesman, Captain Briers, a rank you have yet to achieve. We have yet to see if Miss Murdock's horror is justified."

"Very well."

"And do not tell Mr. Founts about this new incursion. This show must go on."

"I must tell him," Captain Briers said.

"Not before the funeral," Louisa said. "Nothing must disturb it, and we must observe and make conclusions."

The chapel was now packed, and the warmth of bodies gave it a cheerier aspect. The candles lit wheaten and steady, and the altar glistened under the yellow glow. Louisa squeezed past April Birch.

"Do we have full attendance, Miss Birch?"

April lost interest in the proceedings when Louisa spoke into her ear.

"Miss Birch?"

"No, we don't, Louisa. Evie Briers and Miss Nash have yet to make an appearance. That is interesting, don't you think?"

"I suspect Evie Briers will not arrive," Louisa said.

She felt April bristle as though this might be a clue. "And why might that be?"

"She is very fragile, Miss Birch. As I'm sure you, of all people, must know." This took April by surprise, and the notion Evie Briers might be fragile didn't match up with her ability to run the Birch household—or her own.

"How do you mean?" April said, her voice stiff with suspicion.

"I imagine Miss Briers is exhausted, wouldn't you?"

April said nothing, hoisted her Ostrich feather aloft, and batted the suggestion furiously back in Louisa's direction. She looked away sufficiently long to have considered Louisa's advice in full.

"Quite what you mean is beyond me, Louisa."

"A woman of her age, Miss Birch, in service?"

"I have told you about Captain Briers' pernicious meanness. It's surprising the woman has a stitch of clothing."

"I had the same concerns myself," Louisa said. "I cannot make up my mind about Captain Briers."

April turned her gaze, glad the accusation of working Evie Briers to a thread lay behind them.

"As long as he has paper for his ridiculous love letters, I assume he doesn't care if Evie must wash someone else's large kitchen down for the pleasure."

"Miss Chandler may indeed be saving herself some trouble."

"They're not remotely suited, Louisa. Captain Briers is seeking out a servant. Like *most* men." She said the last part with a stinging hiss, one Louisa couldn't argue with.

"Miss Chandler sees me as an abandoned woman. Capable of understanding the years of torment ahead if one doesn't marry well," Louisa said.

"Well, she won't get any sympathy from me," April said with a chuckle. "You only have to look at that dreadful Mrs. Miller to understand why."

"Indeed."

"And to think, June Birch, my own sister, entertains a fancy for the Captain."

"I wonder how real that is, April? Surely, how can I put this nicely? Your sister sees his interests clearly lies elsewhere, even if not Miss Chandler."

"It's entirely foolish. I do humor myself at June's expense over it, though, and it seems to give her great heart lunges."

"She still entertains the idea?"

"Oh yes," April said then: "not enough to kill Miss Collier in case that fanciful notion has crossed your mind. June may be foolishly sentimental, but she is not stupid."

"We do very foolish things in foolish sentiments."

"June would not touch a fly. You can accuse me of it if you like, but not June."

Louisa settled herself, indicating to April Birch she was, for the moment, preferring a stillness to constant chatter. There was a warmth to the air as proceedings got underway. Neither Miss Evie Briers nor Miss Nash made an appearance.

Doctor Jennings arrived with his wife, a rather insipid creature happy to be led by her husband. A somewhat more demure and more diminutive engaging-looking woman Louisa had rarely seen. After choosing a seat, her husband caught her by the arm and led her to the one in front.

"That awful Doctor. Herding his wife around like a prize bull. See Miss

Alcott, why I would not want to be seeking out a husband in Concord."

"Yes, Miss Birch, I do."

"And imagine having to mourn a husband for two and a half years," she hissed. "Imagine if you hated him."

The style of mourning had changed considerably after the war. Set times introduced more extended periods of wearing black for women, children, and siblings. There were numerous etiquette books to be read on the subject, most of which Louisa had happily fallen asleep reading. There were rules around wearing all black, then perhaps a ruffle of white after some time. After mourning ended, the woman was permitted to wear lavender and purple. She was required to remain indoors, not attend any social gatherings, and write on paper lined in black.

Louisa thought the most morbid was adorning oneself with a lock of the deceased's hair. This ornament seemed mildly punitive to the wearer, and a symbol of the hold death has on the living seemed utterly unfair. For many women, the cost of mourning continuously over the war period, or if several family members died, including a husband, became impossible to maintain. It brought with it a depressing of the spirit Louisa saw many women rarely recover from. As if condemned to exist in the world of hollow, humorless people and waiting for the inevitable.

The move from private to public mourning, Louisa thought, brought with it a spectacle most unsuited to the recently bereaved. There was something uniquely intimate about celebrating a person's life with those who knew them best. The ease at which the celebration took place took on a disconcerting political dimension, a statement rather than remembrance. And a new practice emerging was the increasing control the men brought in funeral activity when it was previously a woman's sphere of influence.

As speakers' voices rose and fell, Louisa felt a waft of cold air from behind. April turned quickly to observe the person who had entered. Evie Briers, pale and exhausted in a drab mourning dress, shuffled in. She ambled up towards the top, where Miss Collier lay. Gripped in her hands was a bright red wreath with orange flowers.

"What is this about Miss Alcott, I wonder."

Louisa concentrated on the newly unfolding drama and watched as heads followed her to the top. She extended her arms and placed the wreath across the top of the shining coffin without any ceremony. Whispered a few words into Miss Collier's dead ear, inaudible to anyone, and turned quickly, glancing up once and giving a weary stare about the congregation. After she'd said and done her piece, she shuffled, head up high to the back and left.

A disapproving murmur rose. The bright wreath was visible above all the soft, insensitive drapes of purplish black, as though Evie had marked Miss Collier as a target. Created a centerpiece of her in a most elegant manner.

"Well, Louisa, what do you make of this," April said, squinting through her opera glasses. "Guilt?"

Louisa shifted uncomfortably in her hard seat. It was doing terrible things to her aching limbs, and the cold circulated about her feet like a ravenous monster.

"I have no idea, Miss Birch. I believe she means to send a message to the people of Concord with the wreath. Her words. Now, that's a different matter. If only we could be privy."

The room felt uneasy after this intervention. It was as though it encouraged the wrapping up of events with unnatural speed, and the long speech prepared by June Birch suffered unfair abridgment. She pleaded for justice to seek out Miss Collier's murderer, which caused another ripple of hysteria among the congregation. April rose from her seat.

"June, that's quite enough," she roared from her standing position.

June's alarmed face turned sour, and she finally took her place at the front, a rush of heat entering her cheeks. Captain Briers put his hand gently onto her shoulder, and she smiled. June was about to enter into some conversation when Captain Briers made his way to Louisa and April Birch.

"We must go to the school at once."

"Yes, quite."

"The school? But what has happened?" April Birch was readying herself to move with the throng from the church but was now perched directly between Louisa and Captain Briers.

"Nothing, Miss Birch. We have a rather important meeting to attend to."

Louisa gave the Captain a stern look. He must keep his counsel tighter to his chest if he was to remain a significant investigator in this awful business. She could not—and would not—continue to hold his childish hand.

Outside, a burst of thin lemon sunshine broke through the grey clouds. The air was stiff and frosty.

"Are you seriously telling me there is no form of meeting to convene after Miss Collier's death?" Mr. Miller was saying to Miss Nash, who'd appeared at the end of the service. Her arrival immediately after Evie Briers meant her absence from the service was intended to draw attention away from her presence, which may or may not be wanted.

"Of course, Mr. Miller, we shall be celebrating Miss Collier's life at Hangman's Cottage in fine style."

Mrs. Miller was approaching on her short legs. Her face puce, as though she'd been running or fuming secretly for several hours. Louisa imagined it was the latter.

"There will be no drinking today," she said, glaring at Mr. Miller.

"It would be a favor to the entire community of Concord if they are allowed to mourn her passing, Mrs. Miller."

"It is totally inappropriate," Mrs. Miller said. "Considering."

Mr. Miller batted his wife away. The recent threat to Mrs. Miller's life seemed to trouble Mr. Miller little if the alternative was a party at the Birch Farm. He'd the look of a man who'd waited his entire life for such an event.

"Mrs. Miller," April Birch began, in a voice so meek and mild it was astonishing. "We must mourn Concord's great and good—and not so wonderful—in equal measure."

"Considering the grave circumstances, it would be a terrible injustice to the community of Concord."

"Come now, Mrs. Miller, let's not fret over such a thing." It was Miss Nash.

"I do hope you understand, Miss Nash, your delicacies and cakes will not be served at my cottage today." April smiled evenly, embracing her sister June, who'd emerged from the church doors. Miss Nash blushed and pulled her dark, shabby cloak about her.

"We will certainly not miss your ill humor, Miss Birch, when your time comes."

"Oh yes, I forgot. Miss Nash knows all the village secrets, don't you, Miss Nash?"

"I do not."

"Oh, come now, surely you can't imagine we don't know your little side employment? Rifling through our medical infirmities at the local surgery?"

There was a ripple of indignation from the listening crowd. "I have been doing some research of my own, it must be said."

Louisa moved quickly to intervene. Such loose talk was bound to set tensions above any acceptable level. Add the Birch brandy and tipsy cakes, and it was anyone's guess what might occur.

"Ladies, might I suggest we meet in April Birch's home in an hour or so? The Captain and I have some urgent business to attend to," Louisa said.

The mourners filed slowly down the narrow path, a fine mist of freezing rain finally overcoming the weak sunshine. A truly foreboding feeling in the air, as though, at any moment, it would crack open in a fit of thunder and lightning. Louisa knew this. Her bones were aching, and all she could see in her mind's eye was the warm, blazing hearth and the quiet purring of Hierophant resting near her heel.

She stood under a sizable fragrant yew tree when the first flash of lightning streaked through the sky, cutting it up at the edges.

"What are we waiting for, Captain?'

With that, the resonant crashing of hooves on the ground could be heard suddenly, its din rising to equal the thunder bellowing from the sky.

"Mr. Founts," Captain Briers said. His disappointment matched hers.

"I had hoped we could inspect Miss Murdock's office without his interference."

"Too late now, Miss Alcott."

Mr. Founts descended from his carriage like a Witchfinder in search of evil. He sniffed the sulphury air as though blessed with a feral instinct enabling him to know intuitively where the prey hid. His timing, Louisa imagined, could not have been worse. In the distance, she spied the Miss Birch duo, June and April, speaking loudly with Miss Taylor and Miss Nash. Listening intently to the side was Miss Murdock, pale and in shock. The Chandlers were nowhere to be seen, and Mr. Miller argued in whispered tones with his wife, who was clearly intent on donning her black in peace and quiet for the remainder of the week. Evie Briers was nowhere to be seen either, considering her dramatic—albeit—inappropriate intervention at the service.

Mr. Founts was dressed like a peacock, his elaborate suit of black, complete with onyx fastenings and a tall hat, resplendent with a dark set of feathers that could surely rival April Birch's ensemble.

"I see I have missed the funeral," he said, wiping some stray droplets of rain from his arm.

"I am very anxious to hear of your news, Captain Briers."

Louisa bristled at his exclusion of her presence from the request.

"I trust you had a good journey, Mr. Founts," Louisa said. "I hear dressing for such an occasion can take some time, particularly for a man of your peculiar tastes."

She smiled. Mr. Founts frowned and narrowed his eyes.

"I am not tardy, Miss Alcott, in pursuit of some frivolous or vain activity. Our horse and carriage suffered an accident halfway; it is lucky the poor animal isn't lame. This is a most inclement day for a funeral."

"All funeral days are inclement, Mr. Founts."

He grunted and turned his attention once more to the Captain.

"What updates have you, Captain?"

Captain Briers gave Louisa a sharp look. "There has been an incident at the school we are to investigate and another break-in earlier this morning."

"And what have you been doing about it, Captain?"

"We joined the rest of Concord paying our respects, Mr. Founts," Louisa interrupted. "Surely you did not expect us to forgo such an event of such great importance?"

"No doubt the lure of hysterical keening beloved so much by women was of great importance."

"No, Mr. Founts, but the observation of the suspects in Miss Collier's murder is. And, of course, we cannot be seen to be partial in respect of her character. Whether it was an escaped unfortunate lunatic or one's own flesh and blood, all deserve final respects to be paid. Don't you agree?"

Mr. Founts merely sniffed in faint acknowledgment as one event surely outbid the other in relevance.

"Let us go to the school, Captain Briers. At once."

Just like the consummate gentleman Louisa knew he was not, Mr. Founts did not offer the use of his carriage to make the journey to the school on the sodden road. Instead, they waited for Captain Briers to organize one, the distance far too much for Louisa to pretend to endure. Such foolhardy behavior would mean her feet in a hot basin with salt for many hours. As much as she wanted to run up the hill to the other side of the town and reach the school first, she knew it was beyond her capabilities. At least the Captain, although indeed not the best judge of character she'd ever known, was capable of civility and kindness of the most basic form. Such things were sadly lacking in Mr. Founts.

Once safely inside the carriage and out of a worsening storm, Captain Briers spoke first.

"I do not like his presence here one bit."

"No, of course, it is not the best of things, particularly as I am worried about what we might find at the school."

"Another break-in, surely nothing more than that. Perhaps an opportunistic thief believes their actions won't garner much attention."

"I have a feeling it is far worse, Captain."

* * *

The school occupied the furthest part of Concord, just past the veterinary clinic. It was built to avail of a substantial area of fields, deemed necessary for the children to play in and gain some education in nature. Concord school benefactors prided themselves in knowing this divine purpose was supported by all the inhabitants of the town. It was separated to the west of the village by the river, with its soft velvet banks now reeking of winter decay. As they passed over the bridge, Louisa felt her nose ruffle with the heavy odor of fungal spores. The kind that gave her a monstrous headache. Overhead, the treacherous skies exploded with thunder and lightning, the storm right over them. Bearing down with such force, Louisa momentarily panicked.

As luck would smile, the carriage was able to pull up close to the doorway, leaving little walking to be done, and for this, Louisa was grateful. Mr. Founts, in continuance of his lack of propriety—or common civility- was already in the school when they arrived in Miss Murdock's office.

"Ah. Here, at last, I see," Mr. Founts said.

"We were required to engage a coach, Mr. Founts," Louisa said.

"And leave this unseemly sight for any person to peruse at their leisure?" Mr. Founts said.

"Your lack of manners, Mr. Founts, is beginning to fray my nerves in a most disagreeable fashion."

"The scene you are about to view will fray them further. Look and see for yourself," Mr. Founts said.

At first, the dull room seemed untouched. Miss Murdock's desk was the center of the obscenity, for that is what it was. The chair was pushed back, on which a great deal of blood lay splashed and pooled. Darker blood on the desk, clearly dried, pools on the floor, curdling at their deepest points. Nailed into the soft leather was a note on a yellow piece of paper written in the red ink:

Most evil deeds are not the musings of one diabolical man but many.

Captain Briers stood back.

"This is an outrage," he said in a whispered tone. "What madman has done this?"

Mr. Founts moved closer to observe. "You," he said to one of the guards. "Take some details about this scene. And remove the note."

There was a silence. "Captain, clean this disgusting filth up."

Louisa moved quicker than she'd moved in months.

"You will touch nothing. None of you."

"I beg your pardon, Miss Alcott, but I'm in charge here. I will say what happens."

"Are you qualified in examining scenes such as this, Mr. Founts?"

"I will not be questioned in front of my men by a..."

"Woman? Well, that is too bad, Mr. Founts. I consider myself unqualified, too, but I do know one thing. You must observe and examine this atrocity before simply clearing it away."

"I agree with Miss Alcott," Captain Briers said. "There is much to consider with this new event."

"Like what?" Founts asked, clearly irritated.

"Well, for one, it is clear this sordid affair has to do with Miss Collier's murder," Louisa said.

"And why on earth would that be?"

"Because I heard Miss Collier use this exact phrase before. This evil deeds and diabolical man."

"What nonsense," Mr. Founts said. He was about to reaffirm his instructions to clear the scene when Captain Briers stood between him and his constable.

"I will not have this scene touched until Miss Alcott has had time to examine it. Your guard here will ensure she is left alone to do so and has every assistance."

"I fail to see how this has anything to do with the death of Miss Collier and is pure coincidence," Mr. Founts said.

But even then Mr. Founts' guard was already removing himself from the scene and making his helpful presence known, keeping the door blocked to anyone who wished to enter.

"*Coincidence*? Did you not hear what Miss Alcott said?"

"If you believe this may be evidence of import to Miss Collier's demise, I will not stand in your way."

"But you would stand in my way?" Louisa said, moving toward the table. "Might I suggest you await hearing from your superior regarding this matter?"

"And what shall I hear from my superior, Miss Alcott?" Mr. Founts said.

"I have contacted him directly by mail regarding your lack of cooperation. His response will be with me any day now."

"Of all the impudence."

"No, Mr. Founts, I had my suspicions you would not permit Captain Briers and myself to work on this matter without interfering. The Captain had no hand in it. I had no choice."

"You knew nothing of this impudent act?" Mr. Founts said, addressing the Captain.

"No, I did not."

"And I took the advice of a sound mind in Concord when she said she travels to Fairgreen to send her telegrams. The wisest woman."

In truth, Louisa had used the baker's boy. A young man willing and able to carry out the task without asking questions or nosing into her affairs on the promise of money. Swift delivery of her instructions and a speedy collection of the return mail, without any fuss or bother.

"So, you see, Mr. Founts, we are to be left alone with the use of your men to assist us. You may go now; we are done with this unnecessary wasting of our time. Good day."

There was a great deal of blustering from Mr. Founts, and it seemed word of Mr. Founts' dismissal by Louisa was to reach the ears of Concord residents but not the reasons behind it.

* * *

"Did you really contact the Division Justice?" Captain Briers asked.

"Oh yes. We met once at a party in Boston. He is an avid supporter of the arts, Captain Briers, a man of subtle humor but strong sensibility. He was not an admirer of Mr. Founts," Louisa said.

"I have found him agreeable, I must say," the Captain said.

"The Division Justice was not surprised when I relayed my message to him in short order with few words. He understood the meaning very well."

"Did Miss Collier really say those words," Captain Briers asked, glancing over at the table where the note still sat. Most of the blood was darkened now, a thick crust forming on the surfaces like drying lava. The metallic stench gave way to the cold, wet air coming in through the window upon which deep riparian odors drifted.

"Before I took Miss Birch's advice and sent my telegrams from Fairgreen, I had reason to use Mrs. Miller's post office in town. Most of my correspondence is business-related and of no interest to busybodies such as Mrs. Miller. Or others, for that matter. I overheard Miss Collier using this exact phrase."

"Yes, but to whom?"

"Well, that is the difficulty, Captain. Mrs. Miller was there, obviously. But Mr. Miller was also there. Miss Taylor had just stepped in, and Miss Nash was sending a rather large parcel to the other side of the country. Miss Murdock was setting up the May Day Festival notice on the board."

"Not much help, unfortunately," the Captain said.

"Your sister Evie was just leaving," Louisa said.

"And what was the subject of the conversation?"

"I don't know. I was not long there myself, Captain. I was keeping my own counsel."

His face darkened slightly. "And this phrase, Miss Alcott," the Captain said. "Is it of importance?"

"There is something didactic about this scene. Perhaps a little sinister and dark."

"Mr. Miller is known to have a lively interest in the occult. He often spoke with Miss Collier about such matters, and they shared an interest in the esoteric."

"Well," Louisa said, glancing over at the table. "I think we will find it is animal blood."

Captain Briers nodded his head.

"Unless, of course, we have another victim. In which case, this matter has indeed become very complicated."

"Mr. Miller..."

"Yes?"

"It may not be of great import, but Mr. Miller was at one point cautioned by myself and warned about certain behaviors."

"Well, Captain, please do not keep me waiting."

"He was part of this society which celebrated the Equinox, mid-summer, the old festivals of light and dark. I discovered nothing criminal, but I was concerned to learn that Miss Collier was also a member."

"Well, it's certainly possible dark forces are involved here, but I had hoped it would be plain ordinary evil, Captain. Not some society engaged in ritual practices."

"I don't believe it was anything like that, but I do think we need to question Mr. Miller."

"And you thought nothing of this connection before now?"

"Well, no, I didn't. It all seemed rather harmless. A bit silly, if I might say."

"There are still isolated cases of witchcraft, Captain, or had you forgotten? I hardly need to remind you that isn't far from where we stand."

"I had not thought you were given over to reliving some distant memory of superstition, Miss Alcott."

"I can assure you I am not. But there are others who most certainly are."

"We must keep it quiet."

"I do not want any outside interference in the investigation, Captain. This could ruin our examinations."

They set to work. Louisa insisted Captain Briers take a sample of the blood to ascertain whether it was human or animal. The vet, Mr. Parsons, could easily do this. She imagined if enough whiskey was proffered to keep his silence on the matter for the moment. This made the cost of maintaining livestock prohibitive as Mr. Parsons seemed to find and imagine all manner of diseases, such were his magical powers of diagnoses. He kept quiet in case it caused panic in the community. She took one of Miss Murdock's file covers and placed the note inside for further observation.

There was no specific pattern to the blood, save that it wasn't evident in the area around the door. Neither was it in the hallway nor other parts of the school. Louisa could surmise that it was brought to its location. She imagined it had to be taken in a pail. Otherwise, it would have spilled and dripped and would be evident elsewhere other than on the table. Louisa wondered if there was reason for this.

"Would you please get Miss Murdock here at once, Captain?" Louisa said.

"She seemed shocked, Miss Alcott," he replied. "And is most likely at the Birch place by now."

"I doubt very much the Birch sisters are entertaining her."

"Very well," he said and disappeared.

Louisa walked around the desk to the window to view the scene from behind. The room was practically dark. It was faint, but on the back of the chair, she found some etched symbols. She recognized them immediately: the Salem Hexmark and a daisy wheel. Each is a symbol of protection from evil.

"What is this," she asked herself. She stood back from it and searched around the room. The best thing for her to do was copy the symbols onto a piece of paper. Removing Miss Murdock's chair would not be possible, and of course, Miss Murdock had failed to notice the symbols; otherwise, the gossip would have reached the ears of Concord residents before now.

The Salem Hexmark is used by those wishing to be identified as Godly, not in the grasp of the profane. A sign to the witch hunter that the household rejected the evil doings of witches and advertised their goodness.

The daisywheel was not so well etched. A hexafoil, similar in purpose, protected the building or item onto which it was carved. The Hexmark interested her most: two triangles, the tips connecting at the narrowest parts, with a line drawn through it. Her initial instinct wasn't very clear about this development. A ruse to draw attention away from the actual perpetrator? A method of deflection is indeed the reason why it was so forcefully displayed. The one part of leaving the blood reinforced the possibility of evil forces for the sake of their demonstration of the other.

To divert her and Captain Briers in an entirely different direction from their immediate path. Or historical etchings were a reminder of the prevalence of good over evil in the war between both, and Miss Murdock was still on her list of suspects. Nothing would change that immediately.

She carefully copied each symbol onto paper and stored the evidence in her bag. She would tell Captain Briers about it. But not another soul. As she wished for a carriage to take her to April Birch's, the sound of footsteps rounded the hall and approached the room, and Captain Briers could be heard.

"Just for a few moments, Miss Murdock. Miss Alcott is here."

Miss Murdock rounded the door gingerly, clutching her cloak closed about her. Her eyes darted about and settled on the desk.

"Really, Miss Alcott, must I be here," Miss Murdock said.

"I would not ask if it were not urgent, Miss Murdock. I have put a chair over there," she said, pointing to the one generally reserved for guests.

"Was the school door lock fixed after the last break-in?" Louisa asked.

"I had a man come a week ago, but he indicated there was some item he needed before he could complete the repairs. I may have told him to take his time considering the cost of the item."

"I see, and how was the school secured each day?"

Miss Murdock hesitated. "It was not secured. Yes, that would be the answer."

"I am only inquiring simply to establish that any person could have gained entrance to the building at any time."

"That would be correct." Miss Murdock's lips tightened.

"Was anything else disturbed?"

"I was so completely disturbed myself I failed to check anything else."

"And what were you doing here so early today with no school scheduled?" Louisa asked.

"The answer is simply what you have already discovered. I could not lock the front door, so I check every day, especially when the children are not here."

Louisa slumped into the spare chair beside Miss Murdock and thought for a few moments.

"It is likely the intruder came in during the night. Aware nothing would stand in his—or her—way, they would not feel under any immediate suspicion carrying a pail full of blood."

"Quite, Miss Alcott. Although would it not be difficult for a woman to manage such a task?" Miss Murdock said.

"She has a point," Captain Briers said. "A pail full of blood would be much heavier than water."

Louisa often brought Danny and Doodle's water in pails, and she agreed about the weight. She often had to make a few trips, including any scraps or feed she had to bring.

"It could be a diversion, Miss Murdock. A means to throw us off the scent," Louisa said.

"It has all the indications of the dark arts," Miss Murdock said, now seeming to recover her strength. "A mischief calculated to taunt me."

"You, Miss Murdock, specifically?"

"Well, it's pretty obvious, isn't it, Miss Alcott? Why *my* desk? Why not Miss Nash's desk or somewhere else?" She waved her arm around.

"Really, Captain, must I stay here any longer?"

"One more thing, Miss Murdock. Would you be so kind as to check the records, please, and ensure they are still there?" Louisa said.

She rose from her seat and went to a cupboard, where she retrieved a set of keys.

"Your office door was not locked, was it, Miss Murdock?"

She turned a look of thunder on her face. "No, Miss Alcott, it wasn't. I forgot."

"Was any person aware you occasionally omitted to lock your office door?"

"Miss Alcott, I am not in the habit of forgetting to lock my door, yet I admit I forgot to lock it on this occasion."

"Outstanding, Miss Murdock. Now please check the records," Louisa said.

After she'd left the room, Captain Briers spoke. "Was she the target of this vile act?"

"I am not sure what this act means, Captain."

She took the paper from her bag. "I have copied some symbols I found on her chair, and you'll see they are bizarre indeed."

Captain Briers examined the paper. "Very strange. Are we to assume this is an attempt to divert attention?"

"I think we must assume. And assume nothing in equal parts."

Captain Briers sighed loudly. "We will question Mr. Miller concerning this."

"I think we must, Captain."

Finally, Miss Murdock returned.

"Well, Miss Murdock?"

"There are missing papers. Records of school attendance."

"Which ones?"

"All of them," Miss Murdock replied. "Not only disturbed but stolen."

Miss Collier Speaks from the Dead

Dawn broke over Concord in great swathes of pink. The winter sunrise carpeted the fields and rivers with a low-lying swirling mist. The palette of pink and orange disappeared quickly into grey, as often this time of year. Fingers of frost clawed at the inner corners of buildings and edges of the barns and animal pens. Louisa pulled her aching legs up to conserve the warmth of her body. Hierophant was perched at the end of his bed, his meowing gradually increasing in pitch. "I will venture up soon, Hierophant. Be patient."

She laughed to herself. The animal seemed to understand what she said, and at that moment, she wished the cat could set out precisely what occurred in Miss Collier's living room the evening she met her death. What a joy it would be if animals could, especially for important events such as this, have a human voice for but a few precious moments. She steeled herself against the cold, tiled floor and straightened up. The delicate crystalized frost on the window caused her to shudder and shiver, and Hierophant sprang to the floor, softly making his way ahead of her. She possessed mixed feelings about the previous day. So much had happened, and yet nothing resolved itself in her mind. There was almost a childish demand for attention about the blood-soaked table. An infantile demonstration intended to shock—without any meaning at all.

Missing the Birch after-party was indeed a mistake on her part, but her body and mind thanked her for not drowning it in ill-advised banter. There was enough of this already, mainly as the crowd would be meager. April was wanton in her desire to celebrate Miss Collier's more frivolous side. Others, she would probably discover, celebrated with somewhat less ostentation. Still, the event at the school was alarming; without further prodding, she would not make sense of it, and a decision was required if it played any part and was simply a distraction.

Danny and Doodle awaited her arrival at the pigsty with glorious anticipation. Their loud greetings were accompanied by the usual entreaty for food—of any kind—and some well-deserved water. She'd tended her fire first and put the kettle on to boil, not wanting to leave herself short of comfort when she retired inside to get ready for the day. There was much to be done.

* * *

Kame Bluff was quiet in the early morning light. It never received the slightest warmth from the sun during the winter, protected as it was by a row of grand oaks obscuring the view of the main house. Deforestation was at its height in Concord, and the surrounding townlands were cleared for pasture, tillage, orchards, and buildings. Kame Bluff boasted these fine trees like a provocation to the fell man's ax. A willing swoop would turn them to firewood or a ship's bough. Of course, on this morning, it afforded Captain Briers privacy. He lit a fire in the furthest corner near the old path into Hapgood Wright Forest. There were private documents in his office he wished to burn and remove all evidence of. Some of them were sensitive papers relating to correspondence about town matters. Others exchanged between himself and Mr. Founts, the nature of which were pointless to retain and be tossed into the flames.

Then, there were Mary's endless letters, which continued up to the day before. He wished for her to stop, but Mary was determined to keep writing. He dared not go near Clamshell Farm for even the flimsiest reasons, lest he caused a scene. But Mary's last letter sought a meeting, one which he must either keep or inform her of his refusal.

My Dearest Everett,

I must see you. Meet me at Rosebud Cottage at the beehives at noon Friday.
All my love,
Mary

He sighed long and hard. Mary's determination in the continuance of the affair left little room for her disappointment and proved significantly more advanced than her understanding of the matters at stake. He replaced the letter in the envelope and threw it into the fire. Even now, he imagined her entertaining the Birch women with loose talk and infantile accusations. Perhaps she had something to say about the fateful night to him, which required his presence.

"Everett! *Everett*," Evie's voice came shrill through the air. She wrapped her shawl around her shoulders and stared into the fire.

"What are you burning?" she asked.

"Old papers," he said. "I must clear them out and keep the important ones." She looked frailer than ever. Her eyes were underpinned by shiny purple shadows, as though she had not slept for months. She shivered as the wind changed direction, drawing the fire away to the hedges.

"You'll set us all on fire," she said.

"What is it you want, Evie?"

"I must show you something?"

"Now?"

"Yes."

He stoked the fire flat, quickly placing the last of the papers away from his sister's prying eyes. The house was bordered by a stone wall leading to the back of the milking parlor. Evie scurried ahead, still in her slippers, to the very back near a gate. Right where Scout had hared off the last time, she set eyes on him alive.

She put her arm out and pointed. "Over there."

"Where, Evie? I can't see anything."

"I am not going near it."

Captain Briers glanced at his sister once, then marched in the general direction of the last oak, under which it was on this day almost entirely dark. The first items to catch his eyes were curled and dirty clumps of wool. A stream of dark, bloody entrails, innards, and guts. Finally, the startled eyes in the crown of a dead sheep. He glared back at his sister and then knelt down, the body fresh. No flies. It was recently what? Savaged by a dog?

"Its throat is cut," Evie said in a small voice. "Oh, dear, what are we going to do?"

"Quiet."

There was a clean shear at the throat, just as she had said. The anemic sinews and guts signaled a mysterious loss of blood. The Captain felt his throat tighten.

"Get me my work gloves?"

"Work gloves?"

"Be quick, Evie. Now."

For an instant, it came into his mind that this was most likely the animal whose blood found its way into Miss Murdock's office. He could not be sure; indeed, it was something he should report. But here it was, slaughtered on his land, possibly using any one of the farm tools in an unlocked shed behind him. Kame Bluff had ceased to be a working farm many years ago, but the vestiges of it lay around them like implements in a museum. Once he had covered his hands, he took the animal by its forelegs in one, hind in the other, and carried it to the fire.

Without a second thought, he cast the carcass into the flames and stood back. Unsure of what he'd just done, but with a terrible feeling in his gut, that it *must* be done.

* * *

Mr. Miller hid his illness brought on by Birch brandy behind the *Concord Sentinel*. There came a point the previous evening where he'd no recollection of what had occurred, much to his shame. Compounding his guilt and malaise was the uncannily spritely humor his wife appeared to be in. A heady mix for man in pursuit of some peace and comfort.

"Are you listening, Mr. Miller?" Mrs. Miller said.

"What, dear?"

He felt the wave of dress and underskirts hurtling towards him, threatening to expose the tincture of sherry he'd poured into a glass to banish the throbbing pain in his skull. There was no mercy in Lucy Miller following a night of revelry. The most one could hope for was a diversion, something more significant to occupy her mind than scolding consistently during the following days, as though he'd rode naked through Concord and trampled half its citizens.

"Kame Bluff," she said, as though it should mean something.

"Yes, what about it?"

"I've just told you, Mr. Miller."

"I wasn't listening, Mrs. Miller."

"Of course, you're not. Carousing with any available woman in the town will have that unfortunate effect on a man your age," Mrs. Miller continued.

"I'm not dead yet, in case this escaped your attention. I am very much alive and enjoy being alive. For the moment."

Lucy snatched the paper away, crumpled it up, and threw it on the fire.

"I doubt what happened on Monday is of any use to you on a Wednesday." Before this assault, Mr. Miller had managed to stash his glass away from her view. That tingling relief from a small amount of alcohol gave him enough temper to deal with the onslaught. She huffed loudly and, in her characteristic manner, delayed the purpose of her interaction. Thankfully, for him, this was infrequent. Like any other tumultuous event, the frequency increased as the storm neared.

"Captain Briers was burning documents. Throwing them with free abandon into a fire."

"So what?" Mr. Miller said.

"So what? Lighting a fire at dawn? Disposing of papers like a madman he was."

Mr. Miller wondered where he should begin. The only sure way of removing important information one did not want to be seen or read by another was to destroy them comprehensively in an inferno.

"I often dispose of documents this way, Lucy. Confidential information no longer needed is certainly not required for any reason."

"It was suspicious."

"Suspicious? Well, did you ask him what he was burning? Demand a reply?" Mr. Miller asked.

"Of course not. I was not seen."

"I'm sure if he'd known you were snooping on your unearthly hour of a walk, he might have arranged his affairs in another way?"

"There is no need to be sarcastic."

"Oh, there's every need. What on earth were you doing at Kame Bluff at that hour of the morning?" Mr. Miller said.

"Some of us like a morning constitutional. We're not all beleaguered by headaches from foolish indulgence."

"Am I right in thinking you believe the Captain was destroying evidence?"

"There was a break-in at the school yesterday morning, discovered before Miss Collier's funeral."

This took Mr. Miller by surprise, but it would not surprise him if he'd been informed of this travesty at the Birch cottage and simply forgotten. He felt the sting of being one step behind his wife.

"Even so, I doubt Captain Briers, who is investigating her death, could have possibly had anything to do with the school break-in," Mr. Miller said.

"I don't know what Louisa is doing either. There's that threatening note I received. Anyone could ambush me at the slightest provocation, and it would be my funeral next." Mrs. Miller stood by the fireplace and put her hand dramatically on the mantle.

"You don't care either," she then said.

"Oh, don't be so foolish, Lucy. You shouldn't be walking alone before dawn if you wish to remain safe. Don't you know there's a maniacal murderer on the loose?"

"So, you don't put any store in those threats either?"

"I am simply saying if you were living in fear for your life, you would not be spying on Captain Briers up by the forest. If you go missing, I assure you, a search of those woods will take every able-bodied man in Concord."

Mr. Miller wondered if this news had been spoken of in the Birch cottage, and he could scarcely remember who was there. Miss Taylor was tolerated for a short time, principally on his insistence, he imagined—or rather hoped—but otherwise, the crowd was thin.

"Where were you last evening? After the funeral?" Mr. Miller said.

"Well, it says much for a husband who scarcely cares what his wife is up to during the evening."

"Where were you?" he persisted.

"At the Chandlers. Where all the sensible, sober people gathered to remember Miss Collier."

"With knives to spare, I'm sure. Those people are so sour."

"What is the meaning of that?" Mrs. Miller asked.

"At least I know how to enjoy myself, Lucy. I know it was a gathering in honor of the dead, but really, there's no need to follow them into the grave."

"I suppose Miss Taylor was swaggering around. One would wonder what that woman's motivation is really."

"Well, at least most attendees were not moping about in black. She was there, as a matter of fact. Delightful woman."

Mrs. Miller sniffed and ignored Mr. Miller's all too obvious attempts at hiding the fact he was imbibing sherry with wild abandon. "Lovely woman," he repeated.

As if it would improve Mrs. Miller's mood, Mr. Miller entertained the idea of venturing out again, back to the Birch house. They did know how to enjoy themselves and shore up the lustier side of life. He had no idea how he would survive married life or Concord without them, and life would be much duller.

* * *

Mrs. Miller shelled peas, taking comfort from the rhythmic movements, considering what kind of life she had. Whether she liked it or not, the passing of Miss Collier had brought her out of her familiar role as postmistress into a confidante. It was perhaps something that brought her closer to danger and life itself, something she was not entirely sure she was happy with. The Chandlers were a rather self-absorbed lot. And for such plain people, Mary possessed a histrionic personality that exhausted them, which was quite challenging to achieve in the household. A significant betrayal such as that of Captain Briers must have endangered them as a species. Their affectation was so extreme that Mrs. Miller wondered if Mary Chandler had done away with Miss Collier in a fit of uncontrolled anger. Mrs. Miller's own aversion to the girl was laid bare one afternoon at the post office. Miss Chandler, sure of her ability to blood-suck the most available men within a radius, proved herself practically illiterate. An impediment, Mrs. Miller believed, would surely try the patience of even the most devoted man.

Mrs. Miller was called upon to complete the telegram and could not hide her shock at such willful ignorance in a young woman barely out of Concord school. Of course, under the auspices of Miss Nash and Miss Murdock, any type of arrangement was indeed allowed to occur where Miss Chandler received the barest of tuition to prevent any creasing of her frock. Or stop her admiring herself in a mirror during geography lessons.

Miss Chandler had been wailing most artificially about the fact she was the last person to witness Miss Collier alive. Not an admission Mrs. Miller herself would have considered advisable, and she regrettably told her so. Miss Chandler could procure a look of pure venom with little encouragement, which was the response she received.

Was Miss Chandler so self-absorbed she could write silly love letters but not a telegram? And had she gone back to Miss Collier's Cottage to oversee her earlier evil of poisoning her, see it take full effect?

Mrs. Miller's shelling of peas became so intense she barely realized the job was done. Yes, she was convinced she was very close to the truth, and that is precisely why Miss Chandler had sent the note telling her *you are next*. It was just the type of childish, yet exotic stunt Miss Chandler would be capable of.

"Mr. Miller," she said suddenly. "Stay away from the sherry, or you will not be capable of reading Miss Collier's will."

"I'll be serving brandy at the reading of Miss Collier's will. I think, considering some of the contents, it shall be required."

Lucy rose and made her way to stand in front of him.

"What is in her will?"

"Until it is publicly read, I cannot say a word."

"You are drunk, Mr. Miller. A complete disgrace."

"I sincerely hope so."

* * *

Louisa heated herself by the fire for a few more moments before venturing out. A wild, biting wind rose from the valley and thundered down upon the farm. Her mind was muddled by pain, but thankfully, a visit to Doctor Jennings would not be required as the thought of such a visit was far worse than the aches in her legs and shoulders. Her mood improved once she realized the reading of the will would take place in Mr. Miller's office, a place with homely comforts provided by a man who clearly required to spend a great deal of his time away from home. Of course, being married to Mrs. Miller improved the chances of it doubling as a place to relax and spend some quality alone time. It was barely noon, but she decided to make her way slowly to his offices in a bid to secure a seat by his sizeable open fire, always generously supplied with bone-dry wood logs. There was a notable quiet on Market Street as the wind gusted through the trees and sent shop signs squeaking on their hinges. Danny and Doodle loved the wind and refused to be cooped up in their storm-weather barn for any reason. Perhaps the storm brewing in Mr. Miller's office would be far weightier with these impending omens.

"Come in, Miss Alcott," Mr. Miller said. "You are indeed early."

Louisa moved towards the end of the polished rosewood table where the fire roared.

"Brandy?"

"I'm fond of the temperance movement, Mr. Miller."

"Only thing for this awful business. On a day like today, no amount of brandy is enough."

He poured a rather sloppy glass and chuckled.

"Why would that be, Mr. Miller?"

"I like an audience of gaping, shocked onlookers, Miss Alcott. There are some surprises here this afternoon, and you'll forgive me for being on the verge of complete inebriation in delivering such delights."

"Well, that is certainly an advertisement for death."

"If only Miss Collier were here to see them all."

Louisa had imagined the Captain would make himself available to speak with Mr. Miller and herself before this debacle. Still, the idea would be even less charming after the event. In any case, Mr. Miller might be incapable of being questioned. It would seem this was becoming more and more likely as he downed each glass with alarming speed.

"Wait till you see them all lining up like vultures around a carcass."

"Well, I think curious and nosy might be more appropriate, Mr. Miller. After all, everyone entertains the outside chance of being a beneficiary under a will."

"Not once have I sat in this chair over the last twenty years and experienced anything other than bile and vile hatred. Lingering disgruntlement accompanies all will readings, even if everyone knows the outcome."

"Miss Collier's last will and testament will be more of a surprise. With no obvious beneficiaries?" Louisa said.

"You're angling just like my wife. I cannot say a word until the time is right. My will readings are always at one in the afternoon and no earlier, no later."

"I assure you, Mr. Miller, not one person could take the place of your wife, Mrs. Miller. An ocean of comfort to you."

Mr. Miller grumbled something most likely inappropriate and staggered to a press, which he opened and retrieved eight cut glass lead tumblers.

"Only the best for this occasion, Miss Alcott. Drink up if you fancy it."

As the rain lashed against the window, Louisa enjoyed the peace immensely. Mr. Miller shuffled around the room, taking out papers, arranging his desk, and putting chairs in different places. One imagines this type of affair is similar to preparing for battle or staging a scene in a play. Single chairs for those wishing not to speak to anyone. Double chairs for those wishing to whisper their verdicts into each other's ears, and finally, three chairs in a row for family groupings. Setting a stage was orchestration. Mr. Miller was clearly adept at creating and enhancing it for full effect.

The door creaked open, and the Birch sisters came in, occupying two seats nearest Louisa. "Ah," April thundered. "The brandy is on the go. Well done, Mr. Miller, you never disappoint." She took the liberty of pouring a colossal glass before gulping it down. She poured another and a second one, this time handing it to June. "Now, little bird, get that right into you. Brandy is perfect for shock."

"I'm not in shock, April. Do stop being so obnoxious."

"Of course you are. Captain Briers put his manly hands on your slender shoulders but for an instant, with memories to last eternity."

"Do shut up, April."

June's face soured, and she gave the window her full attention, upon which the most alarming amount of rain pummelled, filling the room with noise.

"I believe the school was broken into again, Miss Alcott."

Louisa stiffened. "That is correct, Miss Birch."

"Once unfortunate. Twice unusual."

"What did Miss Murdock say about the event?" Louisa asked.

"Well, you know a certain type of Concord virgin cannot but help herself in practicing levels of constraint more fit for holy orders. Their gossip is ethical, sparse, and parsimonious."

At this point, June grunted in agreement with her sister's situation summary.

"I'm afraid Miss Murdock preferred the other self-serving Chandler affair."

"So, how did you find out about the school break-in?"

"Oh, Miss Taylor prefers our company naturally enough. Rather in larger measures than we might return the compliment."

"I see."

"Still, I would like to have seen Miss Murdock tell the story because she must now be convinced it was not me she could have seen at the school when she accused me of being a common criminal the first time. It must have been such a disappointment to her."

"And how might she have reached this conclusion? She seemed very convinced."

"Creeping around a schoolhouse at that hour isn't the pursuit of any normal person in love with life. One must be convinced the person who broke in is either very foolish or desperate, and I'm neither."

"Time will tell, Miss Birch."

Louisa was thankful Miss Murdock had not relayed the true nature of what occurred at the school. For this to happen, she believed Miss Murdock to be in a natural state of shock. Deeply disturbed, any person in their right mind must be so. She now regretted not making herself available to oversee the discussions, and it seemed unlikely to have borne much fruit without a reaction.

The Chandlers arrived in a threesome: mother, daughter, and father. Mary Chandler appeared dressed for a wedding in peach with a crimson velvet cloak, soaked to the extremities from the foul weather. Miss Nash and Evie Briers arrived and huddled into a set of chairs nearest the doors. Miss Murdock came alone and sat on a seat nearest Mr. Miller's filing cabinet, staring ahead, her lips set in a grim line. Miss Taylor sashayed in, followed by Edward Lounsey, and they took seats together. There was no sign of Mrs. Miller, and this might have been a Godsend but for Mr. Miller's increasing drunkenness, now practically slumped in his chair. He suddenly cleared his throat, and the low chatter died out.

"Are we all here?"

He checked the large grandfather clock which loomed over the participants beside his bookcase. A gentle chime rang out one gong: it was precisely one in the afternoon, and he made an elaborate lunge for his pocket watch to check it matched the clock. Just as he was about to speak, Captain Briers, accompanied by Mr. Founts, entered the room quietly and stood. The door was closed.

"It is one in the afternoon on Wednesday, December 8th, in the year eighteen seventy."

"Well, there can be no disputing that," April Birch said in low whispers.

"Please be quiet, Miss Birch," he said, with remarkable articulation for a man who'd quickly swam in a bottle of brandy up to this point. "I will now read the last will and testament of Emily Collier of Rosebud Cottage, Concord, in the Middlesex County of Massachusetts."

October 21st, 1870

I hope by the time this will is read out in public I have made it to old age. I have accomplished many things in my life, many of which most people only dream about. But I have so much to do, and yet I feel the impending mortality is something each of us humans on this earth must contemplate.

I leave my farm valued at forty-three greenbacks per acre, including Rosebud Cottage to Maisie Taylor. I leave all my personal effects to Maisie Taylor to do with as she pleases, apart from the listed items below. I leave my dear bees and hives, if they are still thriving, to Miss Louisa Alcott, a tremendous lover of nature and brilliantly independent woman. I want Hierophant, if he is still with us, to live with Miss Alcott; he was so very fond of her. To April and June Birch, I leave my amethyst and diamond gold pendant along with the sum stipulated in this will, which shall remain private. I leave Concord school the necessary funds to carry out all repairs, with the cost to be taken from my estate. I wish to be remembered at the Concord Fete with which I was associated and feel privileged to be associated. I want to also be remembered in whatever way possible at the Choral Society, which vastly increased my joy in life during my time on this great land.

Mr. Miller put his glasses down and laid the paper on the table. Stunned silence in the room created an atmosphere akin to the conduct of a criminal tribunal or court. And yet, there was something justified in the way Miss Collier handled her affairs, all but the legacy to Miss Taylor. This presented something of a curiosity to Louisa, one she could not banish no matter how hard she tried. The will was also recent. Mr. Miller might be able to explain this, but for now, she fretted. Would he be sober enough to withstand questioning?

"Well, there you are, ladies and gentlemen. The last will and wishes of Miss Emily Collier, and I will formalize matters as Miss Collier's lawyer and entrusted executor."

As he spoke, the door creaked open, and a young man in the bloom of his twenties strode into the room. All the heads turned to view his presence, and Mr. Miller's face darkened.

The young man cleared his throat.

"I am Paul Smith. Miss Emily Collier was my mother."

There was a gasping noise that appeared to emanate from Miss Murdock, and a low murmur of voices rippled up.

Mr. Miller sat back in his chair and raised his eyebrows.

"Well, Mr. Smith, you certainly choose your moment. Come in and let us have a look at you."

The young man was acutely aware of the disturbance his presence caused. He took his hat off and cradled it nervously as he made his way to Mr. Miller's desk.

"You have proof of such an assertion?"

He took some papers from inside his coat and laid them on the table. "Yes, sir, I have proof."

Mr. Miller's face betrayed nothing, but Louisa suspected this surprise was one he had not seen emerging, not even in his twenty years as Concord's lawyer. Although, he must have encountered a raucous interruption more than once during his career. Nothing could approach the intensity of this incursion.

He immersed himself in reading and looked up once to see a sea of anxious faces staring back at him. The validity of proof would be verified privately and not under the gaze of persons who'd inherited who might harm this man. Louisa, in particular, wondered earnestly if a beneficiary of Miss Collier's had murdered her. The temptation to assume it narrowed her list of suspects became all too acute, and she exchanged a worrying glance with Captain Briers, who simply and gently shrugged his shoulders.

"For now, I would dismiss you all."

There was noisy dissent, all hungry to hear the man's claim.

"I ask you all to leave in an orderly fashion at once."

He waited for his command to be complied with and then looked at Louisa. "You and Captain Briers can remain."

April Birch could be heard loudly laughing as she swept her velvet cloak about her and examined the young Paul Smith most carefully.

"I do admire a man who puts his hand into the heart of a hornet's nest and stirs with such courage."

"Thank you, Madam," Paul said and gave her a slight bow.

"That is quite enough, Miss Birch. I must deal with this as a matter of urgency. I beg you to take your leave now," Mr. Miller said.

"I am unmarried, Mr. Smith. Hangman's Cottage provides some good conversation and the best sherry in Concord."

As Miss Birch made her way out the door, Mrs. Miller pushed her way past and stalked to her husband's table.

"Is it true?"

"Please, Mrs. Miller, not now."

"I want to know if it's true."

She had barely noticed the young man sitting at the table.

"Is what true?"

"Miss Taylor has inherited Miss Collier's farm and cottage?"

Mr. Miller cleared his throat and poured another brandy.

"I am in the middle of some sensitive business, Mrs. Miller, and I will have to ask you to leave." Mrs. Miller then gave the young man her attention and promptly returned her gaze to her husband.

"I assume it to be true. Will you be home for supper?"

"I doubt it. Not for some time now, please, leave." He did say it as gently as the situation warranted, and Louisa felt a sting of compassion for Mrs. Miller. Her outburst was significantly greater in emotional force than perhaps she'd imagined herself capable of.

She straightened herself, grasping her purse close to her.

"I must speak with you, Miss Alcott, in private as a matter of extreme urgency."

Mr. Miller rolled his eyes.

"I will be home for the afternoon if you'd be so kind as to find the time to pay me a visit."

After she'd left and the door was closed, Mr. Miller spoke. "This is Miss Alcott and Captain Briers, Mr. Smith."

They all nodded greetings. This was an unfortunate time for the young man, regardless of his claim. He seemed visibly disheartened and shaken by the timing of his presence but maintained a type of composure and posture required by the situation.

"I believe your claim based on what you have presented to be, on the face of it, well made. I will have to validate it, of course."

"Of course."

"How did you come to hear of Miss Collier's—your mother's—death, Mr. Smith?"

"The *Concord Sentinel*. I had been looking for her for some time and believed she was in the area somewhere."

"When was the last time you saw her?"

"My father…it was a tough time for her when I was born. I never knew my father, and it was considered best I would be brought up by a relative."

Mr. Miller poured another brandy and slid the glass towards the man. He put his hands up to refuse.

"Go ahead. You'll need it."

Louisa considered how doubly sad this particular state of affairs had turned. A very impossible situation for a young man to be in.

"Your mother was murdered, Mr. Smith."

"*Murdered?*"

"Yes, I'm afraid so," Louisa said, sensing Mr. Miller's increasing discomfort. "Captain Briers and I here are investigating the circumstances."

"How did she die?"

"We believe she was poisoned," Captain Briers said. "She was celebrating her birthday in November and discovered the following morning."

"But who would do such a thing?"

"We are trying to establish this, Mr. Smith. While we have some suspicions, we must continue our work to find out exactly who is responsible."

"I had no idea."

"No, of course, you wouldn't. And your arrival has certainly created somewhat of a stir right in the middle of reading your mother's will, as it were."

"What does that mean?"

"If your claim is valid, which I believe it is, you will have a right to contest the beneficiaries with your inheritance claim."

"What if one of *them* killed her?" he asked.

A perfectly reasonable question, Louisa thought.

"A murderer cannot profit from his—or her—crime. We must be careful in the pursuit of the truth. Your arrival is sure to cause some consternation."

"If I may suggest, Mr. Smith, you should confine yourself to a safe lodging in Concord or perhaps in Bedford or Carlisle. There is a very dangerous individual about."

"I certainly never expected this. Do you think *I'm* in danger?"

"I would imagine you are," Mr. Miller said. "But I'm not privy to all the information in possession of the Captain and Miss Alcott. I would say you must be as careful as you can."

Captain Briers rose and beckoned Louisa towards him, where they counseled in the far corner of the room.

"This could have serious implications, Miss Alcott. Can he possibly lodge at Castle Farm with you and your family? I firmly believe he'd be safer there than in some inn. Now that his claim has been so publicly made, I fear for his life."

Louisa nodded. "I believe this might be for the best, Captain. Besides, he could help us with some chores to earn his keep."

"What are you two whispering about?" Mr. Miller said.

"We have discussed the possibility of Mr. Smith lodging with me during this precarious time. The Captain would prefer he remain in Concord and under a safe roof."

"Confidential, of course," Captain Briers said. "I mean, it would be useful if his whereabouts were not advertised." The unmistakable reference to Mrs.

Miller was fully understood by Mr. Miller.

"I catch the drift of your meaning."

There was a moment of silence.

"Well," Mr. Miller said. "I would like to grant you my sincerest condolences on your mother's passing, Mr. Smith. We shall expedite this matter."

The Society of the Bronze Oak

L ouisa discovered Paul Smith had impeccable manners. He insisted on a carriage to take them to Castle Farm, carefully pulling his hat around his face to avoid drawing attention to himself. The driver barely acknowledged them, and the visibility was poor. The night was ugly. A persistent rain gave way to flurries of snow as the day froze into the evening, the carriage slipping several times as it made its way on the hard, icy ground towards the farm. Louisa paid the driver and ushered Paul Smith into the house quickly. Even in the inclement weather, the gossips were always out and about, prying and snooping. Her isolated farm was no refuge from this until they were safely inside. In the distance, the warm yellow lights of Hangman's Cottage burned, no doubt, with the serious discussion of the day's events.

"I will see to it," Paul said. He lit the fire, hauling in dried logs and some uncut barks he cut in the parlor, carefully laying them out to dry them. It was a job Louisa needed to find someone to do but had of late found no time to engage the services of a woodsman. She set her mind to preparing a stew of chicken, vegetables, and potatoes that would feed a man with the appetite of a horse. The baker's boy had left fresh loaves on the doorstep, which she heated gently and revived them to the point the house smelled gloriously of chicken broth and wheat. Paul sat at the table and clasped his hands, uttering a prayer of thanks before devouring a warm slice of bread.

"I'm so grateful to you and your family, Miss Alcott."

"Please call me Louisa. I consider it the greater respect."

"Thank you, Louisa."

There was something about Mr. Smith that excited Louisa's curiosity. He reminded her of someone but not Miss Collier. Not in the way a son might remind one of a mother. Perhaps her ideas were farfetched, and Paul resembled his unknown father. Either way, from the interactions she'd enjoyed with Miss Collier, there was nothing about the boy—or should she remind herself, man—that resembled Miss Collier. As she predicted, he ate like a man who'd barely seen a plate of food in months. It was satisfying to watch him, even if it meant her own manners were abandoned.

"Someone was seen at Concord school, but the Captain and I haven't been able to establish who it was. Is there a chance you went there looking for someone?"

"I was at the school."

"I see, and what were you doing there?"

"I was looking for my mother."

"At the school?"

"I was told she was a teacher."

"A teacher? By whom?"

"My family, of course."

"But you did not speak to anyone at the school?"

Paul rested his hands on the table. "I was concerned my appearance would cause some distress, and realized my mother probably never mentioned me."

Louisa left Paul to savor his meal. It had been a tiring day for everyone, especially her, and this unusual piece to the puzzle proved to tax her mind into the early hours. Despite wanting rest, she could not figure out where Mr. Smith fit into the whole scheme of things, and the light, bare for December, was crowding the room by the time she nodded off asleep. It didn't last long. She was awakened by a loud banging.

"Miss Alcott," she heard Paul saying from outside her room. "There is a woman very desperate to get your attention outside."

Louisa forced herself into a sitting position. "Paul, you must make yourself very scarce."

When she heard his footsteps fade upstairs, she opened her bedroom window and glanced down the side of the house to see Mrs. Miller, quite puce, about to unleash another round of furious blows to her door.

"Kindly refrain from making such a din, Mrs. Miller. I am coming."

She did, in fact, take her time. Mrs. Miller could wait, and she did, in silence in the cold, until Louisa finally opened the door.

"I see you took your time to light the fire before welcoming me in," she said and walked past her to the fireplace.

"What can I do for you, Mrs. Miller?"

"I don't know where to start, Miss Alcott. Have you considered who made a threat to my life?"

"I had not thought about it for some time." This was not the answer Mrs. Miller wanted. She seated herself, poised bolt upright with her purse nestled into her lap.

"Why not?"

"Because Mrs. Miller, you are still with us, and unless you can tell me why someone would want to harm you, I cannot devote my energies to discovering the writer of foolish notes."

"I see well. You may take it very seriously when you hear what I have to say."

"Can I make coffee first?"

Mrs. Miller's humor wasn't improved by the suggestion, and the idea of making coffee would clearly delay her revelations. Louisa had already left the room and took her time preparing what she felt would ease the conversation and make it feel less like a confrontation. There was her family to consider, also, something which appeared to matter little to Mrs. Miller.

"Now, Mrs. Miller, milk?"

She nodded and then sighed impatiently and somewhat rudely, Louisa thought, but the Mrs. Millers of this world would need to wait their turn, like everyone else.

"Are you aware there's an imposter parading around Concord, masquerading as Miss Collier's son?"

"Well, he may, in fact, be Miss Collier's son."

"Yes, but have you seen this man?"

"He was at the reading of Miss Collier's will yesterday."

"I should have been there," she said, taking her coffee. She sipped at it gently, staring into the fire.

"My own husband would not even tell me. I had to discover it from that snake, Captain Briers."

"What has Captain Briers done to deserve such a designation?"

"What has he done?"

"Well, he's been a very competent investigator of this affair. So far, I see no blemish to his character," Louisa said.

She laid her coffee down and smiled.

"Well, yesterday morning, before that dramatic nonsense at my husband's office, he was out burning documents in a large fire."

"I see, and what documents were they?"

"Well, that wasn't the most disgraceful part of it."

"I see Mrs. Miller, and what was?"

"I continued my walk but decided to go back to have a look. Then I saw Evie Briers and him at the fire, this time throwing a large, mangled sheep onto it."

"Perhaps it had died, and he simply wished to get rid of it?"

"Miss Alcott, I am aware the break-in at the school the day of Miss Collier's funeral was a monstrous occurrence, which included animal blood. All over Miss Murdock's desk."

"And how did you discover this?"

"I asked her. She was far too disturbed the day of the funeral for it to be just someone rummaging in a press. I also understand the school records are missing."

"Well, you are well informed, Mrs. Miller."

"And I believe Captain Briers has something to do with it."

"That is quite an accusation, Mrs. Miller. Unfounded, as it is."

"I think you need to find the truth from him at all costs. If he is to be held up as above the law, he must explain himself."

"I don't believe he thinks he's above the law, Mrs. Miller. I am sure there is a perfectly reasonable explanation for this behavior."

"Well, perhaps he sent me the death threat. After all, I discovered his tryst with Mary Chandler was ended by Miss Collier's death. It is a considerable burden to be in possession of so much knowledge."

"And we shall not forget your keen observance in the matter."

"If you'd observed what I saw, Miss Alcott, what would you make of it?"

"I believe there is but one way of fully ensuring the destruction of papers one does not want to be made public beyond one's study. I dispose of papers in this manner."

"And the sheep?"

"Attacked by a dog or other animal on his land."

"But it looked as if it was deliberately killed."

"That would qualify as odd, Mrs. Miller."

There was a silence, and Mrs. Miller, who had not taken off her coat, drained her coffee.

"I will not be able to impress upon you the importance of this matter. Quite clearly, it features on the lighter side of your priorities."

"It will occupy where it needs to on my list of priorities, Mrs. Miller."

Without a word, Mrs. Miller huffed once, strode to the door, and walked out.

* * *

Louisa felt rattled by the brief encounter. One item was apparent as far as she was concerned. Captain Briers did have answers to give, an explanation possible for the second time, and for one moment, Louisa questioned his motives. She didn't want to fret, but there was something not quite right about how Captain Briers concealed matters. He considered it within his own remit to make judgments he should confide in another about the substance. She could not question his integrity, but the fact remained the situation required his complete transparency. She had to concede Mrs. Miller's point, even if her other grievance was fantasy and pure conjecture. It was also not outside the realms of possibility Mrs. Miller fabricated the threat to her life as part of some broader sinister motive.

She heard Paul moving above, pulling a chair across the floor, and panicked. She wasn't sure if Mrs. Miller was actually gone, and when she glanced out the window, Mrs. Miller was standing at Castle Farm gate, staring up at one of the bedrooms.

* * *

"What marvelous entertainment in Mr. Miller's office," April said, sniffing her brandy. "Such a delight to see Miss Collier's son." She sniggered into her drink. "I only wish I wasn't so damn inebriated."

"Stop being cruel, April," June said. June hadn't found the courage to pour a sherry for herself, worried if she did, she might expose her own feelings and risk opening herself up to more ridicule from her sibling.

"Nothing was entertaining about finding out Miss Collier had a son."

"He didn't look remotely like her, or was I the only person to notice," April said. "As for that, Miss Taylor parading off into the sunset with Rosebud Cottage."

"It's extraordinary."

"Clearly, Miss Collier had lost her mind during the summer."

"What on earth are you talking about?"

"Leaving everything to that deceitful woman. She could not possibly have meant to do such a thing."

"What about our gift?"

"What of it? *We* didn't read the will, little bird, and I suspect Miss Collier changed it a few times. A capricious woman changes her mind often."

June considered this and poured a very small sherry. "Oh, have a decent drink, little bird. That isn't going to do you any good."

"Well, I guess we can afford to now."

April sighed and resettled herself on the sofa. "I hardly think that's the case. And where was that nosy busybody, Mrs. Miller, as the revelations unfolded? Her curiosity must have suffocated her."

"You can be sure she was there after we left," June said.

"Oh, I would imagine she's been like a flea in her husband's ear. I don't know how he tolerates her; she most assuredly knew already."

"I doubt Mr. Miller told her about the will?"

"Mrs. Miller has a way of finding her information, you can be sure."

A pot crashed and whirled about the kitchen. Evie Briers emerged. Her eyes were sunk in pools of dark skin, her hair awry. April waved her arms in June's direction.

"See to it, June. The poor dear."

June sighed and helped Evie over to a chair into which she slumped as though the weight of the world rested on her shoulders. April gave June a concerned look, and June went to the parlor to prepare some coffee.

"What bothers you, Evie?" Apart from being an indentured slave in the Birch homestead, June thought fleetingly as she prepared the tray. It was slightly reprehensible that a woman of Evie's standing was reduced to catering to other people's households. But she excelled at it.

"Hurry up with the coffee, little bird. We're dying in here."

Evie took an embroidered handkerchief from her dress and held it to her eyes and nose, shaking her head gently from side to side.

"I'm so sorry," she whispered.

"Don't be silly, Evie. Anyone who breaks down in misery in my living room requires significant attention." June appeared, and the tea China rattled precariously, stacked on top of one another. April tutted loudly, and in a dramatic move away from her normal stance on these matters, she rose up and grabbed it, placing it down on the table in front of Evie. She felt the pot, as though June was incapable of preparing the coffee efficiently and, satisfied with it, poured.

"Get scones and honey, too," April instructed. Thinking more of herself, if she was honest, as she'd barely had breakfast, and Evie made the best scones. For a moment, wondering if they were safe to eat, she hesitated as June deposited the plate on the table. The unmistakable scent of lavender-infused sweetness filled the room, and Miss Collier's honey was really the best in the whole of Middlesex County. She was glad Louisa would take charge of the hives; she could barely imagine she'd never be able to get such succulent delights.

"Now, drink up and take some scones. You'll feel much better."

When Evie ceased blubbering, she took some coffee but refused a scone, sending April into a quandary once again, only remedied by June snapping one up and slathering it with honey. She ate without any severe consequence, and April was encouraged. April let June deal with the issue of getting to the bottom of Evie's problem. She was so much better at the immediate horrors of female hysteria, but she was adept at solving problems. Her solutions were in great demand, and this occasion was no exception.

"What is wrong?" June said finally.

"I miss Scout."

June glanced at April.

"It must be something more serious than that, Evie?" April said.

"Perhaps that is all it can be," June said, glaring at her sister. "After all, we are not blessed with animals as company. Surely, we cannot understand the sorrow such a death could inflict."

April had suffered the presence of a cat, Jubilee, for a minimal period owing to an infestation of field mice. The cat was extremely hard working to the point it disposed of most of the mice within a week. Miss Collier's cat Hierophant simply stared at the mice and decided he didn't have the appetite for continuous stalking and high expectations placed upon him. Beyond this, April had no interest in keeping animals with all that filth and responsibility. June was much more inclined to keep a pet and was clearly upset when Hierophant went into Louisa May Alcott's care, as though Hierophant knew Louisa was the right person.

Evie engaged in another round of sobbing. "We have no money," she said.

"Evie, that can't be true," April said. "Surely your brother is well provisioned for in his employment?"

"Of course, he is," she said, then bitterly, "he just doesn't spend it wisely."

"Can't you discuss this matter with him?"

There was another round of uncontrollable sobbing, during which April busied herself, pouring a small brandy for Evie.

"Surely, he must know you have to be provided for?" June then asked after Evie, typically eschewing any alcohol, appeared to take it in one undignified gulp. April waved her arms, signaling another round, proffering her own glass first.

"Well," April said, smiling. "Things might improve now that Mary Chandler is off the scene."

"She's not," Evie snapped. "I cannot prevail on him to stop seeing her."

"Have you discussed this delicate matter with him?"

"Of course."

"Well, it seems the Captain is still compromised. What do you think, June?"

June raised her eyes over her glass. She smiled thinly, her eyes greeting her sister with a lingering smirk.

"I'm not aware of the Captain's position on Miss Chandler, I must say."

"Position," April said with a huff. "It's clear the Captain was informed of his duty in the matter. The inquiry into Miss Collier's death must take precedence over any dalliance he's chosen to engage in."

"Dalliance," Evie said, then she too huffed. "If only that were the only mischief he was up to."

April's eyes widened. "Pour," she said to June.

"What mischief, Evie, do be transparent."

Evie accepted another dram, this time taking her time. Her face had taken hold in a swollen grimace, the kind only hours of weeping could create. An odd tightness around her mouth made her seem years beyond her actual age.

"I found a sheep on Kame Bluff. A dead one."

"A dead one?"

"Mutilated. Its throat slashed from one side of its neck to the other."

"A fox or some other horrific night creeping thing must have killed it."

"No," Evie said, her voice strong and determined. "The break-in at the school."

"What about it, Evie? You are not making much sense, dear," April said.

"The day of Miss Collier's funeral."

April and June glanced at each other, this time April pushing the bottle away, and this was no time for a lapse in momentum.

"Miss Murdock was at the school, and there was blood all over her desk."

"She never mentioned it, Evie."

"She said there was blood. All over the chair. All over the desk. She said it was awful."

Evie clapped her hand over her mouth as if the words were themselves full of shame. The brandy worked its wicked way into her system, and April returned to the sofa to capture the rest of the story. Of course, June and she returned to the cottage with other more enjoyable company the night of the funeral. It never occurred to April something more sinister had happened at the school. In their absence, Miss Murdock's alarming disclosure must have been announced that evening. She would not have wanted herself or June to be privy to such information after those trifling accusations of thievery were cast about.

"And what import might the dead sheep have?"

"Animal blood," Evie said, with a superstitious glint in her eye.

"Are you suggesting Miss Collier's murderer is also a satanic fiend?" April said.

Evie shrank back into her chair at the mention of such a thing.

"The blood," she said. "It must have come from the sheep," Evie said.

"And you believe your brother, the Captain, found the animal whose blood was poured over Miss Murdock's desk?"

"Yes, and then destroyed it. Makes him look very guilty."

April took her time before phrasing her next question, which in the asking might cause some consternation.

"Have you some concern over this burning of the carcass?"

"What if this was the evidence, Miss Birch?"

"June, call over to Miss Nash and have her take Evie home."

"Why can't you call to Miss Nash?"

"I cannot think and walk at the same time. Unless you wish to accompany Miss Briers back to Kame Bluff?"

"Yes, I think I will. The air will do us both good."

April scoffed at the air being good. Nothing was good in Concord now; it was positively rancid. This new information made her giddy, and she wondered if Louisa was aware of this treacherous news.

"I need to keep my chores here," Evie said, much to April's relief.

"Are you sure, Evie?" June asked.

"She's sure," April said. "Quickly now, both of you. I must make some notes."

* * *

When Louisa was sure Mrs. Miller had left and was not skulking about the property, she checked on Danny and Doodle. They nudged and nosed their way to the side of the pen where she stood, filling their trough with water. There was something odd in how Mrs. Miller told Louisa of her concerns and as though she knew quite some more details than admitted.

Paul came out from the door behind her and offered to help with the evening feed.

"Who was that woman?"

"Mrs. Miller, the postmistress."

"I see. What does she want with me?"

"With you?"

"I'm afraid she saw me in the window as she was leaving."

This put Louisa instantly at ease, not having to worry whether or not Mrs. Miller might have seen Paul wandering about. There was nothing to indicate Mrs. Miller already knew but more than likely will have burdened her husband with disclosing it. What was concerning was Paul's identity. Louisa was sure his mother *was* in Concord; it was just not Miss Collier. This had been noticed by a number of Concord residents. His presence, a challenge to Miss Collier's will, would complicate matters, and Louisa felt it her duty to protect him.

"Do you know anything else about your mother?"

"Apparently, she never married. I, of course, was not spoken of."

"Nothing after that?"

"She moved here. I'm afraid I know nothing more."

"Would your family know more about her?"

"I get the impression, Miss Alcott, you don't believe Miss Collier was my mother?"

"I'm not sure she *was* your mother."

He stopped turning the hay over in the pigsty, resting his arm on the pitchfork. There were signs of disappointment on his face, as though he knew this affected things, including his place in the order of inheritance for this woman, Miss Collier. As if his move to Concord took a considerable amount of thought and planning which now amounted to waste.

"Do you think my mother is still alive?"

"Yes, I believe she is."

* * *

Louisa wrote a note for an appointment with Mr. Miller. She assumed he would be fully back to his senses, fully recovered from his previous indulgences, and she would discuss the matter of the strange symbols with him.

The second was for Captain Briers. He would accompany her to question Mr. Miller, and if in the knowledge of some matters odd and unusual, his behavior would dictate how she would handle his continued pursuit of the culprit, for if he was tainted by some wrongdoing, he must not persist. She entrusted Paul Smith with both missives, instructing him to call to the Captain first.

* * *

At Kame Bluff, Captain Briers knelt beside the spot where the mangled sheep breathed its last. Or so he'd assumed to be the case, not equipped with any knowledge to the contrary. The area bore no footprints but was crowded with rough grasses and roots. There was no other indication it died there or, indeed, was killed on his farm. He cursed himself for not taking it to vet Parsons, who might, with some investigation, have been able to determine if, indeed, its blood was on the school desk. Evie had returned in a state of complete confusion, her mind poisoned by the deed beyond any logical operation, for he knew the feeling of dismay she'd experienced.

She trusted him, and in the current climate of violence, she had no choice. But lately, he found Evie distant and suspicious. Had he given her reason to be so? As he stood up from his inspection, he spied Paul Smith, the inheritance claimant and alleged son of Miss Collier, striding purposefully across the field towards him.

The air had warmed, and a thin grey mist swirled around like tiny ghosts. The stink of acrid wood hung in the air, and resonant heat radiated from the dead fire. It was comforting in a small way, except when he saw a tiny curl of wool snagged to an unburnt twig. Evidence of what he'd done.

"Captain?"

He recognized him at once.

"What are you doing here?"

"I have an important message from Miss Alcott."

"And she sent you?"

"Yes," he said, holding an envelope out. "Urgent."

Captain Briers kept his eyes on Paul as he tore open the missive.

"Are you not concerned for your welfare? Strutting about like this?"

"Miss Alcott seems to believe I am safe, and I have contained myself to her farm. I have barely ventured out until this very moment."

"Yes, yes," Captain Briers said as he read the letter. He turned it over and then returned it to the envelope.

"Am I to join this meeting today?"

"I have not read the contents."

"I'm sure you would not advise me even if you had."

"Why are you so hostile?"

Captain Briers smiled. "These are testing times, Mr. Smith, and someone with an unknown agenda has thrown Concord into turmoil."

"And I have no doubt made matters worse."

"Yes," Captain Briers said. It was said cheerily as though Paul answered correctly in a school examination. "Well, I must respond to the summons, Mr. Smith. I must thank you for your attention to the matter."

"May I accompany you to town?"

"How do you know I must go to town?"

"I have another message for Mr. Miller."

"Well, come, hurry up."

* * *

Mr. Miller waited until just after lunch to receive his unexpected visitor. He made a point, except at home, in punishing those who arrived unannounced or aggressively disrupted his routine. Although frequently engaged in nothing in particular and spectacularly industrious at it, his mind was always busy. There were always minor items to be attended to, completing wills, adjusting fees, and amending maps. Some of this work occurred strictly outside of client instructions. He found the average mundane resident of Concord practically impossible to educate. There was simply no explanation simple enough for some of the more assertive fools he'd the displeasure to contend with.

"Come in, Miss Taylor," he said, delighting in the time-lapse he'd managed to impose. Miss Taylor walked in, and although made to endure a wait in his anteroom, he'd decided not to light a fire. The possibility of enrichment by Miss Collier's estate seemed to warm her bones sufficiently.

"Take a seat," he said. "Brandy?"

"Why not?"

Neither made the requisite eye contact, the sort that gets down to business. Mr. Miller was naturally excited by her presence; she was of different humor and one certainly more curious than triumphant.

"I take it you're here about the legacy?"

"Well, no, I'm not," she said, swirling the liquid about her glass. "I'm here to find out how serious this son of Miss Collier is. If indeed he is her son."

"Everything points this way."

"Have you noticed he resembles nothing of Miss Collier?"

"I myself did not resemble my mother or father. Or siblings, for that matter," he replied. "Thankfully."

"I think you'll find other people found the dissimilarity, Mr. Miller," Miss

Taylor said.

"Is there a specific reason for your visit, Miss Taylor?" he asked, of course, hopefully. On the last occasion of their meeting, a somewhat different range of emotions unleashed themselves. Her aloofness and distance disturbed him slightly, and her current business-like manner was off-putting.

"I am here to ensure you understand Miss Collier's will must take effect."

"I assure you the law and justice will be served."

"Meaning?"

"If Mr. Smith has a valid claim, this will have to be investigated. His arrival at this point is somewhat awkward, but it will be thoroughly examined for now."

"It is not simply awkward. It is regrettable."

She said this with her characteristic smile and a grimace of sweetness sure to captivate all who encountered it, but the undercurrent was unmistakable. Mr. Miller felt her whole meaning. But he was not in a position to agree with it.

"I'm not sure I understand you?"

"I'm sure you do, Mr. Miller." With a swift movement of her hand, she had finished her drink and replaced her gloves on her slender, delightful fingers.

"I will be available to sign all the paperwork as soon as it is ready."

Mr. Miller sat back in his chair. An odd sensation of defeat overcame him, one he was not accustomed to. He was, of course, where Mrs. Miller was concerned but never in his realm, his world, where he enjoyed autonomy and freedom to decide precisely how matters should play out.

Was this a direct threat from Miss Taylor? He'd seen this type of vicious hostility play out before, an avaricious horde of grasping relatives ready to slit the throat of the other over a parcel of land not fit to grow a row of carrots on. This was an entirely different matter. He made a note to discover more of Miss Taylor's intentions to bring the case forth. Make it impossible for her to blur the issues and use her wiles on him. He ought to be ashamed, but he didn't get the chance. Another unwanted missive arrived.

"Sir," Paul Smith said, marching directly to his desk through the door Miss

Taylor left open.

"An urgent message from Miss Louisa May Alcott." The letter contained some facts dressed up in riveting prose with some scurrilous flourishes, none of which could be described as anything other than evil. An accusatory tone mixed with a type of sympathy about the edges. He balled it up and threw it into the fire. Again, his brief reflection was tainted by another intrusion. This time Louisa herself was accompanied by the Captain.

"I apologize for the interruption, Mr. Miller, but we must speak with you."

She seated herself, a wave of cold air wafting from her clothes. Captain Briers' cloak emitted a burnt stick odor, which made him sneeze.

"I would have preferred if you had made an appointment, Miss Alcott."

"Yes, we did, but under the circumstances, prior notice won't suffice."

"I see."

"The Society of the Bronze Oak," Louisa stated in what might be the start of a bleak discussion. It conjured all manner of an oddity, the very sound of it. Society was a word associated closely with secrecy. People became angry and envious all at once at the thought of being a member of society, depending on whether one was in it or not of course. Committees were arduous, thankless, and irritating endeavors; societies were exciting and mysterious.

"What about it?"

"I told Miss Alcott you were a member. She's curious about it."

"There's nothing to tell."

"I wouldn't ask Mr. Miller if I wanted to be fobbed off."

Louisa gave him a short, dark smile. A spiky tone in her voice. She refused to be misled on this account; it was too important.

"You're aware, of course, that animal blood was spilled over Miss Murdock's desk at the school. There were symbols carved into the back of her chair. Thankfully, it appears they were unnoticed by her, so their presence has not circulated about the town," Louisa said.

"And you imagine the Society has something to do with this?"

"I imagine nothing."

"The Society is an earth appreciation group, and it's not a mystery." He gave the Captain an agonizing look of innocence, for as sure as anything, knowledge of the society's existence to Miss Alcott was indeed his fault.

"I don't see how it can possibly have anything to do with this." He then thought, of course, Miss Alcott possibly visualized members, naked, adorned with branches and twigs, wandering around the forest chanting like heathens. Perhaps sacrificing animals to eight wood spirits trapped in the soil whilst drinking wine from gold chalices.

"Who are your members?"

"Miss Collier, of course. April Birch. Some academics, cartographers, diviners. We didn't conduct rituals, Miss Alcott. It isn't some occult fantasy."

"But what is its purpose?"

"Preservation of rare plants and, of course, the trees. Which are being felled at a furious rate and will be so difficult to replace."

"And animals?"

Mr. Miller leaned forward. "We don't kill things, Miss Alcott, we preserve them. Our goal is conservation and studious research, none of which involves murder."

"And where do you congregate?"

"At Hangman's Cottage. Here. What does it matter? Is there a point to this questioning, Captain?" Mr. Miller said.

The weight of his question was directed solely in Captain Briers' direction, who felt it heavily.

"Do you record attendance and minutes, Mr. Miller?" the Captain asked.

"No, we do not." His answers were to become as stiff as his brandy, and Louisa could feel the Captain moving uneasily beside her. A late blast of sunshine illuminated the room, and it felt deeply uncomfortable for a moment.

"Well, if I might ask, what activities do you engage in?" Louisa asked.

"Oak trees in Concord. There are not many, as you've noticed. In fact, the Captain and Evie live in one of the few remaining properties with excellent examples. Kame Bluff. We discussed how we could better conserve. How to deal with diseases of the bark and leaves. Some other activities."

"Specifically?"

"I'm sure the prevalence of Lady's Slipper or Hairy Arnica is not relevant to a murder investigation, surely?"

"So, it is rather a social gathering, you would say?"

"Occasionally, we venture out on field trips."

"I see. Go on."

"There's nothing to tell Miss Alcott. Traipsing around fields. Lurking in damp, wet habitats or on the side of railway lines isn't for everyone, and it can be very tiresome. You could hardly imagine April Birch being a member if it were up to her to rummage in the undergrowth for rare plant species."

"Are animals involved?"

"Concord is populated with farm animals and domestic animals. Hardly in need of preservation? There are too many damn cats if you ask me."

"How do I become a member?"

"Now look, Miss Alcott, we don't initiate people if that's what you're getting at. No secret bloodletting or mantras, none of that nonsense."

"On the subject of blood, you're aware from my letter that animal blood was found on Miss Murdock's desk at the school. Along with the theft of records, this is a bizarre occurrence," Louisa said.

"I neither knew—nor know—anything about it."

"You know nothing about the blood, or you had no idea there was blood on her desk? Which is it?"

"On both accounts, Miss Alcott." His patience returned. With a studied, unruffled look, he managed to resume control of matters, and Louisa resolved to bring the conversation back to a more mundane topic.

"What will happen to the estate of Miss Collier?"

"I advised Miss Taylor that if Paul Smith has a claim, it will be investigated. I have assured Mr. Smith if his claim is bona fide, he will prevail. There is nothing more I can do. My duties are to carry out Miss Collier's wishes. This can often be complicated by operation of the law."

"Miss Taylor has already been here?"

"She is entitled to know what is happening, Miss Alcott. After all, currently, she is the sole heir to Miss Collier's estate."

"How come Miss Collier agreed to sell Rosebud Cottage to Edward

Lounsey only to change her mind?"

Here, the obstructionist returned. Mr. Miller shuffled his feet under the table, his eyes growing small and mischievous with each moment that passed, fully aware he could no longer protect in confidence the affairs of a woman who was now dead.

"I am well aware of the circumstances, Miss Alcott. The deal soured a few days before it was due to be formalized, and it was Miss Collier's right to withdraw."

"And she made her will less than two months later? I am correct in thinking the will was dated October?"

"Correct. The sale was due to close in August."

"And she gave no reason?"

"She gave me no reason, Miss Alcott."

"Was there a previous will?"

"I destroyed it."

"Yes, I'm sure that's the practice, but who was the original beneficiary?"

"I am not at liberty to say. It is completely unimportant now, with the current situation. I'm sure you'll understand."

"You must not hide behind formalities, Mr. Miller," Louisa said.

Louisa felt worn out by his obstructionist behavior. And yet she needed his neutrality—even if forced—to ensure she heard and saw what he did, even if relayed in a somewhat grumpy, uncooperative way. She suspected his mood and ability to be civil might improve if he knew that it was her belief—and she was positive she was correct—the note Mrs. Miller assumed was for her, threatening her life, was most likely for him.

The Bees Buzz

Captain Briers pulled his boots on two hours before the sun would breach the horizon, that is, if it rose at all. The moon's nocturnal shadow was visible between the oaks, and he could see the night brought a heavy coating of snow, and it glistened under the pale blue light. Delightful from the warmth of his bedroom where the fire smouldered. Much less gruesome than the storms coming in January. The low stone walls resembled fruit cake with pure white icing, and the tree branches strained under the weight of ice. The wind howled down the chimney, and the windows rattled. He glanced at his desk, where the ink had spilled a large pool of dark liquid the night before. He'd composed a letter to Mary Chandler, the content of which would probably send her into an infantile rage. In fact, he'd written several and crumpled them up one after the other to throw on the fire, settling on one with the aid of a bottle of Bourbon.

He swayed between meeting her as arranged at noon at Miss Collier's beehives and wondering what had come over her to request the meeting. By turn, each letter agreed to the meeting, and the next refused it. Part of him was curious; Mary was more likely to use the word "noon," yet his recollection was she'd written 12 noon. He'd given up at one point, and the floor became littered with cast-off paper—expensive paper—which he'd have to ask the ever-complaining Evie to replenish.

Was love worth this torture? His anxiety around the issue seemed to have burned out with the candle in a circle of dried wax. Another excuse for further complaints in the need to conserve the candles and paper. Captain Briers wondered if he'd ever write anything if he couldn't make mistakes and destroy his own words with a powerful gesture in the constant need to be conserving paper. Obviously, he shouldn't. Evie would undoubtedly be relieved. Evie wouldn't moan about stocking the pantry with equal force as his paper. He thrived on writing his thoughts down. Envied Louisa May Alcott for the ease with which she plied her trade and wrought success. The injustice of it all.

There was little to be done that early. He checked the outbuildings, most of which had fallen into a state of sullen disrepair. Standing in the cold air, he breathed deeply, letting the flurries of snow land and melt on his face. A cleansing of the soul. He remembered the fire and took a pitchfork to break up the embers and twigs. With one swoop, he picked the white curls of wool and hurled them over the wall. There was little to do. The snow had taken care of most of it, but still, he needed to disperse it. There was something uneasy in his mind about the whole business. He glanced back to the house. A light had come on upstairs, and no doubt Evie would be in to wake him and come across the room littered with paper. He decided to walk. There was nothing for it but to take the crisp air and fill his lungs with retribution.

* * *

Mr. Miller endured the freezing flagstones for one reason: to ensure the pot of water was firmly on the fire for coffee. He despised snow. Mrs. Miller perched herself in the window seat and declared the post office closed for the day. No reasonable, decent person could venture out in such weather without some mysterious agenda. People indulging in inclement weather were devious and untrustworthy.

"Why are you up so early?" she demanded from the upstairs room. Mr. Miller stood as close to the fire as possible, still in its infancy and barely heating the room.

"I have an early start."

"Madness going out in that weather."

"Some of us have appointments to keep."

"Why are we talking through floorboards?"

Mr. Miller re-read the anonymous note he'd discovered left on the doorstep.

Meet me at Emily's Cottage near the beehives at 12 noon Friday.

He wasn't sure, of course, what it meant or whom it was from, but certainly, one thing was certain. It was a trap. He'd resolved himself to that, but his curiosity raged at a fever pitch. Who would dare suggest a meeting with him to which he'd not agreed? Who on this infernal earth would expect him to keep such an appointment?

"Joseph?" came Mrs. Miller's insistent voice.

He made the coffee. Carefully measuring out the ground pieces. A man would always keep this information close to his heart, for his life depended on it. He'd no choice but to be accommodating to his wife's needs, even if, for want of a blunt instrument, he'd instead murder her this morning. The idea, for it was not a thought, floated around his idle brain for more than a moment.

"I'm bringing the coffee, my dear," he said. Mrs. Miller muttered something, and he set about keeping her out of his counsel on the message. How he longed for his office on a morning like this. A lively fire kept alive by his occasional assistance from a spoon of sugar or splash of brandy. A flaring and quick reminder of his freedom. For now, he was distracted by a meeting with a murderous lunatic on the loose around Concord.

"What is so important you must leave today?"

Mr. Miller deposited the coffee on the nightstand and poured it for his wife. Buying himself the time he needed to lie. Part of him wanted to disclose the nature of the communication but felt the best way to avoid any complication was to keep it secret. Perhaps he could bring with him a knife. What he needed most was a musket that would draw attention to himself, ensure the mystery stranger would see he meant business, and intended to protect himself at all cost. The Birch ladies had a well-stocked arsenal. He'd often wondered about the wisdom of that, but right now, asking for a weapon would undoubtedly raise suspicion.

"Mr. Miller?" Mrs. Miller said, irritated. "Where is your mind?"

"What?"

"You're distracted."

"I have papers to review this morning. Urgent matters."

Sufficiently vague to keep the woman at bay. He shared coffee in silence under the intense glares of his wife. "No breakfast?" Mrs. Miller said out of the blue.

"Not today. I'm feeling off."

"Not for you. For *me*."

Mr. Miller shuffled back toward the parlor and poked his nose out the back door. The hens seemed delighted pecking at the hard ground, and he pulled on his house shoes to finalize the task of finding eggs. The air was still and cold, a faint brightness struggling to open the curtains of clouds. A burst of snow flurries started, and he shuddered. Four eggs, enough to make Mrs. Miller her breakfast. It was not far off noon, and his misgivings increased by the minute.

* * *

Captain Briers walked to Rosebud Cottage and, much to his relief, didn't meet a soul. He could feel the intense, calm stares of sheep behind the low walls as though they knew about the massacre on his own farm. Their slow, purposeful chewing of icy hay, watching him pass. Unreasonable and irrational guilt engulfed him, and he knew at once concealing information from Louisa was a foolish error. It would only be a matter of time before she would discover it, and yet again, he might have to explain himself in the presence of the insufferable Mr. Founts.

He'd barely considered the consequences for his career, but now was not the time to entertain misgivings or quandaries. For what he was about to do now, meet Mary Chandler, was adding to this woeful display of bad behavior and bad judgement. He needed to recuse himself from all further dealings with her and, as much as he could resist, the possibility of meeting in secret. For there was something in Mary's character that made it quite impossible for her to understand the very concept, never mind exercise it. No wife at all was preferable to an indiscreet one. Such sentiment might easily win him some favor with the distinctly uncordial Misses of Concord but bode particularly ill for him now.

His future plans might not involve a Concord lady at all. If only he could persuade Evie to leave Kame Bluff and lure her to Boston, their lives might be more manageable. His connections would run deeper. The excitement of a larger home unburdened by acres of the useless land they possessed. He could not prevail upon her to see the value of such a move. In fact, it caused numerous disagreements when Evie reminded him that the farm was also hers, if not in law but by a divine source of justice, which prevented him making decisions alone, affecting both of them. It was her home. The excessive attachment to Kame Bluff distinguished and set them apart, common with siblings of a remarkable age difference. His modern views and rational thoughts clashed with her intolerable refusal to see the benefits of anything other than isolation in Concord.

There was much in the miserable woman he despised, despite being kin. And with misery came a sort of hell on earth acceptance with no desire or imagination to alter it. He pulled his coat tight around him as he approached the cottage. It did not have the look of a place where violence occurred. It looked unlived in, for any time he passed and Miss Collier was there, a warm glow of candles and hearth illuminated it. Now, the windows resembled the dead eyes of a skull, black and shiny with hidden depths. Like the fields and outhouses, it was smothered in soft white snow. No footprints. He did wonder—or suspect—if Mary would abandon their meeting. Her fragile disposition was rarely given to walking except in a carriage or cleaned hallways. And she must know he had to reiterate the relinquishment of their relationship was the only thing to do.

The gate was recently opened, and he now saw footprints to the side. Of course, Evie had undertaken to put the hives in the shelter and care for them. Maybe assumed she'd inherit them until the reading of Miss Collier's will indicated she would not be their carer for much longer. The role of the beekeeper changes each season. Miss Collier gave a talk in the Concord town hall in August, explaining to anyone interested how the bee community thrives—and dies. In spring, the bees swarm. In summer,

Miss Collier explained how she fed the colonies. In winter, mites, illness, disease, and turmoil were the fate of hives. Bees don't hibernate. Their instincts are to survive, but without nature's cull, the land would be infested. Most poignant, she explained a custom in England of telling the bees when someone had died. Bees were part of the family and considered valued workers within the family itself. If not informed, they would either die, or leave entirely.

It was enough to calm the fears of some of the children yet to understand the necessary cruel cycles of nature. A colony should not die from poor husbandry, and every effort should be made to protect them during the harsh winter until February when spring awakens.

Did they leave when Miss Collier died? Evie hadn't said anything. And with Mr. Lounsey's help, she'd moved them to a well-ventilated dry outhouse and bored holes in the hives. Evie swept up the dead male drones, evicted by the females during the autumn. A very fitting end for the poor creatures in Concord, Captain Briers thought. He heard a faint hum as he approached the back of the barn. The door was slightly ajar, but there was no sign of anyone. He checked his pocket watch. It was almost noon, and the wind picked up, hitting him with chilling blasts. He was about to leave when he heard determined footsteps coming from the front of the Cottage, scrunching the ice into the ground. A man, no doubt. He had no choice but to look for cover and moved around the side away from view.

It was Mr. Miller.

What was this?

He waited in hiding for several moments. Mr. Miller marched impatiently back and forth.

"What business have you here?"

He spoke as Captain Briers emerged into the light, and Mr. Miller was startled. He squinted in the freezing onslaught of snow.

"What is *your* business, Captain?"

"I have an appointment."

Mr. Miller gave a humorless smile. "Well, it is a popular location, no doubt. I received an anonymous note to meet at Miss Collier's beehives at noon." He stared at the Captain with an air of suspicion. "Did you order me here, Captain?"

"I did not summon you. I can assure you of that."

"Well, I assure you I did not come here to meet you."

For a moment, both seemed locked in increasing fear, each suspicious of the other.

As they stood there, a riotous humming erupted.

"What is that?" Mr. Miller said, walking towards a hollowed-out trunk. Both men moved towards it and shrank back.

"Do bees swarm in winter, Captain," Mr. Miller asked, starting off across the clearing. As he reached the other side, he stopped and made a little ducking and dodging movement of his head.

"There are so many bees here, and I didn't notice them until now," Mr. Miller said.

A moment later, he pointed to a crevassed trunk in the bare apple tree. "Oh, look in there. That's where they're all hiding. Captain, I think we should leave here. I don't like this at all."

Captain Briers stepped a tiny bit closer. "They've swarmed, and they've ended up in here," he said. "Be still."

Why did they swarm? It was highly unusual.

As he finished speaking, a bee alighted on Mr. Miller's bare hand. He flinched and flicked it away. When it didn't move, he brushed it off with his hand. As he did, he felt the sudden sharp pain of the sting in his flesh.

"Oh God, it's stung me. *Dammit.*" His words were barely out when he felt another sting, this time at the back of his neck. "Oh," he cried out. "Captain, let's go."

There came another sting and another. Mr. Miller, shrieking and raising his hand, brushed another from his cheek. Captain Briers watched as a hazy dark fog rose from near the dry serrated bough and moved closer to him. Mr. Miller looked down at his hand, where a dozen clung to his skin. Frantic and terrified, he let out a terrified shriek.

In a second, Captain Briers was at his side. Desperately, he brushed and slapped at his body while the bees swarmed in a darkening cloud. They were everywhere, and the air became filled with the sound of angry buzzing and of Mr. Miller's desperate cries as he tried to ward them off. They multiplied over his body, every inch of his unprotected skin.

"Keep still, Joseph," Captain Briers shouted. In his desperate, growing agony, Mr. Miller turned and ran. Heedless of his own danger, Captain Briers ripped off his coat and shirt and tried to throw them over him as a shield, but now his arms flailed uncontrollably, and he knocked it aside. In seconds, his arms and face were black with a sprawling mass of bees. A moment later, his terrified screams filled the air, and he was running. As he ran, the bees followed in a methodical fuzz above his head and a long undulating trail behind.

Leaping forward, Captain Briers fell over the root of a tree. Scrambling to his feet, he ran on. Mr. Miller rushed blindly forward among the trees and could barely be seen through the bees.

Captain Briers was within a few feet of him when in a small clearing, Mr. Miller suddenly halted, staggered, spun in a full circle, and fell backward onto the ground.

Gasping with horror and at his own exertion, Captain Briers stood back as long as he could until it was safe, then lunged to his side, breathing so hard he could barely think.

When he reached Mr. Miller, the bees rose up and away from his body. A moment later, there wasn't one bee to be seen. On the rough ground, Captain Briers knelt beside him. He was on his back, his face turned away, his legs twitching spasmodically, while his swollen fingers curled and uncurled. His bare flesh was hideously swollen and discolored in large black welts.

"Joseph...oh God, *Joseph*."

At the sound of his voice, Mr. Miller slowly turned his head towards the Captain, and he knew he couldn't see him; his eyes were swollen shut, tiny slits in the massive swelling of an unrecognizable face. He tried to speak, but his mouth and throat were so swollen that he struggled to form any words. With difficulty, Captain Briers parted his lips, and a dead bee fell from his tongue. Arching his back, he let out a short, hoarse, agonized sound as he tried to fill his lungs with air. Captain Briers bent over him, pinched his nose between his finger and thumb, sucked in air, and clamped his mouth over his. Desperately, he tried to force air into his mouth, but it was useless. His mouth was swollen, and the air went nowhere. As he tried to pump more air, he felt a sharp shudder go through Mr. Miller's body like a lightning shock. Captain Briers leaned back, lifted Mr. Miller's limp wrist, and felt for a pulse.

He knew it was pointless; he had no doubt at all that Mr. Miller was dead.

* * *

Hangman's Cottage was ablaze with heat. April Birch propped herself up on her pillows and wondered when it would be appropriate to call on Evie Briers to return to her duties now that she'd had a night's rest. There was so much to be done, and June complained all morning about having to set the fire and prepare food when Evie had her hysterics the day before. It was most inconvenient. She wanted her ostrich feather sewn to her funeral wear, but in such a manner she could still use it to fan herself, or issue instructions with it should the need arise. She had a feeling deep down she'd need her funeral black for more untimely demises sure to occur, and it must look its best. There was no knowing, with the climate of violence in Concord, what would happen next.

"Little bird, what are you doing?" She waited for a response, but June didn't respond. April assumed she was in a huff over scrubbing pots or the floor or demeaning tasks of an erratic nature that come with running a household. She hated being confined to the outer reaches of the Cottage, where it was damp and unpleasant.

"June?"

"What is it, April?"

"Be a lovely little bird and fetch my blanket. I'm rather cold."

June reached across to the other armchair and held it out. She snatched it back just as April put her arm across, and she did it again.

"Don't be so childish, June."

"You are demonically lazy, April," June said. "You summon me for what appears to be an emergency but is merely an attack of sloth." She eyed the open brandy. "And greed."

"And what is your complaint precisely?"

"Complaint? You need a full-time domestic. Possibly a slave, resigned to a life of joyless indenture."

She left the room and deliberately pushed the doors open to ration the heat out towards where she continued, noisily, to perform work beneath her status. There was one she relished. She pulled on some old boots, still encrusted with dirt from her last venture outside. She was about to leave the door to the yard open, but this was counterproductive. She, too, would suffer from the icy blasts and swirling snow that continued to assault the countryside. Some feeble complaints emanated from April, but she ignored them.

She entered the potting shed, which hadn't seen much use in ten years. Not since April refused to pay the handyman for whom it was a workshop had they found any alternative function. In summer, it was cool and helpful in storing pantry items if they were kept above the shelves and away from vermin. For now, it was a convenient place to store unwanted items from the Cottage.

Like a water pail encased in dried blood, for example.

She'd left it steeping with water in the window, where it would not be discovered. She took a scullery brush and scrubbed the brown stains for all she was worth. But it was, in the end, pointless effort.

* * *

Louisa rose late that morning. Her limbs ached, and she immediately knew the source of her troubles when she looked outside. As she stared at the blankets of snow, Paul knocked gently on her door.

"I've lit the fire, Miss Alcott."

"Thank you, Paul," she said. "I will need the doctor today."

"Are you ill?"

"In a manner. Nothing serious."

There were a few moments of quiet between them, and Louisa contemplated the arduous business of readying herself for a trip to Market Street. Sending Paul to summon Dr Jennings seemed like a sensible course of action. But then, so was keeping him here to feed Danny and Doodle and attend to the wood cutting.

As this conflict raged in her mind, he returned with coffee. This seemed to calm her significantly, but she wasn't sure if summoning Dr Jennings was fair due to the inclement weather unjustified by any sort of emergency. The idea of struggling in pain to Market Street didn't appeal much to her either. But she had questions for the Doctor that would not be well answered in the presence of a listening ear such as Paul Smith's, and on balance, she decided to make the journey.

Market Street was predictably empty. One set of carriage tracks traced its way along the white roadway, all but now covered in fresh snow. She was practically frozen and in terrible pain by the time she reached the surgery, which thankfully had signs of life. It would have been easier for Dr Jennings to confine himself to the lower level of the building for occasional invalids such as herself, and it took her several minutes to ascend the staircase. It turned out to be fortuitous, if not tortuous, as at the exact precise moment she reached the first landing return, a blazing row was unfolding ahead of her. A tempest of raised voices and accusations.

"Miss Nash, if you must be here, at least ensure the patient folders are kept in order." Dr Jennings said.

"If I was asked in a timely fashion to attend the surgery, I might just be able to assist with these matters. As it stands, I cannot keep up with your unreasonable demands."

"They are not unreasonable demands, Miss Nash, and they are the requirements of the position."

"Even so, if you allow your wife and children to run riot in the office, I cannot be responsible for what happens to patient files."

"What exactly do you mean by that?"

"You know perfectly well what I mean, Doctor. This isn't the homestead, and neither is it a nursery."

A door slammed quite deliberately, and Louisa heard movement. She hurried her pace, which all but destroyed her knees, until she came face to face with Miss Nash.

"I must see the Doctor, Miss Nash. Is he available?"

Miss Nash's sour face was drawn and ashen. In her arms, she carried a pile of papers, some in disarray and requiring sorting. Louisa could only assume she was seeking out a table on which to finish the job. She sighed rudely and pulled her woolen shawl closer with her free hand.

"Of course, Miss Alcott, come with me."

She hauled her up the stairs as though Louisa was most definitely in the final stages of immobility in such a rough fashion she wondered if she might collapse. Although not required, Miss Nash had no bedside manner when dealing with patients, and Louisa flinched several times to get the message across.

"Take a seat," she said. "I will let Dr Jennings know you are here."

She said this like she was required to enter a chamber of horrors, never to return. Louisa, meanwhile, had the disturbing burning sensation in her hands and fingers when one is obliged to be out in freezing conditions for more than a few moments. Nevertheless, the pleasing sensation of heat calmed her nerves somewhat.

"Miss Alcott," Doctor Jennings said in as convivial a tone as possible, considering the altercation. "I was not planning on seeing patients today, but as you're here."

Louisa gave him a poisonous stare.

"And what else might you be doing, Doctor, if not seeing those who have entrusted you with their health."

"Well, on a day such as this…."

"On a day such as this, people become ill, Doctor. Possibly more so than when the sun is splitting our rocks open."

She rose awkwardly and made her way toward his office. This insolence was not acceptable in a man handed a practice of an entire town without so much as a struggle to secure it. The country Doctor was not a role one should lightly assume, she imagined. Although a recent addition to the community, she was convinced the heart and mind of Doctor Jennings were elsewhere. His commitment to his duties was hampered by a rather lazy attitude to service and dedication. And practically no sense of duty.

"I have a tincture which will help your knees and ankles," he said. "There isn't much more I can assist with. The weather affects us all in this regard."

Louisa let out a slight laugh. "Wait until you reach my state of dereliction."

"Yes, I really ought to know better."

"It would be useful if you made house calls," she said. "Then half my troubles could be avoided by the travesty of having to attend in person."

"Yes, Miss Nash?"

Miss Nash had entered the room with her cloak and hat on. She lifted her chin in an imperious manner.

"I am due payment."

"Ah, can we discuss this perhaps tomorrow?"

"No, we cannot. The weather is due to worsen tonight, and I shall not be available to trudge all the way here to suit you."

"Ah, yes."

"I would like to run some errands before heading home, and while I do not have to explain myself to you, I need payment now."

There was an awkward silence into which neither party wished to step, and Dr Jennings, like many professionals of his type, appeared to believe Miss Nash could survive on thin air. Her arguments were well-made and balanced. But clearly, the Doctor had not provisioned for such a trivial item as the woman's wages. His begrudging manner was deplorable.

"I would assume my fee for today and such sundry items I require could cover Miss Nash's dues? At least until you can satisfactorily settle this matter?"

A look of relief washed over the younger man's face.

"Miss Nash," Louisa said and turned slowly in her chair. "I would also like to know something now that I have the pleasure of both your company?"

"If I can be of help, of course."

"Miss Taylor," Louisa started. She felt a rush of suspicion from both of them but proceeded anyway. Such was her need to have a factual matter resolved.

"What about her?"

"I believe Miss Taylor has a child."

Miss Nash looked at the Doctor for his approval or simply an answer. Doctor Jennings had been most evasive on the last occasion, and between the two, she hoped to rush them into a response.

"Well, yes, she does."

"And have you the details of this offspring?"

"It's not my place to discuss patient's private affairs, Miss Alcott."

"I do have a valid reason for enquiring," Louisa said.

"She has—had—a son."

"And do we know anything more about this son?"

"It is a rather delicate matter when a child is born without a father."

Louisa wanted to laugh at this suggestion.

"Every child has a father, Miss Nash. I think your suggestion is the child's father abandoned his duties to the infant."

"He'd be an adult man now, I'd imagine."

"And do either of you have any further information to add to this?"

"I'm afraid not, Miss Alcott," Miss Nash said.

"You're quite sure?"

Again, there was an exchange of glances. Louisa allowed this silence to deepen, and as one part of the official investigation, she imagined this was the only reason she was not asked to leave the office.

"It's not well known, I guess," Miss Nash said.

"That Miss Taylor had a child?"

"That too, I imagine."

"Come now, Miss Nash, this isn't a dentist. Am I required to continue extracting the information like an infected tooth?"

"Miss Taylor is married, Miss Alcott."

"Is she now? And to whom is she married." Louisa was sure most of Concord was aware of this, but it was useful to have the situation confirmed.

"Edward Lounsey."

"Ah, thank you."

Miss Nash frowned slightly and was about to reiterate her need for payment when Louisa reached into her purse and took out some coins.

"I would love a nice sponge, Miss Nash. Do you think you could see to it I get a nice cake from your industrious endeavors? I would like that very much."

Miss Nash looked surprised—and complimented—all at once.

"Not oat squares, if you don't mind," Louisa said.

Miss Nash smiled nervously and took her leave. When the door was closed a sufficiently safe amount of time, Dr Jennings smiled and seated himself. He'd been standing for the duration of her interrogation of Miss Nash, surely a giveaway for his nerves.

"You got what you came for?"

"Why didn't you tell me this information, Doctor? I asked you about Miss Taylor or Mrs. Lounsey, some time back."

"I was not aware Miss Taylor was married, Miss Alcott. I would have given this information to you if I'd known."

"I don't believe you, Doctor. But anyhow, you knew she'd an adult son?"

"So," he said. "I am not an information point, Miss Alcott. I do have a duty of confidentiality, as you are well aware."

"There are consequences if you withhold vital information, Doctor. You should be well aware of that."

"I wasn't aware Miss Taylor's private affairs were of any importance."

"I'll decide that. Besides, you cannot have been living in a tree trunk these last few days. Surely you know a man has appeared in Concord claiming to be Miss Collier's son?"

"And what are you suggesting, Miss Alcott?"

"I haven't the faintest idea. To discover who is behind the murder, I must know everything."

There was an agreement in gesture from Dr Jennings, who'd taken the time to remove his glasses and clean them pointlessly while considering his own position. His impertinence would not have bothered Louisa as much if the timing of the information was so poorly received. To know of this completed at least one small part of the picture, and like many shards of information in Concord believed to be unknown or obscure, quite the opposite appeared to be the true position.

Louisa glanced out the window at the near-blizzard conditions. "Please be so kind as to arrange a carriage to take me back to Castle Farm."

* * *

Captain Briers sat in the kitchen of Kame Bluff, awaiting Mr. Founts' arrival. He'd sent one of his guards from the school to fetch him, to see the scene up at Rosebud Cottage for himself in all its elaborate and grim details.

Evie had disappeared inexplicably. Her absence from the house was only noted as he finally made his way to the upstairs landing after calling on her several times and receiving no response. Believing she was ill, he'd rushed from room to room. The fire had all but died in the grate. She must have gone out for a good reason, unprepared for this weather and indeed not a willing journey to make in such a blizzard. His worry was compounded by the fact he must choose between his duty to investigate and anxiety should Evie get into difficulty.

He heard the muffled sounds of carriage wheels outside and went down to greet Mr. Founts, whose countenance was frostier than the weather. He descended the steps to the ground, eyeing up the endless white sky with horror.

"What is this business, Captain, about Mr. Miller?"

"Have your driver bring us to Rosebud Cottage," the Captain said.

Inside the carriage, Mr. Founts turned his unimpressed face to the Captain. "Where is Miss Alcott?"

"I have not advised her of the incident yet."

"And who is advised?"

"No person at present."

"And why am I here? In such dreadful weather?"

"Because I had no choice due to the unusual set of circumstances."

"Huh. I see, and I suppose Miss Alcott will have a perfectly reasonable explanation for this when she considers it?"

"You shall have to see for yourself, Sir."

Mr. Founts raised his large eyebrow upwards. He'd never seen an investigation so shoddily carried out and vaguely referenced through sheer ignorance of facts. He was, of course, ready at any moment to step in, but for his daughter's wedding in a few days, which seemed unlikely if the bride was to be blue in the face throughout and in a constant state of distressing complaint. He sighed loudly, and just as he was about to ask how remote Rosebud Cottage was, they came upon it.

"Why do people live like this," he muttered as they rounded the carriage and entered through the gate. The stillness of the scene caused Captain Briers to shudder. He was, he imagined, in shock and needing some warm stew and a toaster of whiskey. His guard rode ahead and covered the body with sackcloth. Mr. Founts pushed his cloak aside, knelt down, and uncovered the corpse with the tip of his walking stick.

"Good God," he said. "What happened to this man?"

"Does he need a doctor, Captain," the guard asked.

"Don't be stupid, man. He's clearly dead."

Captain Briers explained the circumstances briefly. There was, of course, the issue of his rendezvous with Miss Chandler, which he could not disclose for the sake of his standing and worth. And his employment.

"Why were you here?"

"I received a note asking me to meet here at noon."

"From whom?" Mr. Founts asked impatiently.

Captain Briers clenched his fists behind his back. "I do not know."

"And Mr. Miller was here when you arrived?"

"A few moments later."

"Well, spit it out, man. Had Mr. Miller any idea why *he* was here?"

Captain Briers lifted his head. "No, he did not."

Mr. Founts tutted, moving the sackcloth entirely off the bloated body of Mr. Miller.

"Do bees swarm? In the middle of winter?"

"I don't know, Mr. Founts."

"Does anyone know anything about this occurrence? Or are we to stand

151

here and assume it was a freakish will of nature?"

"It was very odd, Sir."

"Very odd," Mr. Founts said under his breath. "I must see the scene for myself."

They moved towards the outhouse, where the hives hummed quietly in the darkness. A distinctly lower amount of noise, unquestionably, a lot of the colonies were either dead or had fled.

"Get some light," Mr. Founts instructed. The guard returned with a lantern, and Mr. Founts strode around the hives one by one.

"Are they supposed to be open like this?"

"I don't believe so. My sister Evie has been engaged in the husbandry, and Miss Alcott was entrusted with them under Miss Collier's will."

"We will need your sister to verify some important facts, Captain. Surely, they are to be contained during the cold months." He said this more to himself and suddenly turned and walked out.

"These notes. Where are they?"

"I burned my note."

"What would make you do such a thing? Surely you must have asked yourself the question, man? What would I be doing meeting an anonymous miscreant for no good reason? You are investigating this matter. You would have been better served being accompanied; any manner of madness might have befallen you."

Captain Briers understood his foolishness only too well. He must be convinced that Mary had no intention of meeting him more than ever, and he must keep her name from the matter at all cost. It was a trap, for which he'd no reply as to the details.

"Well, it's quite clear I must remain here now," Mr. Founts announced. "I have little confidence this awful situation is being managed properly." He ordered the guard to remove the body, which would have to be arranged by use of a cart from a neighboring farm. This did not delight Mr. Founts, and he was met with a tirade of insults.

"We shall have to inform Mrs. Miller," he said. A thought that instilled Captain Briers with dread.

"We need to inspect his home and find out if the note is there."

"And if it is not?"

"Are there some details about this affair you are privy to, Captain, which you'd rather not tell me?"

"Of course not. I would imagine Mr. Miller destroyed his note. Just like I did."

"Even so. We require your sister's expertise in the matter of bees to better understand what has occurred here."

* * *

Louisa was relieved to be transported directly to her door. It was a treacherous journey, if not that far by carriage, and she was significantly consoled by the thought of her warm house and some sustenance to revive her. The ordeal of winter aches and pains was something she'd rarely considered slowing her down quite as much as it did, but she must live with it. Live with the irritating nuisance the climate had on her body.

As she alighted, she spotted a bright crimson cloak blowing in the wind. Miss Chandler was standing, frozen as a statue, at her front door. Rather than her usual sullen countenance, she smiled broadly when Louisa walked the short distance to greet her. She was pale, but a slight rose color lit her cheeks up, and when she took Louisa's hand, she was warm and soft.

"I really must speak with you, Miss Alcott."

"We shall speak inside," Louisa said, ushering her ahead. It could only be assumed Paul Smith had spied Miss Chandler outside and, taking his need to remain undiscovered seriously, had simply refused to let her in. It was warm and welcoming in the house, and Miss Chandler walked into the living room, seating herself gingerly on the edge of the sofa.

"I'll make some coffee," Louisa said, hoping a perhaps eavesdropping Paul would oblige.

Mary smiled awkwardly as if the last thing she wanted was coffee. Louisa was reminded of her previous visit and anxiously searched her mind for one possible reason for Mary to make the trip, on foot, in such miserable conditions. It hardly struck her as something she'd be capable of, at least voluntarily.

"What can I do for you, Miss Chandler?"

"I hope you recall my last visit, Miss Alcott?"

Louisa nodded. "Well, I recall some of your last visits, and you insulted me."

Mary's smile vanished and replaced itself with a concerned look, a rather childish look Louisa found strangely endearing.

"I had no wish to insult you, Miss Alcott."

"We often do things we're unaware of, Miss Chandler. Especially if we don't possess the acute emotions of the other person on whom we inflict such behavior. When I was young and rather more foolish, I too was capable of such insults without realizing."

Mary seemed perturbed and yet unsure as to what the whole meaning of Louisa's statement might be. There was a deflated air about her now as if some triumphant disclosure she wished to make was somewhat blunted by Miss Alcott's sly ambush.

"I will get the coffee."

When she returned, Mary was in precisely the same position and waited patiently until a small cup and saucer came in her direction, from which she gratefully sipped.

"I have some serious information, Miss Alcott. Something which unfortunately touches off your investigation."

"I see."

"Well, no, you don't really. Not the way I see it."

"Please do enlighten me."

"I explained on the last occasion I was here that I saw someone at Miss Collier's cottage after I left her."

"But you couldn't identify this individual?"

She replaced her cup gently on the table. "Not exactly."

"Exactly what, Miss Chandler."

"I knew who the person was, or should I say, I saw who it was."

Louisa waited impatiently for this information. Of course, Miss Chandler must be aware that the circumstances of Miss Collier's death were now greatly more complex than the first few days of revelations had led any of Concord's innocent residents to believe. Sadly, Louisa thought she could not trust Miss Chandler's sources, such as they might be compromised by her indulgences and fantasies, which, left unchecked, might get her into serious trouble.

"It was Edward Lounsey I saw," she declared. "I'm quite sure of it."

"Sure of it now, Miss Chandler, or sure of it then?"

The younger woman's eyes widened.

"I am telling the truth, Miss Alcott. You must believe me?"

"Oh, I am more than sure you are telling the truth, Miss Chandler. Then why did you lie to me?"

"I did not want to accuse him of any wrongdoing."

"Surely that is for the Captain and me to decide?"

She flinched at the mention of Captain Briers and took her cup into somewhat shaky hands to take another genteel sip. It was Louisa suspected, more to employ her fingers than to savor the coffee. She said nothing for a few moments. It was as if her plan of revealing her information was either not welcome or believed. Or worse, not a surprise.

"He must have killed Miss Collier," she then stated. "The facts point to such a case."

"Well, not exactly, Miss Chandler. There has been some new information that might account for Mr. Lounsey's presence, if indeed he was there."

"I knew you wouldn't believe me."

"It's not saying that I don't believe you, Miss Chandler. As you describe it, this fact must be put to Mr. Lounsey, and he must have an opportunity to explain himself."

"What else would he be doing there but up to some mischief?"

"Well, you have admitted being there too, Miss Chandler."

Mary put her cup down with a degree of violence that almost shattered Louisa's good China. There wasn't much left after her family's move, and this display of anger was expected, if not warranted.

"I see I was wasting my time."

"Miss Chandler, I will speak to the Captain about what you've said to me. But I warn you. Making such claims must be backed up by some evidence, and I have your word alone as to what occurred that night after all the others left."

"I see."

"Do you?"

"Thank you for the coffee, Miss Alcott. I must be on my way."

"I would ask you to keep this matter to yourself, please?"

"Why should I? Everyone in the town is terrified of what is happening."

"Yes, I understand, but hurling accusations around will not help matters."

"Has nothing I've said been of assistance?"

"It might be, Miss Chandler. Time will tell."

After this exhausting visit, Louisa did wonder if Miss Chandler's version of events could be authentic. She did not want to alarm Miss Chandler, but neither did she want her loosely disclosing this business out of some vindictive revenge. For it was indeed a possibility Edward Lounsey may have been there on account of Miss Taylor. There might be any number of reasons he could be there, not least to again use the occasion to implore Miss Collier to sell her property to him. And perhaps, in not liking the response, decided on a much regretted course of action.

Captain Briers is Censured

Daybreak broke above Concord only briefly the following day. Snow whited out the sky all night, and where drifts reached the upper ledges of doorways, it laced the walls and fields in fine, luminous sheets. A sensation of warmth filled the air as if the cold had moved on. The sounds of mourning and grief, which had started earlier the previous day at the Miller homestead, continued that morning. Mrs. Miller wailed her way through the night and found herself devoid of feelings and numb as she sat by the fire. She was still in her nightdress, and between curled, frustrated fingers, she clutched Mr. Miller's toupee.

She mourned that very few people in Concord would even believe he'd been slightly bald. These incendiary matters would, of course, become public knowledge, mused upon, ruminated upon as though it were everyone's entitlement to know. Mrs. Miller was far beyond caring what people thought. She'd been drinking vast amounts of Mr. Miller's brandy since dawn.

"He loved his hair so much," Mrs. Miller said amidst a gasping and sniveling round of cries. She'd summoned Miss Nash and Miss Murdock to be by her side. Not for comfort or even the merest pretending at grace or humility but for witnesses. Indeed, she imagined that people thought she'd ordained his death in her grieving fantasy. Some mysterious angels of misfortune had landed upon their roof and led directly to his untimely demise. Maybe it was his fault for mixing his business with pleasure and hers for turning a blind eye. It was her fault. All of it.

Everyone in Concord would think she'd brought this to her own house.

Like a plague of biblical locusts descending and feeding on her as their right. She was doomed to meet her maker as the instigator of her husband's death. She must be next, she thought. She has to be next.

"You're being ridiculous, Lucy. There's no possible way Mr. Miller was murdered," Miss Murdock offered. "How could anyone know he was to die in such a hideous manner?"

Mrs. Miller roused herself from reverie.

"He brought demons into our house. He consorted with a devil, and they made it so."

Miss Murdock glanced at Miss Nash, who sat quietly through a round of coffee and cornbread without muttering a word. She raised her eyebrows and forgot to let them fall. The cornbread had far too much salt, and she put it back on the plate and wondered who would bake such an atrocity. She could only trust herself when it came to the purchase and mixing of ingredients and to be sure she knew the constituents.

"I'm sure you agree, Miss Nash," Miss Murdock said.

"Agree with what, exactly?"

There were disapproving glances from both women, and Mrs. Miller continued on her path of destruction by eating large chunks of cornbread washed down by glass after glass of brandy. Now, she bemoaned Mr. Miller's habit of storing his best brandy at his office. She convinced herself she was sure to be murdered if she ventured out of the house for any reason.

"Mrs. Miller must abstain from dulling her senses as though she was in the Birch household. A touch of sherry is most important, but a batch of glasses is not helpful," Miss Murdock said to Miss Nash.

"I'm sure she can be allowed an indulgence on this occasion. If anything, you'd need it for digestion purposes. Of all types."

With that, Mrs. Miller held up a piece of bread to inspect it and then let it drop from a height. It crumbled into tiny pieces on the plate and the floor.

"My God," she said. "Have I been poisoned? Who made these?"

"Evie, I suppose," Miss Nash announced unhelpfully. Mrs. Miller stumbled off the sofa and up the stairs towards the restroom, where she could be heard inducing sickness. Her choking, gasping sounds could be heard all over the house.

"You really are a foolish woman, Miss Nash," Miss Murdock said.

"Well, she did ask."

"She has just lost her husband in the most mysterious of circumstances. In the middle of a murderous rampage of the most awful criminal behavior. The least you could do is hold your loose tongue."

When Mrs. Miller appeared, Miss Murdock rose from her seat and guided the stricken woman back to her sofa, where she propped up some pillows and covered her with a blanket. She then nudged Miss Nash. "Fetch a pitcher of water, please."

Mrs. Miller regarded her with red-rimmed eyes, and a few silent tears flowed down her cheeks, which she rubbed away quickly with the back of her hand.

"You must compose yourself. There is a funeral to arrange," Miss Murdock said. She was sure Mrs. Miller would be in no fit state to organize the upcoming arrangements, which required a significant urgency in management. She was, of course, the ideal person for the role. With Miss Nash, of course, if Miss Nash could control her emotions and keep her thoughts to herself. The Birches would no doubt stick their noses into the proceedings, but of course, Mrs. Miller could be prevailed upon to steady herself and take the best advice available. Her standing would demand this, and as a widow, she was required to observe all the formalities and ignore the frivolous suggestions put forward by less well-intentioned residents of Concord.

When she appeared to be less wild, Miss Murdock handed her more water, insisting she drink as much as she could manage.

"My life was threatened," Mrs. Miller said suddenly. "I got a note."

Miss Murdock slowly placed the glass back on the table and glanced at Miss Nash.

"And what did it say?" Miss Murdock enquired cautiously.

"You are next," Mrs. Miller said in a low voice. "Who would write such a note?"

"Surely it was some vile person out to upset you, and it can't be anything else," Miss Murdock said.

Miss Nash kept quiet.

"And why was Mr. Miller up at Rosebud Cottage in the middle of a snowstorm?" Mrs. Miller said.

"It doesn't make any sense, dear. You mustn't upset yourself further," Miss Murdock said.

Mrs. Miller waved her handkerchief at Miss Murdock as if to dismiss her or make her disappear.

"I'm telling you he was lured up there for some mischief."

"Now we don't know that's true," Miss Murdock said. "There could be any number of reasons for his appointment."

"Why did he lie?"

Mr. Miller was rather well known for lying to Mrs. Miller in respect of his whereabouts. Regrettably, it was one of his tiresome legacies, and practically everyone was aware of this proclivity. Most of the time, it was perfectly harmless, but on this occasion, even Mrs. Miller would have to admit she was unable to verify his story. There was no way she'd venture out in freezing temperatures just to prove a point. Mr. Miller was so much less controversial when he was alive, but this new concoction of horror was almost too much for Mrs. Miller to take.

"Will I call to the church?" Miss Nash asked in a small voice.

"I haven't decided what to do with him," Mrs. Miller said.

"What do you mean?" Miss Nash asked, a little alarmed.

"Captain Briers will be investigating the circumstances of this suspicious incident," Mrs. Miller said.

"We don't know if it was suspicious," Miss Nash said. "Are you convinced something untoward happened, to Mr. Miller?"

"Are you stupid?" Mrs. Miller said, rounding on Miss Nash. "It's self-evident he was murdered. He was allergic to bee stings, I'll tell you. I should know. What do you think, Miss Murdock?"

Miss Murdock was knee-deep in some reverie.

"*Sylvia*," Mrs. Miller said, with as much force as she could muster. Now Miss Murdock appeared lost in thought.

"Yes, I think you should consult Captain Briers and tell him everything you know."

Miss Nash moved uncomfortably in her seat. She could not stop her mind from repeating the phrase Miss Murdock had used. *Appointment.*

* * *

The sun burst out unexpectedly just before noon that day. A bright orange glow filled the horizon, gradually turning to bronze over the quiet snowy fields. Louisa felt a jolt of joy at it and sat on her bed as she did on cold mornings, in no hurry to get up. Paul had lit the fire and fed her pigs. Danny and Doodle had taken to simply glancing at her and then turning their heads away in disgust as though she'd abandoned the creatures. It didn't help Hierophant would wind himself around her legs, making it quite clear he'd found a cozy home with her, soaking up her attention like a brittle dry cloth does water. It seemed to insult the pigs deeply, this shirking of her duties and the favoritism.

When she'd roused herself and come downstairs, Paul had chopped enough firewood to last until February and made coffee and fresh bread. His skills knew no bounds.

"There was quite a fuss in the town earlier," he said. "Something happened yesterday causing quite a stir."

There was no time to respond. A persistent banging on the front door nearly lifted it off its hinges.

"I'll go," Louisa said. "You stay in the kitchen." The pounding continued, and Louisa felt her nerves upset.

"I'm coming," she shouted. "Who is it?"

"It's Captain Briers, Miss Alcott."

He swept in, bedraggled as if he hadn't slept. A blast of cold air accompanied him as though he'd been in the weather and damp for some time.

"I must speak with you."

"You look positively deranged," Louisa said, leading him to the sitting area

161

where a large fire burned. He took his gloves off and heated his raw red hands over the flames.

"What has happened, Captain?"

"Mr. Miller is dead," he said, without ceremony.

"What happened to him?"

"He was at Rosebud Cottage. Miss Collier's bees swarmed and killed him."

"What was he doing there?"

Captain Briers hesitated, and Louisa could see him calculating the answer, which didn't materialise.

"Mary Chandler was here for a visit. Now suddenly, she's disclosed the identity of the person she saw after she left Miss Collier's cottage," Louisa said. There was a deafening silence. "Did you hear me, Captain?"

"I heard you, Miss Alcott," he said, in almost whispered tones. "I was at Rosebud Cottage when Mr. Miller died."

"Whatever for, Captain?"

"I received a note from Mary to meet her there at noon yesterday."

"And where is this note?"

"I burned it."

"Ah, the mysterious fire witnessed by Mrs. Miller. You have much to disclose, Captain."

"I was just as surprised to see Mr. Miller there as he was to see me."

"The reason for his attendance?" asked Lousia.

"He received a note. Identical to the one Mary Chandler sent me, and it is most bizarre."

"What is most bizarre, Captain, is you would agree to meet Miss Chandler."

"I know."

"Especially considering she is a suspect."

Captain Briers looked directly at Louisa. "On what grounds is Miss Chandler, a suspect?"

"You were not listening, Captain. Miss Chandler claims to be the last person to see Miss Collier alive. Now she has also accused Edward Lounsey of murdering Miss Collier."

"Perhaps she is right."

"Captain, you cannot allow your feelings for Miss Chandler to obstruct your good judgment."

"My good judgment remains intact."

"Or I will exercise good judgment for you," she said, as if ignoring his statement.

He resisted the temptation to argue with her. His feelings for Miss Chandler had diminished, and this was not something he'd had an opportunity to tell her in person, although he worried such a meeting might have caused more significant harm than good. Despite the tragedy, this was one positive thing to be glad of.

"The same words were in each note?" asked Lousia.

"Yes."

The Captain seemed a little unsure what to make of this, but Louisa had some ideas. "Are you sure Miss Chandler sent the note?"

"I'm positive. Or at least, I am fairly sure."

"Strange, she never mentioned it when she came here, Captain. I mean, you do know her handwriting, I'd assume?"

He hesitated. Men were not great on details, Louisa believed, unless they regarded affairs of state or politics. Or religion. Or creating impossible general rules for other members of society to abide by, but never themselves. The finer details seemed to evade them.

"You've received notes from Miss Chandler before?" Louisa asked.

"Excellent, Miss Alcott, you've made your point. I could not be fully sure the note was from Miss Chandler," Captain Briers said.

"She cannot have had any reason to meet Mr. Miller, surely?"

"Nothing surprises me at this point, Miss Alcott."

"Well, it seems to be some mystery individual who lured you both there. Or indeed, if Miss Chandler did write the note, this mystery individual wished them to be there at the same time as you were."

"It's certainly possible."

"Bees do not hibernate, Captain," she said, setting her coffee down. "The winter is a challenging time, and if disturbed, they make for vicious enemies."

"Evie will assure you are correct."

"And we will discover no doubt Mr. Miller has an intolerance to bee venom. And that remains to ask you, Captain?"

"As me what?"

"Have you an intolerance to bee venom?" asked Lousia.

"No, I have not."

"That you know of?"

"I don't recall an occasion upon which I've been stung recently, Miss Alcott."

Her questioning appeared to irritate him.

"Perhaps it is recorded somewhere?"

"Well, it's possible," he said. "But where?"

"With a doctor?"

"Doctor Jennings?"

"He took over the practice Captain. His archives would include your details. And Evie's. We must ask Miss Chandler if she wrote both summons."

"We cannot ask Mr. Miller about his note Miss Alcott."

"We can ask Mrs. Miller, I'm sure. If she is not consumed with hysterics."

* * *

The summons from Mr. Founts was not far behind the Captain's visit to Castle Farm. Louisa prevailed upon him to accept her hospitality and come to visit them both at the farm. Her motives were far-reaching and selfish, and she maintained the advantage of being on her territory. Having grown accustomed to having a household rather than being alone. She must control the impulses of the Captain, for he was a dangerously weak link. A very resourceful and cunning enemy lay in wait. If not the enemy, there might also be more than one. Enemies or those unaware they're playing into the hands of the enemy. Information played a great deal of importance in the hands of a perpetrator. She castigated herself for not realizing this sooner, and her father would no doubt agree with her conclusion.

Mr. Founts kept them waiting for the more significant part of the afternoon before arriving noisily close to four. He descended his carriage and took his time to look around Castle Farm while the Captain and Louisa observed him from the window. He stood, arms behind his back, glancing at walls and trees and finally visiting the pigs.

He took his cane to the door and knocked loudly and continuously until Paul Smith, dispatched by Louisa, opened it.

"And who might you be?"

"I thought I knew Sir, until recently."

Mr. Founts moved Paul aside with his cane and proceeded to the drawing room where Louisa and the Captain were seated.

"Who is that insolent servant you have receiving guests?"

"Do come in, Mr. Founts. It is so delightful to see you once again." Louisa said and smiled, and Mr. Founts made himself taller, finding a straight-back chair to rest himself on. He chose the only one with armrests and balanced his cane on the back before inspecting it for stains. He rubbed imperiously at the worn green velvet covering it and then collapsed like a weary traveler.

"I'm afraid I'm not fond of drinking, but I keep a cabinet for guests. Would you have sherry?" Louisa said.

"Absolutely not," Mr. Founts said. "Dulling the senses will do none of us any favors. And judging by the events of the last week, there is much to discuss with all the senses required." As he said this, his beady stare rested on the Captain and finally on Louisa.

"I've read some of your stories, Miss Alcott."

"And articles, Mr. Founts."

"And articles, of course. I believe you've had some of the best creative minds and intellect around you from an early age."

"It surprises you because you did not know or not thought it possible?"

"*Plots and counterplots*, Miss Alcott, very much interested me. I understand your knowledge of this area is somewhat more developed than I had imagined."

"Sensation stories are written in half the time and keep the family cozy, Mr. Founts. Wouldn't you agree?"

"I don't read frothy rubbish, Miss Alcott." Mr. Founts declared.

"English writers choose Italian dungeons and misty European forests. It does sell rather well, Mr. Founts."

"*Perilous Play*, for example, Miss Alcott." he said. "There's a story you couldn't write in an English country garden, eh?"

"Your perception Mr. Founts, astounds me."

"I'm much more grateful you're involved with this sad mess now that I know you could imagine such tales."

"My heroines are forceful, independent, sexually demanding, and rarely concern themselves with housework."

"Yes, I can only imagine if the collective time of American housewives were freed up to indulge such ridiculous fantasy."

"You've come to the wrong place, Mr. Founts, as Concord is a veritable den of perilous play. I'm sure you wouldn't argue that point."

"Your writing is indeed good."

"They're rubbishy tales, Mr. Founts, born of will and desire to be prosperous."

Such declaration of intent did not appear to alarm or frighten Mr. Founts. Hiding behind her pseudonym saved her the moral duty to instruct tiresome ladies in domestic responsibility, and she could hardly expect a man such as Mr. Founts to understand this subtle point.

"Will fiction entertain us or instruct Mr. Founts?" she asked. "Or does it very much depend on what sex we are?"

Mr. Founts tapped his fingers on the sides of his chair.

"One thing I do believe, Miss Alcott. I have possibly read something accomplished, and it was probably penned by you. I may not have realized it at the time."

"Again, very astute, Mr. Founts."

As they basked in this unexpected blaze of mutual admiration, the Captain made his presence known by clearing his throat.

"Speaking of domestic, romantic pap," Mr. Founts said, with a mock amused look on his face. He glanced faintly in the Captain's direction.

"I want the full details about your presence at Rosebud Cottage yesterday, Captain. No lies."

"I've never intended on lying," Captain Briers said.

"Not much intending on telling the truth either, Captain."

"I received a letter from Miss Chandler asking me to meet her at the beehives up at Rosebud Cottage at noon yesterday."

"Oh, for heaven's sake, Captain. Are you still lusting after that deranged sprite?" Mr. Founts said.

Louisa ruffled at the description. However, it reminded her of one of her own characters. A rather evil ballerina. There were similarities.

"No, Mr. Founts, I am not lusting after her, as you put it. I was hoping to end our liaison and put a stop to her delusions, but she did not arrive at the appointed time."

"You are sure it was yesterday?"

"The message read Friday at 12 noon."

"And you are positive it was Miss Chandler requesting this appointment?"

He glanced at Louisa and then his own hands.

"I am as sure as I can be."

"What on earth does that mean, Captain?"

"It was possibly her writing, but I can't be positive."

"We get closer to the truth. And what was Mr. Miller's excuse for showing up at the beehives?"

"A similar note."

"What an idle mess," Mr. Founts muttered. Louisa agreed with his summary but for different reasons.

"What do you make of all this, Miss Alcott?"

"I think the Captain has another piece of vital information he has not shared."

The Captain took on the silent demeanor of a punished schoolboy and did not respond with any meaningful gesture.

"Then there was the incident at Concord school the day of Miss Collier's funeral," Louisa said. "You will recall a great deal of blood was found in Miss Murdock's office. Miss Murdock attended the school early owing to a broken lock and previous break-in."

"Yes, a very odd state of affairs," Mr. Founts said.

"Miss Murdock did not disclose the details of what occurred widely, and so we considered it safer not to panic the residents of Concord unduly."

Captain Briers finally lifted his head and directed his attention to Mr. Founts.

"I found the carcass of a mutilated sheep on Kame Bluff. It was discovered by my sister Evie as I burned some papers."

Mr. Founts' eyebrows sailed upwards, one arching in disbelief.

"Well, you were very busy, Captain. I take it Miss Chandler's note was sacrificed to this fire? A purging of the soul? Or the truth?"

Captain Briers hesitated once more. "Yes. And the dead sheep, sir."

"I see. So, you've been industriously derailing this investigation with ill judgment and rash decision-making. Burning evidence, my word what a mistake that was. I was given assurance none of this would occur."

There was a silence.

"Not even Miss Alcott is rallying to your defense, Captain. What do you have to say about that?"

"I know I have shown poor judgment, Mr. Founts, but I assure you I am not compromised in my personal motives."

"You can see the difficulty, Captain," Louisa said suddenly. She felt Captain Briers bristle. She'd provided her unwavering support to him, and now, she must say what she felt was the truth. Part of the theatrical display was to ensure Mr. Founts did not carry out an instruction from his superiors which is what he might be capable of. Remove Captain Briers from all his duties until this idle mess was over, as he so accurately described it. For in chiding the Captain, she hoped to arouse some sympathy in Mr. Founts– and not arouse his desire to involve himself more directly.

"You describe a note from Miss Chandler, and yet during her visit to me, she mentions not one word of it. The note is burned on admission by you. Mr. Miller is dead and unable to verify any of your fairy tales. He presumably behaved as he always did and kept Mrs. Miller in the dark?" Louisa said.

"Perfect Miss Alcott, I was ruminating on the same series of obvious facts," Mr. Founts said.

"Obvious facts?" the Captain said.

"And we shall no doubt discover Mr. Miller has no tolerance for bee stings. I suspect the vet has been a very busy man and will tell us your bloodbath belongs to the sheep, and your notes belong to your imagination," Mr. Founts continued.

Captain Briers' lips trembled.

"You must see it from our angle, Captain. I have long been an ardent admirer of your capabilities, but even you in the cold light of day must see there are inconsistencies in your statements," Louisa said. "Add to this the knowledge of bees of your sister Miss Evie Briers," she continued.

"Oh, what might that be?" Mr. Founts asked.

"Evie had nothing to do with this," the Captain said.

"She guided the bees through the winter and must know many of their proclivities during these harshest times," Louisa said.

"Oh yes, the Captain mentioned that. His own sister has access to the bees and would surely know how to stir them to a frenzy," Mr. Founts said, smiling slightly.

"Miss Alcott, I had nothing to do with Mr. Miller's death," Captain Briers said.

Louisa rose awkwardly from her chair, the effort paining her beyond all limits. She retrieved her notes from the school incident. She handed them to Mr. Founts, who gazed at them with expressionless eyes.

"The Society of the Bronze Oak, I assume, " Mr. Founts said, and gave a dry smile while handing them back.

"You are aware of the Society?" Captain Briers said.

"Of course, I am aware of them. I was hauled to Bedford a year ago to inspect similar symbols carved into trees on a farm."

"And what was your conclusion?" Louisa asked.

"Thoreau enthusiasts. Perhaps a little too much brandy after reading *The Succession of Forest Trees*."

"That is a fine essay," Louisa said.

"If you condone drunkenly trespassing into private property to inspect seedlings, perhaps," Mr. Founts said.

"There is far more to it than that, surely," Louisa said.

"This Society is nothing more than fools parading around after dinner on other people's property in pursuit of the nature of trees. Such deliberate nonsense is of no interest to me."

"Yet, Mr. Founts, these were found on Miss Murdock's chair?" Louisa said.

"Was Mr. Miller a supporter of these lunatics?" Mr. Founts asked.

Captain Briers cleared his throat, and he'd been sufficiently removed from the center of attention to dare re-enter the conversation.

"He operated the Concord branch."

"Clearly some form of misdirection, Captain. The Concord *branch*, you say? At least someone enjoys a joke around this stuffy little enclave," Mr. Founts said.

"I believe this is a misdirection," Louisa said. "What I do not understand is the use of animal blood."

"We are not far removed from dragging people out of their abodes and burning them on the pretense of banishing witchcraft Miss Alcott. When people utter the word *society*, all clandestine images are conjured up. Animal sacrifice being one. Perhaps these ingrates graduated to humans. Or someone wants us to believe it."

Louisa considered this. Mr. Founts possessed a far more outstanding intellectual faculty than she'd previously given him credit for. It more than compensated for his intermittent irritating nature.

"Are you suggesting it is symbolic of some misdeed perpetrated by Mr. Miller?" Louisa said.

Mr. Founts smiled.

"It may have been poured over the desk of a hard-working head teacher such as Miss Murdock, but I have no doubt the implications were of a very different character."

"The records at the school were disturbed first," Captain Briers said.

"And stolen this week," Louisa added.

"Clearly, we will not know what interested the culprit," Mr. Founts said.

"Indeed," Louisa said.

At that moment, Paul entered with a large tray festooned with bread and cold meat. He left and returned with a hot pot of coffee, replacing the cups and moving a small table to accommodate Mr. Founts.

"This is Mr. Paul Smith, Mr. Founts," Louisa said.

"Do you always introduce your servants, Miss Alcott."

"I'm not a servant," Paul said perfectly mannerly. It was said without the slightest bitterness.

"Well, you're not here for the good of your health, I'd imagine," Mr. Founts said, blowing genteelly on his cup of coffee. Paul glanced at Louisa as if his presence was a mystery, to him included.

"Mr. Smith arrived the day of Miss Collier's funeral. He believes he is her son." Louisa said.

Mr. Founts frowned. "I see. Would somebody care to inform me about the facts?"

"I have been told my mother is Miss Emily Collier of Concord. I came here looking for her."

"And arrived in the middle of her funeral, that must have been interesting."

"At the reading of her will, actually."

"Even more scandalous. I suppose now you're a challenger to the estate of Miss Collier. That must have set some wings flapping."

"We believed it probably would," Captain Briers said. "It's not safe for him here."

"Indeed. No wonder you're hiding out up here, acting manservant. You'd be better served in Boston. And what precisely do you mean, you believe you are Miss Emily Collier's son?

"Mr. Miller was checking the details of Mr. Smith's claim," Captain Briers said.

"If I understand correctly, your mother may be here but may not be Miss Collier?" Mr. Founts said.

"I'm not sure."

"But who told you Emily Collier was your mother?"

"My family. In Boston."

"Miss Collier's extended family?"

"No. My adopted family."

"They might have been told anything at the time," Mr. Founts said. "Not unusual under the circumstances, isn't that right, Miss Alcott."

"I am beginning to believe Mr. Smith's mother is in Concord."

"But not Miss Collier. Why did you decide to come here?"

"I found out she'd died."

"Not murdered?" Mr. Founts said.

Paul glanced nervously at Louisa and the Captain.

"I'd no idea she was murdered until I got here."

"Well, luckily for you, your mother might be still alive. Unlucky for your coffers though."

Louisa figured this an unnecessary and cruel embellishment to an otherwise tragic story. She was sure Paul Smith was a man of integrity, and his beliefs were honestly held. Nothing about his demeanor gave her any reason to believe otherwise, and yet, there was something deeply shrewd about Paul Smith. As if he knew precisely how to play his situation to the best advantage. Whether this was simply good manners or not, it was either fooling or delighting her, nothing in between. She sensed Mr. Founts' misgivings and felt she must be led to at least some degree in the direction he might go.

"There is the uncomfortably obvious, isn't there, Mr. Smith."

"Sir?"

"You murdered Miss Collier to get her fortune."

"How could I possibly have murdered her when I didn't know her?"

"You could have been in Concord well before your sensational appearance at the reading of the will. Show yourself off at the most opportune moment. In front of practically all the residents of Concord who knew Miss Emily Collier."

"We do have only your word, Mr. Smith," Louisa said. "You were seen at the school the day of the break-in. You admitted it to me."

"I see," Mr. Founts chimed in. "Now we are getting somewhere. You can't be oblivious to the fact your presence here is badly timed, Mr. Smith. A wild allegation Miss Collier is your mother might also induce you to kill Mr. Miller."

172

"With respect, Sir, that is utterly preposterous."

"I inspected your papers at Mr. Miller's office. I was aware of your presence before I even arrived here, " Mr. Founts said, with a rather smug look on his face.

"What of it? Mr. Miller was going to check my claim thoroughly."

"I'm sure he was Mr. Smith. He would undoubtedly confirm one of your previous occupations as a beekeeper in a large holding south of Boston."

Mr. Founts clearly had the upper hand, and this revelation took Louisa and Captain Briers by embarrassing surprise.

There was a significant silence.

"And you, Captain, were so determined to get here to spew your silly confessions to Miss Alcott before I arrived, you could not or would not assist me earlier today. If you had, you would have known this man had motive and opportunity to carry out such a heinous attack. Unknown to the community and lurking in Concord well before Miss Collier was murdered" Mr. Founts continued.

"For what purpose?" Paul Smith asked. His voice deepened, a man under some threat for sure. "What possible reason would I have to murder Miss Collier or Mr. Miller?"

"Perhaps you knew you were not Miss Collier's son. But an imposter."

"My claim would still have to be verified on her death. Or shown to be false by another."

"Or perhaps it has nothing to do with Miss Collier's estate?" Mr. Founts said.

Again, there was silence. Louisa enjoyed the concept of another motive entirely, one she'd been giving significant consideration to herself but his last point lacked any rational basis. Mr. Founts' tactics were ham-fisted and awkward, but within them were the seeds of renewed ideas. And yet there was something rehearsed and officious in how he delivered his accusations.

"Well, I assure you, I want the truth as much as we do here. If Miss Collier was my mother, I will challenge this woman, this Miss Taylor, and prove I'm entitled. I think I would be justified," Paul said.

"Quite right," Mr. Founts said, which drew a shocked expression from Mr.

Smith.

After a short silence: "I think I will retire to read, Miss Alcott."

"You do that, Mr. Smith. Because it appears you will be waiting a good deal of time before this matter is satisfactorily settled. It was so nice to meet you," Mr. Founts said.

After he'd stormed out calmly, if there was such a thing, Mr. Founts sat with a satisfied look.

"This Miss Taylor who's inherited the estate, Miss Alcott. What do we know about her?"

"She masqueraded as one of what we call the Misses of Concord until I discovered she was married to Mr. Edward Lounsey. It was no secret generally, but I was not aware of it."

"This Edward. He's the farmer to whom Miss Collier promised to sell her farm?"

"Yes, he is. He also sold me my pigs."

"Oh, of course, he did. Set himself up to be the good clay and salt type. Has nothing but good intentions. Wouldn't be hardly able to slaughter one of his own pigs, let alone a human being. A bit conversationally challenged. Does that describe him?"

"I don't know him that well, Mr. Founts," Louisa said. In her defense, she didn't, until now, figure him much in the picture at all. She did recall him kissing Danny before they left to do the business of payment, and this seemed slightly odd at the time.

"And now he has what he wants. Through his marriage to this Miss Taylor."

"Yes, he does."

She was about to say something else when Mr. Founts continued his musing unabashed.

"And the noxious streams of other Misses of Concord?"

"If the crime were pure hatred, any one of them."

"And with Mr. Miller's demise in what must be determined suspicious circumstances, we have no immediate hope of knowing which hated Miss Collier more. I cannot get out of my mind the possibility Mr. Miller's position made him privy to large volumes of confidential information."

"Quite so, Mr. Founts. But do we really believe Mr. Miller's death has anything to do with Miss Collier's?"

"I profoundly disliked Miss Murdock and Miss Nash. They're the school mistresses, eh?"

"They concern me," Louisa said. "Both are very close to events. The birthday party. The school. It seems they're frequently on the fringes of the tragedy."

"Miss Murdock strikes me as a very sly woman. There's something very secretive about her manner. As if she'd, in fact, killed Miss Collier and feared detection every time someone addresses her."

"The blood was on *her* desk. Not Miss Nash's," Louisa added.

"Perhaps a witness or someone with knowledge of the murder warns her by breaking into the school and letting the entire town, sure to hear it, know of it."

"Miss Chandler, the Captain's love interest, has come to me on three occasions. First to inform me she'd been the last person to see Miss Collier alive, her second visit a vain attempt to firmly root in my ideas she'd seen another person after she'd left her. Finally, she named Edward Lounsey," Louisa said.

"The pig seller again," Mr. Founts said, without any specific meaning. "Miss Chandler strikes me as the worst possible candidate for a wife. The fleeting fantasy of lust maybe, but for the sturdier business of exchanging vows, she's hardly solid gold."

"She would not kill Miss Collier," the Captain said.

With no visible or audible support from either Louisa or Mr. Founts.

"But she could have," Mr. Founts said.

"She knew Miss Collier was not going to support your marriage, Captain," Louisa said.

"And you advertise your business around Concord," Mr. Founts said. "No, I think Mary is an outstanding suspect. A firm sense of entitlement in that one. She could have brought the poison with her, surely. And just as Miss Collier polished off the last of her birthday treats, slipped her some of it."

"There are the Birch sisters," Louisa then said tentatively.

175

"You cannot be serious, Miss Alcott?" Captain Briers said. "They have never expressed the slightest word of violence against Miss Collier. They were not at her birthday."

"Captain, you must refrain from limiting your thinking," Mr. Founts said, pointing at his skull in a derisory fashion.

"One is as insane as the other," the Captain said.

"You must resist resorting to archetypes, Captain. There is a great deal I like about the Birches, and I must refute your charge of insanity on their behalf," Louisa said.

"I must meet these women," Mr. Founts said.

Captain Briers let out a long, ill-humoured laugh.

"You will not get much from them, Sir. The mad have mental faculties stronger than most when it comes to hiding the truth."

"Or they possess significantly more intelligence than those about them," Mr. Founts said.

Louisa let out a disappointed sigh. She pulled herself from the chair to ensure she could still walk and put two logs on the fire. She needed more coffee as if it would improve her mood and give her a reason to ask Mr. Founts to excuse Captain Briers from the investigation. It was pretty clear he was not only incapable of being impartial, but he was also irrational himself. A most compromising situation.

During her absence, the conspicuous lack of conversation from the drawing room worried her. She expected some chatter to flow, but it appeared keeping Captain Briers involved was now out of the question. Mr. Founts seemed to intensely disrespect him, and she sensed he was a man of instinct. Even if he refused to acknowledge it.

"This postmistress," Mr. Founts said once she returned.

"Mrs. Miller?"

"Yes, the dead lawyer's wife. Is she capable of some part in all of this?"

"She received a note."

"Our killer is fond of writing letters? More than doing away with people?"

Captain Briers sat back in his seat and gave Mr. Founts a neutral stare.

"What did the mysterious author have to say?"

"*You are next*," Captain Briers said. "It was received some time ago."

"Indeed, the woman who intercepted your foolish telegram, Captain."

"Yes, it was her, but what has that to do with my telegram?"

"At first, I assumed it was some sort of plea for *my* attention," Louisa said. "There was something odd about it."

"But then?"

"Mrs. Miller does see and hear a lot in her role as postmistress. She could have overheard something, perhaps not even known its importance, and it was more of a warning."

"She's still alive. Her husband is not."

"And perhaps the summons Mr. Miller received was for her, Mr. Founts", the Captain said. "He may have intercepted it and assumed it was for him."

"We may never know," Mr. Founts said. "But I hardly think one would be in a hurry to keep an anonymous appointment when your life has just been threatened? No, it seems more likely Mr. Miller viewed it as a clandestine invitation he'd be unable to ignore."

"I should be most careful in suggesting that Mr. Founts. On account of Mrs. Miller's fragile state," Louisa said.

"I agree, but unfortunately, my superficial inquiries suggest Mr. Miller was fond of the ladies in Concord. Married or not. Attached or not."

"That is hardly a crime," the Captain said.

Mr. Founts gave him a disconcerting glare.

"Could I have a word, Miss Alcott? In private?" Mr. Founts said.

Louisa roused herself and led the way ahead of Mr. Founts to the kitchen. She seated herself, inviting him to do so as well. He closed the door gently behind him.

"I'm aware we got off on the wrong foot, Miss Alcott," he began.

"Well, you needed to ensure matters were being pursued sufficiently. And efficiently."

"Of that, I'm sure in respect of your involvement, Miss Alcott."

"Please call me Louisa. I'd be much more comfortable."

"Louisa," he said deliberately. "Of course."

"You have some concerns you do not wish to share with the Captain?"

"Quite right, Louisa. In fact, I believe the Captain is compromised by his personal involvement."

"I see."

"His critical ability appears to be in question, and he is just short of being a complete fool."

"Some of his actions appear dubious, Mr. Founts."

"Jeremy, if you wouldn't mind."

Jeremy," she said. "I have my own concerns. Particularly over the past few days. It isn't clear to me if the Captain is aware his actions cannot be excused by merely apologizing. I would certainly overlook mistakes if not continuously made as if he was unaware of what he was doing."

"Or Louisa, he is involved in this matter more than he would admit."

"I'm not sure it runs that deep. You don't think he's directly involved?"

Mr. Founts let out a sigh and then checked his pocket watch. "If not, the hand that does the acts, he is very close to the matters giving rise to them."

"If he would simply tell me the truth as it occurs, instead of concealing matters, it would certainly improve matters. I am not as mobile as I would like, as you can see, and I cannot be in every place as quickly as a young man is capable."

"Your mind moves to those places rather quickly, Louisa," Mr. Founts said, with the unmistakable undertones of affection. "The measured and considered approach is the best. And your approach is beyond reproach."

"Shall I break the bad news to the Captain?"

"No, I will. It has already been more or less decided by my superior, known to you as you made quite clear."

Louisa felt a sudden rush of pride. She decided a very long time ago not to be dissuaded by modern expectations upon her to be ridiculously refined and domesticated. Her characters' frivolous behaviors displayed enough of this, and she was thrilled for them to be confined to print on paper.

"I doubt he will be pleased. Will it affect his chances of advancement?"

"I'm afraid it does, Louisa. We are servants of the people. But we're not that civil when it comes to advancement. One has to have a certain discretion and resolve, good decision-making skills and ethical standards below which we dare not venture."

"I must agree with you there. Depending on one's standards, that is."

"Privately, one may do what one likes, provided no individual is harmed. However, if given over to the tasks involved in government, the probity and fitness of an individual can make the difference between swimming and sinking."

"Is the Captain to lose his posting?"

Mr. Founts sighed and raised his hands as if there was nothing he could do.

"I have no guarantees for him. My superiors would not take kindly to personal involvement once it has been discussed. The Captain doesn't appear to understand. Even honest contrition at this level means you can never again be trusted, despite demonstration to the contrary. But to conceal evidence is not acceptable. The whole sheep burning business moves this quite beyond my control."

Louisa felt despair for the Captain. Despite her own relief, he would no longer be capable of making matters more complex than necessary. Mr. Founts made some astonishing statements, most of which she regrettably agreed with.

"Do you really think he concealed evidence?"

"It appears that way, Louisa. And that is the problem."

When they returned to the room, the Captain was standing by the fireplace, facing the window. The snow had melted outside, and the grass was visible under patches of thin ice, transparent and clear. The fire was comforting but not fighting the intense cold.

"We shall have more snow," Mr. Founts said, reaching for his cane. "I can certainly feel it in my shoulders."

Captain Briers glanced over at him and then looked absently into the fire.

"So, my good man," Mr. Founts began. "You are absolved from any further involvement in the investigation of Miss Collier's murder and other matters until further notice. Unless of course, we require you for someprocedural matters on the fringes."

"Do you agree with this position, Miss Alcott?" the Captain asked.

179

"Yes, Captain, I do. I could forgive the initial mistakes, but recently, there have been too many."

He nodded despondently but refused to look at Mr. Founts. Instead, he took his gloves out and pulled them on violently, preparing to walk out.

"I'm very sorry my assurances are not enough."

"Shall I give you a carriage to Kame Bluff?" Founts asked.

"No, Sir. I can walk. It is punishment enough."

He nodded his goodbye to Louisa and marched out.

"Let him go, Louisa," Mr. Founts said. "I only hope he does not compound his misfortune by continuing on the road he's embarked on."

"Would you stay for dinner, Jeremy?" Louisa asked.

"I would, Louisa, but unfortunately, I must report to my superiors. However, another time. I will return soon. We have much work to do."

* * *

On Sunday morning, the snow returned. Miss Murdock glanced out at the large flakes tumbling from the sky, glad it was serene and quiet. She could still see breaks in the clouds, which meant it would be on and off. Unlike the blizzards a few days ago. She'd prevailed on the goodwill of a local locksmith to repair the broken one at the school, scowling at his pride in community spirit voiced several times. She alone understood the meaning of community spirit in a den of vipers unfamiliar with any form of charitable consciousness. It was one thing to have a conscience. Another to exercise it consciously in the world, as though it were your last day on earth. A tawdry businessman selling his wares for free when he could easily afford it did not qualify as a man in possession of community spirit.

Her nerves bit at her. She wasn't quite ready to go into the school building. It was bad enough the children must stay out of it while the cleaning of the hideous mess took place, but to face the desecration of the school's records, a matter she simply couldn't repair, was beyond her. And that insidious Miss Louisa Alcott would no doubt be snooping around. As she crossed the courtyard, she was slightly grateful if she admitted it to herself that the weather would keep Louisa at bay for some time. There'd be no surprise visits. All she had to do was retrieve the church hymn booklets from her office and deliver them to the service in an hour. Normality was essential now, even a practiced artificial kind sure to put everyone at odds. The consistency of good hymns and chanted prayers would surely keep her from going mad.

When she reached the door, it was open. She handled the lock as if it was something strange and unusual in her hands. The hair on her neck and arms stirred and spiked. An irrational shiver of fear embraced her body, and she stood away for several seconds. As she did, a densely black raven landed on a naked branch near her and squawked. She pulled the door open and entered the cold, still atmosphere of the school. She hurried to her office, hoping the lock had sprung open somehow due to faulty craftsmanship. Perhaps she could get the smith back to fix it, test his community spirit to the hilt. As she approached her office, she heard something drop and turned pointlessly towards the empty corridor.

Her own door was locked. She opened it and held her breath, closed her eyes tight. When she opened them, it was as if nothing of the horror which had been there barely a few days ago remained. She closed the door slowly and moved towards her desk. A thorough job had been done, even to her critical standards. The faint ammonia smell lingered, a pleasing, cleansing odor that gave her more comfort. Then she noticed the envelope on the desk, obscured by the school bell, holding it down like a paperweight.

She removed her gloves, taking the bell away and observing what lay in front of her. A plain, expensive cream envelope, with her name in an exaggerated script of red ink, tiny feather flourishes. It was intended to be disguised, she imagined, and her heart thumped furiously in her chest. She breathed in deeply and opened it, taking the short letter out. Yellow paper, written in red.

You must not keep secrets forever.

She felt herself unconsciously inhaling and realized she'd kept her breath in for several tense moments. As she contemplated the contents of this communication, her door opened gently, and Miss Nash appeared.

"I thought I heard you come in," she said casually. "Are you well, Miss Murdock? You look as though you've seen a ghost."

"I might well have seen a ghost, Miss Nash."

"Would you like some coffee?"

She smiled, and Miss Murdock reluctantly returned the favor, if briefly.

"What are you doing here, Miss Nash?"

"The post," she said innocently. "The school has been closed for several days, and I thought I should see if things were in order."

Miss Murdock felt the letter burning on the desk in front of her as though it would catch fire any moment. She swallowed deeply and allowed the anxiety which engulfed her to subside.

"Everything is in order, Miss Nash. Would you kindly get the hymn booklets so I may take them to the church?"

"I can take them if you like Miss Murdock."

"Would you please do as you are asked, Miss Nash."

"Are you sure you are all right?"

"Please leave them at the door. On your way out."

As always, Miss Nash nodded in a manner that should be subservient but managed to take on the character of rebellion.

When she heard the outer door shut, Miss Murdock rose from her desk, feeling weakness in her legs as though she was about to wade through seawater. She could feel Miss Nash had left, the odd sensation confirming it. She took the envelope and placed the letter back inside. There was nothing more to be done. Why was this happening now? Hadn't she cooperated to the very best of her ability?

* * *

Hangman's Cottage was a miasma of muffled sounds in varying degrees of hostility. The death of Mr. Miller propelled April Birch into a manic moment of creativity from which she felt she might not emerge.

"Really, April must you make so much noise," June said as she replenished the fire with some wood. It spat liberally and forcefully, causing April to shriek dramatically.

"Will you make sure you choose the dry kindling little fool? Are you trying to set the house on fire?"

"Yes, I am. We shall burn in eternity for our collective sins. You and I, screeching in pain for our foul deeds."

"You really are a fool, June. Get me more brandy. I can't complete this score without assistance from the divine."

June slammed a bottle of brandy on the table and disappeared in a silky mist of expensive nightdress adorned with oriental flowers.

"You could at least pour it, little bird," April said. "You know I'm creating."

Evie Briers emerged from the kitchen, her face a sweaty, harassed mess.

"Well, Evie, I see you must be feeling much better?"

"Not much, Miss Birch. I feel as if I've been run over by a train."

"Wonderful news," April said and continued marking up the parchment before her in deep, inky letters, curling upwards and downward in such a dramatic fashion, April felt she could die and be in heaven all in the exact moment. As she contemplated her notes, she'd inscribe a feather in red ink at the top of each page, reminding her to keep the musical notes light and airy, just like her best humor.

There was a knock at the door. "Be a dear Evie and see who it is?"

"Not at his hour, surely Miss Birch?"

"I love night visitors. Let them in, please?"

"It might be anyone, Miss Birch."

"I know the mystery is killing me."

Evie reluctantly put the cloth she'd been using to polish the Birch silver, which rarely saw any activity, over her shoulder and walked into the hallway. She knew who it was immediately and hesitated.

"Who is it, Evie? Hurry up, dear."

Evie opened the door, and a smiling Miss Nash stood in front of her. In her hands, she carried a plate covered in muslin.

"Who is it, Evie," April's insistent voice came from the drawing room.

Evie stood aside, and Miss Nash walked in, greeting April Birch with the same smile.

"Miss Nash? To what do I owe this dubious pleasure?"

Her glasses slid down her nose, and she observed Miss Nash as if some curiosity in a zoo.

"Miss Alcott's generosity is surely a great thing. I was able to make us some fancy cakes."

She handed the plate to Evie and took her coat off without being asked to stay. April Birch enjoyed a late visitor, but she wasn't sure about Miss Nash. Her usual puritanical gaze and miserly clothing always ignited April's unease.

"What do you want, Miss Nash?"

"To visit an old friend."

"I am quite lost, Miss Nash. I am not old, and we are not friends."

"I was at the school earlier, and I must say Miss Murdock got quite another scare, so to speak."

April observed Miss Nash with renewed interest. It appeared something—or someone—had ruffled her feathers recently, in a pleasant sort of way. She was unsure if this was a painful or pleasurable experience, but one thing was beyond doubt. Miss Nash appeared like a lady for the first time, a sparkle of revolution in her eyes, the kind April liked to observe.

"Shall I cut the cake, Miss Birch," Evie said, reappearing into the drawing room.

"Oh heavens no. I'm not that desperate for sugar, eggs, butter, and poison."

Miss Nash simply looked at April Birch, and Evie remained standing with the plate in her hands.

Finally, Evie took the cake and returned to the kitchen, where she placed it on the counter and stared at it. She lifted the muslin—a delicate blue with tiny daisies sewn into it, a soft yellow frill around the edges. It looked so harmless. She examined the cake and turned it around. It smelled of almonds, with fruit and icing on the top. It looked good enough to devour. She was in the Birch household, so she must obey what April said if she wanted to receive her stipend. April was clear that she would, of course, have June inspect her work and see if it was satisfactory. And the truth was, June barely looked and usually paid her immediately. But today, April informed her she would personally venture to the kitchen and have a quick look over the various chores she carried out to see if they were to her liking.

A sort of inspection on June's assessment. Not that it was much use as April rarely knew what to look for and sometimes pointed out flaws that pre-dated Evie's arrival. Such as the big pot, covered in black burns at the bottom. Evie nicely told April that this was unavoidable and the only way to get rid of the stains was to throw the pot out and buy a new one.

Evie suddenly thought of the pail with dried blood she found in the shed.

There was nothing to do but destroy the cake. The shovel was heavy—a man's implement—not for the weak of heart. She'd removed some of the cake and crumbled it on the plate. The rest she wrapped in paper and tied with a string. She couldn't let this happen again, absolutely not. She chose a spot on the other side of a wooden fence to the back of Hangman's Cottage. It was overgrown with weeds that still managed to thrust up through the snow. The ground was rock hard, but nearby there was a tiny hillock Evie sometimes used to drain off hot fat from the roasting meat. It made a kind of soft paste of the clay. It was easy to dig. If the cake was gone, it wouldn't harm anyone. If April or June asked, she'd say it fell onto the ground due to her clumsiness, and there was no way to save it.

When she returned the shovel to the shed, the pail on the ledge once again caught her eyes. It might be anything—used to make blood pudding. Used to wipe up blood after a chicken or rabbit slaughter. But April and June were not up to wringing a chicken's neck or skinning a rabbit. And they rarely went outside—especially the back. It was none of her business, she decided. She took one quick look. The blood gathered on the top in oily pools. The rim was covered in rusty brown residue.

Inside, she cleared the plate to the side of the table and covered the tiny pieces left with muslin. The sound of voices, low and determined, came from inside. She prepared a tray with cups and pot, sugar, and honey. It was the last thing to do before seeking June out and being paid, the last thing she would do before heading back to Kame Bluff and more work.

April and Miss Nash's conversation ceased immediately after she appeared.

April's face flushed with heat—or anger—and she closed her eyes in exasperation once she heard the cups clattering on the tray.

"Get me a sherry, Evie," she said.

"I'll have coffee Evie," Miss Nash said and smiled. Evie's trembling hands struggled to lay the tray down quietly, and it crashed onto the table, evincing a sigh from April. She poured April a large glass of sherry.

"Find the little bird," April said, "she will see to your wages, Evie."

After Evie left and closed the door, April sipped her drink, giving Miss Nash the odd sly glance.

"What is it you want, Miss Nash?" April said. "I haven't the slightest idea what happened to Miss Murdock. I don't know how many times I have to tell you."

"Oh, come now, April, the letter."

"What letter?"

"She got a letter. Written in big scrawly writing just like yours."

"Really, Miss Nash. First, Miss Murdock accuses me of stealing school money and loitering about the place. Now I'm supposed to have written her some poison pen letter? Where is this insanity to end?"

"When you confess to killing Miss Collier," Miss Nash said. "Nobody believes you had nothing to do with it."

"And why might I want to off a spinster like myself? Someone I relied upon for sensible discussions with an excellent range?"

"Well, who else can it be?"

"How am I supposed to have killed her, Miss Nash? I rarely leave the house, and you know it takes me months to work up the courage to attend the winter Festival and suffer the riffraff of Concord sneaking and spying on me?"

"Very convenient, April," Miss Nash said. She lifted her coffee and sniffed it.

"Oh, don't be ridiculous. It wasn't my baking skills that poisoned Emily. And now you think I'm busy infusing your coffee with cyanide, I suppose?"

"I might never know."

"Well, Miss Nash, as tempting as it is to put you out of your virginal boring misery, I can assure you I had nothing to do with it. I wasn't even there, which, if you will notice, is something rather important according to Miss Alcott and Captain Briers."

She took another gulp of sherry and searched about for the bottle. "Be a dear and fetch the bottle. You see, I am guilty of laziness so extreme; I could not possibly drag myself off the sofa to do away with Miss Collier."

Miss Nash retrieved the bottle and slammed it on the table in front of April.

"You didn't have to be there to do it. You could have had June's help."

April laughed so much that she thought she might expire.

"Now," April said when she'd composed herself. "What did this letter say."

"Why should I tell you," Miss Nash said. "You already know."

"I don't. And I need another good laugh. The first one just warmed me up."

"*You can't keep secrets forever.*"

"Well, well. Why doesn't it surprise me that Miss Murdock keeps secrets? Have you found out what they are?"

"It's too late, April. They all know."

"Know what?"

Miss Nash didn't say another word. She took her coat off the back of the sofa and put it on.

"What are you talking about, Miss Nash?"

She glanced back once and then left the room.

* * *

Louisa settled herself in front of the fire to write. It wasn't the most opportune moment or the most comfortable way to approach her work, but the office she'd set up was like an icehouse, and she couldn't bear to work in it. What a splendid way to pass the time, and amused herself with the truth that when creating, her mind worked altogether in a more productive manner than would otherwise be possible. She felt a thrill of excitement at the thought of Mr. Founts respecting her work. Not her investigation skills, no, the work she tirelessly struggled with to get her message out to the world. He was a man of better quality than she'd at first imagined. A man who was willing to inspect life's peculiar occurrences with both humor and wit. Something rare in a man.

Her writing allowed her mind to expand to numerous possibilities, and the working through of different emotions on the likelihood of other actors in this sorry saga suggested an entirely more complex set of circumstances than she had initially thought. She'd just settled into her proper flow when there was a knock on the door. She sighed loudly and got up to respond, and she predicted who it was.

Miss Murdock, with a terribly concerned look on her face, that cold, grim line of the mouth. Her hands were clenched in front of her in the perpetual motion of wringing, something Louisa found so disconcerting.

"What can I do for you, Miss Murdock?"

She barged past her into the living room, making herself comfortable, which for Miss Murdock meant sitting upright and stiff, similar to the position she required of her students. As if her visit augured a certain austerity which expected all about her to obey.

"Blood on my desk Miss Alcott is bad enough. Then there was a letter this morning."

She opened her purse and removed the envelope in which she'd received her missive. "When is this awful business going to end?"

She handed it to Louisa, who read it and then examined the envelope and paper.

"And?" Louisa said.

"Well, did you read it?"

"Yes, Miss Murdock, I did. What do you want me to say? *You can't keep secrets forever.* I'm afraid I can't help you if you can't tell me what secrets it refers to?"

Louisa's patience abandoned her, and she rose to walk around, something she never did. She always felt more in control sitting at rest. But Miss Murdock got on her nerves.

"I have no sympathy for anyone in this town, Miss Murdock. I assume you will tell me things you ought to have told me weeks ago?"

"No, I am not. I have no idea what this means."

"There has to be a reason, Miss Murdock, why you are being targeted by an unknown individual? And why would this person, if indeed it is the same person who left a message on your desk and I quote, *most evil deeds are not the musings of one diabolical man, but many*."

Miss Murdock appeared to be heavily engaged in thought as Louisa retook her seat. "Can you tell me what that means? Well, can you?"

There was no answer.

"Yellow paper, written in red," Louisa said. "Very like this one."

"There was a note the day of Miss Collier's funeral?"

"Perhaps I should ask the questions, Miss Murdock?" Louisa said.

"Of course."

"Yes, there was a note written almost in the same hand."

"Miss Collier used that phrase about diabolical men. Some say she was wronged very deeply by a man or men in her time."

"She never explained it?"

"She refused to explain it."

"To whom did she say it?"

"You were there, Miss Alcott. In the post office. Everyone was there, Miss Alcott. Any number of people overheard her. At a meeting of the school finance committee, she used it again."

"Who was there on that occasion?"

"The Birch sisters, of course. Miss Nash and myself. Mr. Miller and Lucy Miller. Evie was sweeping something up as usual. Miss Taylor came in halfway through, and I couldn't be sure if she was there when Miss Collier said it. Really, it's not much use to you because there were other people present for the vote, like Captain Briers and Mrs. Chandler. We had to have all committee members there for certain items on the agenda. Miss Collier just kept talking about evil men and their diabolical deeds."

Louisa thought about this. It surely meant something, but what, she could not be sure.

Miss Taylor and the Forest Nymph

Monday morning gave Louisa the new impetus she needed to engage her mind thoroughly. A temporary thaw was underway in the laneways and fields of Concord, and although ice clung to the corners into which the sun could not reach, it seemed a good deal warmer. Perhaps her mood heated up. As she sat fully dressed and ready to go out by ten in the morning, she felt as though some of the threads connecting this tapestry of this tragedy were beginning to form a picture. From up close, the picture made no sense, but once one stood back and viewed it from afar, the contours betrayed their shapes. The images sprang out and disclosed their meaning with full force.

Paul tended the fire in the living room, and Louisa decided it was time to see if the young man was calm and at peace. Especially with the treatment he received at Mr. Founts' hands the previous day. It was a time of turmoil, something Louisa understood only too well, not just the immediate after-effects but how it can cripple one's emotions. Make one feel desperate and alone. To arrive in a triumphant state of mind only to find yourself under suspicion. She knew the feeling all too well.

"What will you do if you cannot challenge Miss Collier's estate?"

"You mean Miss Alcott if I am not who I've been led to believe I am?"

"Unfortunately, I do mean that. You must understand Mr. Founts was theorizing and voicing his thoughts, and he is responsible for bringing the culprit to justice."

"And his theories no doubt include me."

"If it assuages your fears, I don't believe you had anything to do with it."

Paul gave her a genuine smile and placed a log judiciously to make the most of the heat. He was a Godsend, and she and her family would miss him terribly if he left.

"Will you leave after this is over?" she asked. "Despite recent events, it's by no means the worst place you could find yourself."

"I could stay in Concord if I could find work, Miss Alcott."

"I see," she said. Now her mind was razor sharp. What better position could Paul hold than with her for a while? She had the means to pay him and needed the assistance.

'I was hoping you would consider a position here. Some chores and, of course, the pigs require tending to. I will have Miss Collier's beehives too, which need to be nurtured. I understand you have experience in that regard."

The man's eyes brightened.

"It would certainly sustain you until something more appropriate came along?"

"Yes, Miss Alcott, that would be a great opportunity if your faith is strong in my ability."

She considered herself fair and modern, a combination in short supply in Concord these days.

"I will arrange papers to cover our arrangement. Perhaps six months? You may, of course, have lodgings here and a wage?"

Paul nodded with the enthusiasm she hoped and reached out, shaking her hand vigorously, a genuine smile on his face.

"Well, that's settled," she said. Deep in her mind, she hoped that Paul Smith had nothing to do with this sorry mess. She was convinced of his innocence but positive he fit in somewhere in this sad saga. And if his part in the tragic performance was unknown to him, having sight of him would ensure she knew it before it became common knowledge. For someone in Concord knew precisely why Paul Smith was here and who exactly he was. Of that, she was positive.

"I will not disappoint you, Miss Alcott," he said.

And she figured he wouldn't.

Before she finished her coffee, Paul answered a knock on the door. Evie

Briers swept in on a gust of icy air, talking like the possessed.

"I must see Miss Alcott," she said with labored breath. As though she'd run from Kame Bluff at full speed without taking the slightest break.

"Miss Alcott is taking her breakfast," Paul said with the air of a house butler. "Perhaps you could wait in here."

Louisa wasted no time receiving Miss Briers. She'd a busy schedule to keep that morning, and no doubt Miss Briers' visit would be fraught but short.

"Evie what is troubling you?"

Evie, expired of breath still, inhaled and exhaled as though calming herself. Paul handed her a cup of coffee and left the room.

"Miss Alcott," she said. "I must tell you about something I've seen."

"Well, you must tell me everything. Please calm yourself first," Louisa said. She didn't want Evie passing out with her exertions, and the possibility of inviting a third party to the proceedings didn't excite her much. And although Evie didn't occupy the top of her list of suspects, there was hardiness and resilience about the woman, which paused ruling her out entirely.

"I was at the Birch sisters' house," Evie began. "Yesterday."

She took a sip of coffee, and a standard color replaced the ashen horror which etched her face moments ago.

"Miss Nash arrived," she continued. "With a cake." She paused again to take some more coffee and glanced at Louisa as though the mention of a cake signaled something sinister.

"A cake?"

"Yes, her jam sandwich."

"Makes a considerable change from oat squares. I suppose we should congratulate her for the expansive repertoire," Louisa said and smiled. Still, Evie's face took on the usual pained expression of a woman burdened by endless phantom horrors she alone must live with.

"I offered to cut the cake," Evie said. "But Miss April Birch said she didn't want *butter, eggs, sugar, and poison*," Evie said this in a measured fashion, out of character, Louisa thought.

"April implied Miss Nash wanted to poison her?"

"You know Miss Birch," Evie said. "Her manners."

"Yes, I know what you mean, Evie. Miss Birch is not one to mince her words, and it is less her manners than how she expresses herself."

Evie waited for Louisa to say something more.

"Is that it, Evie?"

"No, Miss Alcott. I went to the kitchen," Evie said. "I took the cake outside to bury it."

"I see Miss Briers. Why?" Louisa asked.

"I agreed with Miss Birch. I thought it better to be safe."

"On a literal reading of the situation Miss Briers, I suspect you did no harm. I doubt Miss Nash would be so obvious firstly, and no doubt she would not be aware you buried her cake?"

Evie put her cup down. "That's not all."

"I see."

"The shed. I went there to find a shovel," Evie said, much to Louisa's surprise. "Full of discarded items."

Louisa's patience would remain intact, but for a short while. She sipped her cold coffee and nodded in encouragement to Miss Briers, now entirely in charge of her story.

"I saw a pail on the ledge full of water, and there was blood in it."

"I see, Evie, do continue."

"There was talk after Miss Collier's funeral about the blood at the school, and Miss Murdock mentioned it. She said there was no blood anywhere else, and I think whoever put it there must have used a pail."

"You certainly have put some thought into this, Miss Briers."

"It's logical, Miss Alcott."

"With respect, Miss Briers, did you discuss this matter with anyone?"

"My brother mentioned the possibility."

"I see. And what do you make of this, Miss Briers?"

"Everett—Captain Briers—burned the sheep, you see."

"I see."

"I found it on the farm, Miss Alcott. There was no doubt it was killed."

"No, there must be no doubt it was killed."

"How can there be any other explanation for the pail in the Birch shed?"

"We mustn't claim conclusions, Miss Briers. The pail might have been there for any number of reasons."

Evie shook her head in disagreement. She was sure what she'd seen must be of the most incriminating nature. And while this was a puzzling development, it wasn't clear to Louisa what the offending item could possibly be doing at Hangman's Cottage.

"I don't believe the Misses Birch would have a good reason for it, Miss Alcott. They're not conventional ladies by any means," Evie said.

"Perhaps some unknown person left the pail in their shed. We are isolated, and isn't it possible this is the case?" Louisa said.

Evie thought about this, but such was her determination—and apparent dislike of the Birch sisters—she was convinced. It wouldn't do to have this matter swimming up the tide of accusation, feathering the nest of suspicion. Louisa's first concern was the damage this revelation might do if it became common knowledge. And with the propensity for chatter and gossip, not to mention Mr. Miller's death, this was very likely to spread like fire.

"I doubt the Misses Birch venture regularly to the shed, Miss Alcott. They have me do that for them, and I doubt they've been outside since summer."

"I well believe that, Evie," Louisa said. "Could I ask a favor?"

Evie straightened up to the critical task, whatever it might be. Rarely did she get to do any favors for anyone, her life an endless set of chores.

"Of course."

"I need you to keep the existence of the blood-stained pail quiet, and I don't want details of it getting around Concord. Do you understand?"

"Yes, Miss Alcott. I understand."

"Thank you for bringing the details to my attention."

After Paul saw Miss Briers out, Louisa wondered why the Birch sisters had such an item in their shed. The discovery by Miss Briers offered no comfort, particularly when she learned of the visit from Miss Nash at the same time. And she thought about the cake she'd commissioned from Miss Nash, which now would probably end up buried just like April Birch's jam sandwich. There was simply no way to know where the threats were coming from, Louisa thought.

"Paul?" she said, gathering her purse to leave.

He appeared out of nowhere. "You weren't eavesdropping, I hope?"

"I was, Miss Alcott. I'm most humbly sorry."

"There's no need to be. If anything arrives for me, can you kindly put it in the kitchen until I return?"

"Of course."

"If it's a cake, don't eat it?"

Paul looked at her strangely. "I did hear about the cake. However, I would never help myself to a cake, Miss Alcott."

"I would normally not care, Paul; you may eat what you like. But if a cake arrives attached to a lady named Miss Jean Nash, kindly leave it for me to inspect."

He nodded in agreement if a little confused by her instructions.

* * *

Louisa braced herself for the journey into Concord. The beauty of golden sunshine, low in the sky over the frozen fields, filled her with joy as she approached Market Street. She didn't mind the long walk, not if it was still and quiet and her joints obeyed her. And it was deserted on the street, with no signs of life. The death of Mr. Miller propelled residents into mourning, so soon after, Miss Collier died, for which they were unprepared. This created a subdued atmosphere and a general feeling of malaise. Louisa noticed the Concord Festival's date moved twice, with no sign of preparations taking place. May Festival began days before, and the carnival atmosphere accompanied it. An undercurrent of joy pervading the community, palpable in everything. None of this was evident.

Miss Taylor wasn't delighted to see Louisa.

Dressed for an elegant ball rather than a Monday, she glanced at the grandfather clock before admitting her. A gracious reception-style smile on her face, rather than any fond and sincere feeling.

"I was on my way out," she said, leading Louisa towards her drawing room. Once again, a seat appeared recently vacated. Breakfast for two dishes were still on the table in the kitchen, where Louisa glanced moments before finding herself comfortably installed on Miss Taylor's sofa.

"I won't keep you long," Louisa answered.

"Coffee?"

"No, I've just finished my breakfast, thank you."

Louisa waited for her host to settle herself. A stack of papers on the table indicated Miss Taylor had been studying before her arrival. She closed an open journal with detailed notes before giving Louisa her attention.

"The will reading was interrupted by Paul Smith, you recall?"

Miss Taylor's practiced smile vanished and replaced itself with a scowl. "How could I forget?"

"He's still in Concord, and I plan on keeping him on for a stipend."

"His claim will fail, Miss Alcott."

"I see. Is that because Paul is your son and not Miss Collier's?"

Miss Taylor regarded her as though she'd attempted her murder. Her elegant face twisted with rage. "How dare you suggest such a thing?"

"You have a child, Miss Taylor?"

"How did you find out?"

"I'm investigating Miss Taylor, or should I call you Mrs. Lounsey?"

"Miss Taylor will do. How did you find out?"

"Is Paul Smith your son or not?"

"No, he is not. I have a son since you won't answer my question, and he's a good deal younger than Paul Smith."

Louisa was far from satisfied by Miss Taylor's response, but for the moment, she had to accept this was the case. It ceased to have any significant impact on her inquiries, as it appeared one way or another, Paul Smith's claim would indeed fail. It was a side matter that required further explanation, but as of yet, she had no clear idea if it had anything to do with Miss Collier's death.

"And when did you marry Edward?"

"Fourteen years ago," she replied. "I met Edward at a fair in Boston."

Louisa struggled to put a pair such as Miss Taylor and Mr. Lounsey together. It was one of those strange attractions in life that defied explanation but made perfect sense to each of the parties involved. An odd coupling. And although she'd never seen Edward with her for any significant period of time, she felt it wasn't quite right. Perhaps a marriage of convenience, where comfort wasn't the most apparent reason to the onlooker. And she figured she wouldn't get to observe them together under normal circumstances any time soon. Funerals could only do so much of the work, and people tended to be formal and ceremonial at these events. Not natural.

"Why the secrecy, Miss Taylor?"

"Secrecy?"

"I have called you on two occasions, and both times, you appear to have a visitor hotfoot out the door before I come in."

The gracious smile returned, and Miss Taylor seemed more relaxed. "Edward and I live almost separate lives. I am an independent woman, and I don't want him living here."

Louisa hid her surprise.

"I see, and how does that work, Miss Taylor?"

"I have Market Street, and frankly, I loathe farmland. I didn't want Miss Collier to know my business. I'm sure you, of all people, understand."

"And now Mr. Lounsey has the way onto his farm he so desperately wants?"

"Yes, it was very generous of Miss Collier, Miss Alcott. But I don't wish the great and good of Concord to know my business."

"Why did she leave the Cottage to you? Mr. Miller wasn't sure, and the sudden change in Miss Collier's desires to sell this summer is most odd."

"A spinster, Miss Alcott, has few options. No offspring and not many friends. That's how I'd describe Miss Collier, and I was one of her friends."

"Who were you afraid would know your business?"

"We all need our privacy, Miss Alcott. Just because Miss Collier decided to make me her beneficiary does not mean she owned me in life. There were sufficient reasons for her to be concerned about what might happen to her property should she die, and she had no legal heirs."

"And so, she did die. Very soon after."

"An unfortunate tragedy."

"A pressing motive for murder."

Miss Taylor's smile failed to diminish.

"Such a state of facts certainly presents a motive, Miss Alcott. Is it far too obvious in your opinion?"

"Nothing is too obvious, Miss Taylor. For example, your obvious and very noticeable departure from Miss Collier's soiree might be such a fact. Or that your husband stands to gain a great deal and improve the value of his estate now he owns Rosebud Cottage."

"And who said he owns Rosebud Cottage? It is a gift to me, so I may acquire ownership."

"And this Market Street house?"

"Yes, well, because of marriage, Mr. Lounsey is the legal owner."

Louisa was reminded she was gifted Castle Farm by her father, who acquired it with funds she provided to him. The obvious arrangement was for her family to live with her, but Castle Farm had sufficient room to accommodate all. A ludicrous situation but one that couldn't be helped—until something brought about a change for women who decided not to have their nerves frayed by the institution of marriage and chores attached to such an endless and tiresome state. The potential to live a great deal longer than a husband was incentive enough for most unmarried Misses. Such transactions had to be carried out months apart to avoid any suspicion of collusion and were not without risk.

"And you are sure there's no other reason Miss Collier bestowed her worldly goods on you, Miss Taylor?"

"I assure you there's no other reason, Miss Alcott. And don't forget, you've inherited the bees."

Which sent a shudder down Louisa's unstable spine. The murderous bees to which she'd been assigned ownership felt wrong and outside of her area of competence. Paul Smith had experience in the matter, but still, the fact remained they'd been responsible for Mr. Miller's death, and she shied away from taking on the responsibility. The whole idyllic concept turned poisonous in her mind. There was nothing romantic about swarming angry bees, and she doubted it would taste the same from her farm. Rosebud Cottage was surrounded by lavender and rosemary bushes, infusing the delicate golden honeycombs with aromatic sweetness. She had pigs and grass, and she wasn't a plant lover. The aroma of pig slime seemed less attractive in a delicacy such as honey.

"Was your husband at Rosebud Cottage the night Miss Collier was murdered?"

"I was ill, Miss Alcott. And it wasn't that kind of party. I'm sure I've told you that."

"I'm aware you left early, Miss Taylor."

"Why would Edward be there?"

"I don't know why; that's why I'm asking Miss Taylor."

"I can't answer for him, of course."

Louisa took this as less an admission than familial obstruction, for which any wife might be guilty.

"Is he here?"

"No, Miss Alcott, he's not."

"A witness saw him at Miss Collier's Cottage the night she was murdered. After the party."

Now, a genuine look of confusion took control of Miss Taylor's face. She straightened her perfectly unruffled dress.

"Who is this witness?"

"I can't say."

"He wasn't there, Miss Alcott."

"How can you be sure? You have just asked me why he might be there."

She stood up and walked to her window. A solitary carriage trundled past the window, a reminder of life continuing outside, and she turned to face Louisa.

"I can't be sure, Miss Alcott."

"If he was at Rosebud Cottage, what might he have been doing?"

"You'll have to ask him yourself. I believe any other course of action is either hearsay or rumor."

Louisa imagined she would find Edward Lounsey scarce after this conversation. A legitimate query regarding her pigs would undoubtedly be an opportunity to interrogate him. But despite her curiosity, she was tempted to disregard Miss Chandler's assertion she saw Edward the night in question. There was something in Miss Taylor's demeanor less concerned that her husband might indeed have been at Rosebud Cottage, more disappointed the possibility was real. Or for what reason he might have been there.

"When will I have the pleasure, Miss Taylor?"

Miss Taylor proceeded to leave the room. "You may let yourself out."

Louisa gladly left her company. Miss Taylor was less Mrs. Lounsey the more she considered it. Not expecting to be enlightened about Edward's movements, but neither expecting obstruction. She was sure that Miss Taylor would take delight in frustrating the investigation of that one point. Miss Taylor gave herself to quiet rebellion as if it were her duty to propagate it like climbing flowers. Such behavior required little encouragement in Concord.

* * *

Louisa's next stop was Mr. Miller's office. She'd avoided Mrs. Miller for the time being, as funeral preparations were sure to be fraught with hysteria and meddlesome interference at every turn. In this case, it was less about Mr. Miller's passing than her reputation following his death. Mrs. Miller regarded her position in marriage more important than anything, even that of postmistress, from which she derived more pleasure than marriage. Louisa expected her to remain in mourning as long as possible to remind Concord residents of her previous status. Widowhood will be unbearable for everyone associated with Mrs. Miller. Death in such circumstances obscures the facts surrounding tragic events in a manner disagreeable to Louisa, making individuals unavailable for the most rudimentary comment or unwilling to cooperate with the most essential tasks. A paralysing of the senses appeared to be acceptable to all civil society under the guise of grief. One which made getting business done practically impossible.

When she finally ascended the stairs to Mr. Miller's office, she found Captain Briers.

"What are you doing here, Captain?" She regretted her rather accusatory tone, and he looked up from the desk bemused.

"I am here at Mr. Founts' request."

"I didn't mean to sound unpleasant," Louisa said. "Is Mr. Founts here?" A door opened slowly, and Mr. Founts shuffled out.

"I'm here, Miss Alcott—eh Louisa, so not to worry."

Captain Briers scowled and continued stacking papers. Mr. Miller appeared to have his own filing methods proving impossible to decode. Sifting through another's private papers was terrible enough without having to make sense of a personal filing system requiring at least some organization, forgotten or abandoned years previously. Louisa thought of her untidy desk, for which she alone understood the nuances. The key to understanding where each item lived was perspective. Sitting at a desk may sound relatively stationary and non-eventful, but many things occur when one does. The movements, the particular angle of books and pens, the favored drawer from which one could open and retrieve items without even looking. The shelving behind, where one could locate that one book sitting there because it has always sat there.

"Louisa?" Mr. Founts addressed her as though she was miles away, which she was.

"Yes, apologies. I was thinking how difficult it must be to arrange Mr. Miller's office now that he is gone."

"Quite. But I have been here all morning, and with Captain Briers' help, we have put some order on things."

"You understand the contents of Mr. Miller's papers?"

"I am a lawyer, Louisa," Founts said. "I have some experience of disarray. Feeble-minded clients were my specialty and a host of rich imbeciles with nothing better to do than argue over nothing. Hence, my valuable practice was sold for a fortune."

Louisa seated herself as Captain Briers separated stacks of papers, with no specific visible order beside each other, sending clouds of dust into the air. Mr. Founts curated a smaller bundle, each with a red ribbon tied around them, and carefully separated them again. It appeared to be work that required immediate attention, the paper folder containing the estate of Miss Collier written clearly atop. The next pile had many files with a blue ribbon attached and were works in progress. The final accumulation caused Mr. Founts to smile.

"This," he said, placing a hand gently on top of the largest pile, "are those cases which keep one indebted to the fight. No other explanation is needed. The longer they remain, the more money flows like a river bursting its banks after a deluge."

"I'm glad you enjoy such monumental misery, Mr. Founts," Louisa said.

"The ones which cause heartache are fewer. We rid ourselves of these as quickly as possible. In Boston, where I had my practice, this was easier. Find an unsuspecting victim, thirsty to make his name and thrust it upon him. Before he knows it, he has landed in a pile of cow pat. Likely to relieve the poor fool of more money than he'd profit."

"Very unethical, Mr. Founts."

"Not once you've traded for a while. Then the more difficult cases arrive worth the trials, bringing out the spiritual side of any lawyer."

"And the first pile?" Louisa asked, eyeing up Miss Collier's.

"Land and property. The heart of evil in the civilised world. The greatest turmoil known to man since he first fenced off an allotment and put cattle and crops on it. A complex arrangement never ceases to swell the bank account."

"And in this case?"

Mr. Founts hovered over the papers for a moment without replying. His initial rudeness in this regard appeared more of a habit, cultivated through the advocacy skills he'd clearly possessed in his youth and only slightly tarnished in his twilight years. He'd retained some of his brilliance. But this required long pauses and raising of the head in search of invisible answers. A type of silent pontificating calculated to impress or intimidate an audience,

202

and she believed his prowess on this front must have been quite something in his day.

"There is nothing untoward in Miss Collier's will."

"And Paul Smith?" Louisa asked.

Mr. Founts rounded the desk and sat down, placing his hands in front of him and smiling ceremoniously. It didn't bode well for Mr. Smith.

"I'm afraid his claim cannot be proven and, in any event, appears negative. Mr. Miller made some soft inquiries into the matter but closed it out. I checked his diary, and it seems his reluctance to continue with the matter coincides with a visit from Mrs. Maisie Lounsey. Might I suspect Mr. Miller had unhealthy favoritism for Mrs. Lounsey or Miss Taylor?"

"I would imagine so," Louisa said, aggrieved on Paul's behalf. Her instinct on the matter had been proven right, but nobody clearly believed Paul Smith was Miss Collier's son.

"Miss Collier had no children. I conducted the relevant searches and made the fullest investigation, whereas Mr. Miller did not. Or, perhaps, struck down in the middle of it by the swarm. But I have my suspicion he reached the conclusion within reputable boundaries, and for that, I must be satisfied." He eyed up a bottle of Mr. Miller's brandy and poured some, a look of smug approval on his face as though resigned to ending ten years of sobriety.

"Clearly, he didn't want to be in other areas. Captain? A glass?"

"No, Sir," Captain Briers said. "Will you need me much longer, Sir?"

"Why? Have you a pressing engagement tearing you away?"

"I must see to my sister. She was ill this morning."

"Is she ill, Captain?" Louisa asked.

"None more than the usual."

"Before you go, Captain," Mr. Founts said, rising from behind the desk and moving to the door, which he closed gently. "I found something of interest here."

Captain Briers glanced at Louisa, a look of annoyance on his face. Louisa disliked Mr. Founts' surprises as much as the Captain. Mr. Founts reached for a set of papers in a drawer and opened them. The paper was dense, with inky notes and underlined passages.

"I asked Captain Briers to find Concord's general records, and they detail one murder in the last five years."

"Is there any connection to the school records?" Louisa said.

"I'll come to that. The murdered man was a farmhand on Kame Bluff named Samuel Wilson."

Louisa looked at Captain Briers as Mr. Founts stopped to deploy one of his dramatic and irritating pauses he was so fond of, but not anyone else.

"He wasn't killed *on* Kame Bluff." Captain Briers said.

"A Concord unsolved mystery, eh Captain."

"I do not like your tone, Sir."

"Better get used to my tone, Captain."

Captain Briers turned to Louisa. "There was a brawl. He'd been drinking illegal liquor and returned to Kame Bluff, where he died."

"Recollections about this brawl vary, Louisa. Samuel Wilson breathed his last on Kame Bluff, time and circumstances unknown," Mr. Founts said.

Captain Briers became visibly agitated. "It's clear, Mr. Founts, that Samuel received the injuries that killed him elsewhere and returned drunk. He died. Slumped against a wall, but he was not killed at Kame Bluff."

"I see," Mr. Founts said and clasped his hands before him. "You might have disclosed this matter before now? Are you aware of facts that dispute the official record? A fact which discloses this man was indeed murdered?"

"No, I do not. It has nothing to do with Miss Collier's murder. I can tell you that much."

"I made some inquiries, as seems to be necessary regarding this matter. Wasn't Samuel Wilson rather fond of your sister, Evie?"

"A scandalous rumour."

"And yet your sister claimed never to have seen Samuel before once his cold corpse showed up on Kame Bluff."

Captain Briers trembled with anger. He clenched his fists and raised one to his chin, willing himself not to speak, for he knew, as sure as day broke each day, if he stood up, he might strike Mr. Founts with such force, Mr. Founts may not survive.

"Why didn't you tell us this fact, Captain?" Louisa asked.

"It is completely irrelevant, Miss Alcott. And Mr. Founts knows it."

"Why did your sister claim not to have known Samuel?"

"I have no idea, Mr. Founts. You may have to ask her yourself."

There was an agonizing silence, and Mr. Founts shuffled some papers around, raising his head occasionally and referencing the written notes a few times before rising and standing by the window, glancing out. Mr. Founts began laughing to himself and rather discourteously allowed himself to be consumed by it.

Captain Briers waited until this rude fit had subsided, then said coldly: "I am delighted this matter amuses you, Sir. Perhaps you could show some decency by informing me what is so damned funny."

"The school records, Captain. They have, of course, been rifled and stolen, but Miss Sylvia Murdock informs me Samuel Wilson performed some repairs at the school. She remembered him well, a man in love with ladies of all types. Could barely keep his hands to himself."

"I believe we are wasting our time on such matters, Mr. Founts," Louisa said.

"I am merely exploring all possibilities."

"There is no connection between this man and Miss Collier. Nor has this matter anything to do with my sister," Captain Briers said stiffly.

"Perhaps," Mr. Founts said. "I'm suggesting there was a great deal more information in those school records than we know."

"Now that they are gone," Louisa said. "Surely you tried a criminal case in your time, Mr. Founts?"

"I'm happy to report, Louisa. I haven't."

"It shows, Mr. Founts."

Mr. Founts' smile dissipated.

"I don't mean to be rude," Louisa then said. "While I enjoy your possibilities, as you so fondly call them, I cannot help but conclude the school records which are of interest relate to a child. Or perhaps children."

Mr. Founts gave a dismissive sniff. "Nonsense. My money is on Paul Smith or the Captain here, a man consumed by a few affairs close to his heart, with something deep and dark to hide."

Louisa put a defensive hand towards the Captain, who appeared to be about to leap across the desk and throttle Mr. Founts. There was impotent violence in the air, and she was determined the Captain would not sully his character to the point of no recovery. His passions betrayed him so often, and Louisa wondered if Mr. Founts was quite aware of the disturbance he caused with such loose talk and accusations.

Louisa sighed loudly. "We will adjourn, Mr. Founts, as these possibilities are becoming rather sharpened to a point. We must be careful not to wander down the obvious paths before us when our cunning enemy is hiding in the undergrowth. And I believe requiring the Captain to perform such ridiculous duties having dismissed him is inappropriate."

"Very well, Louisa," Mr. Founts said, resuming his composure. "But I will say," he said, glancing at Briers, "this is a land deal gone rotten. Or a love affair that has gone sour, and I'm rarely wrong."

"Rarely, Mr. Founts implies *occasionally*, if viewed in the number of such investigations you've undertaken," Louisa said. She now smiled and rose. She ushered the Captain to the door, as nothing would be served to leave him within the grasp of such an impossible situation. The only person in the room capable of rational thought was herself, and she freely admitted to it silently. She agreed with Mr. Founts on both points, but not for the reasons he might think.

"I will have to close matters out for Miss Taylor, and she is now the rightful owner of Rosebud Cottage," Mr. Founts said.

"Life must continue, Mr. Founts," Louisa said. "But encouraging disharmony achieves nothing."

Mr. Founts cleared his throat. "Until this matter is resolved, you will find the Captain and myself in Mr. Miller's office. This will be our headquarters, Louisa."

* * *

Miss Taylor stopped in her hallway to admire the new coat she'd ordered. A deep green velvet with a bow the texture of ceremonial decoration ribbon.

A piece of gently ribbed and delicate fabric in sage green reflected the light in shades of dark and light, depending on which way she turned. A perfectly delightful addition to her winter wardrobe, equally suitable for the approaching spring. Very few ladies in Concord could afford such delicious pleasures, most consumed with envy as they darned and stitched their way through winter after winter in the same acceptable dark brown shades which showed few stains. But were formal enough to go unnoticed on a dull December day and looked marvelous in a graveyard.

She despised extreme doom and gloom, and the Misses Birch also hated it, and if all three of them were to be murdered, Concord would become a hellish pit of colourless despair. She took her new blue umbrella with her, the threatened rain already floating in the wind like tiny pins thrashing her face with each gust. She wore her black leather boots, another wise acquisition for the winter highways when one was forced to travel on foot anywhere.

At least the Misses Birch were civilized like her and not resigned to the muck and filth on the farms dotted about Concord. It was always a challenge for her when forced to attend business miles from Market Street, and the unpredictable circumstances always filled her with horror, and today was no exception.

Market Street was pleasant before noon as it was. The road was dry, and the sun rested in lemon shades on the corners of buildings. Waterfalls of melting ice spluttered around her as the sun tried its best to rid Concord of the recent snowstorm, and the trickle of water soothed her.

Hangman's Cottage appeared deserted at this hour. At least the Misses Birch maintained a suitable entrance, clear of snow and dirt, for her to safely reach the door. She glanced up at the windows, the sun's glare beaming outwards, and saw nobody. She knocked and sighed. Indeed, there was no hour the Misses Birch considered appropriate to visit except for late at night.

A window opened abruptly above.

"Who is it?"

June Birch peered out, then moved forward to get a better look.

Miss Taylor shielded her eyes; once a Birch was agitated, it was difficult to tell them apart.

"Just me, dear," she said.

"Who is me?" June repeated.

"Miss Taylor," came the reply, equally agitated.

June rolled her eyes heavenward and slammed the window, leaving Miss Taylor wondering if the damn woman would actually open the door. No doubt a second opinion was required of the other one before she'd gain admittance.

As she waited impatiently, she thought about her trip to Rosebud Cottage. Should she have gone there to rescue the amethyst and diamond gold heirloom Miss Collier was so keen the Misses Birch should receive? Maybe she should have gone there right away and visited Hangman's Cottage on her way back.

"Miss Taylor, do come in," April said, making a rare appearance in person. She smiled broadly as Miss Taylor entered and led her towards the drawing room. Miss Taylor wasn't sure if she'd ever seen April walking before and wasn't likely to see it again.

"To what do we owe this great pleasure?"

April took her seat as she always did and immediately uncapped the brandy, feebly offering Miss Taylor one with a raising of a glass and a shrug.

"You are amusing, April," Miss Taylor said.

"How so, Miss Taylor?"

Miss Taylor pulled her gloves off and gave her umbrella a shake over the Persian rug. The act itself failed to elicit any reaction from April Birch.

"Great pleasure?"

"A milder turn of phrase, you'll agree. I'm not so gracious to other people," April said.

"I'm here because of a diamond and amethyst pendant?"

"An ugly trinket, Miss Taylor. Hardly worth the waste of ink in Miss Collier's will, wouldn't you say?"

"I'd hardly describe it so, April. It is worth a great deal of money."

April smiled. "June dear, be so kind as to close the door and not listen."

A scowling June Birch did as she was requested, and once the door closed, April took a refresher of brandy.

"Be so kind not to misconstrue what I'm about to say," April said, smiling insincerely. "I'm under no illusions about what you're capable of. Or what you've done, let's say."

"What would that be?" Miss Taylor asked.

"Some of us know what you've done and are keeping our mouths shut out of courtesy."

Miss Taylor raised her eyebrows and smiled. "I simply came here to tell you I'm going to Rosebud Cottage to get your *ugly little trinket* for you. I don't understand what else could be important to you now."

"Miss Taylor, the continuous inference that myself and the little bird are impecunious is nothing short of scandalous. That I should rest my fortune on a minuscule donation from Miss Collier is insulting, and that Miss Collier somehow found herself indebted to you seems highly unlikely. And I wonder if Edward Lounsey knows about your secret little hobbies?"

"What can you possibly be referring to, Miss Birch?"

"When that awful virgin Miss Murdock accused me of being a thief and a liar, I'd never considered you had any part to play in this terrible, confusing tragedy. I forgave you because you have an air of civility so lacking in the married women around here, even though you have that burden to bear."

"What are you insinuating, Miss Birch?"

"Where's the real *will*, Miss Taylor? What shady misdeeds of Miss Collier's were you and Mr. Miller privy to that forced Miss Collier to change it?"

Miss Taylor laughed. "Really, Miss Birch? You think I persuaded Miss Collier to change her will?"

"Oh yes, I do."

"Did I murder her also?"

"Most likely," April said.

Miss Taylor pulled out her gloves and snatched her umbrella. "I guess, Miss Birch, now we shall never know."

"Indeed, we will. I have every intention of disclosing my theory to Miss Alcott, possessed as she is of a singularly brilliant mind. If I were you, I would have left Concord well before this. But greed is an easy mistake to make."

"You are as ludicrous as ever, Miss Birch," Miss Taylor said.

"I'm right, as ever, Miss Taylor."

"I'll leave the pendant with June, and I've no intention of darkening your doorstep again if I'm branded a murderer. You'd best be careful to whom you say such nonsense, or you might find yourself stripped of your mysterious fortune."

"Is that a threat, Miss Taylor? I do hope so. It will make my story more interesting for Miss Alcott when I get around to discussing this with her."

"The money will be paid to you on the account. Some matters were taken care of before Mr. Miller's untimely demise."

"I wonder who you prevailed upon to do away with him?" April said.

"I cannot summon a swarm up, Miss Birch. Your ridiculousness knows no limits. Good day."

After the door shut firmly, June Birch entered her sister's realm, where April remained lost in thought.

"What a hateful woman."

"If she sues us, we're done for," June said.

"She knows it's the truth. Were you listening, little bird?"

"Do you really think she killed Miss Collier?"

April's face flushed with anger and alcohol, but this only encouraged her. "I don't know, June. But I know her secret trysts with Mr. Miller moved his hand the wrong way across Miss Collier's will. There is no way Miss Collier would bequeath her entire estate on Miss Taylor. If she wanted to assist the two-faced snake, she could have given that husband of hers the right of way into the farm."

"I used to like her so much," June said absently.

"You must get Miss Alcott to come here, and she must hear my theory. At once, little bird."

June sighed loudly and confiscated the brandy bottle. Which they were running rapidly low on, and now the source, Mr. Miller, would no longer be able to procure any. As if she'd read June's mind, April shouted after her.

"If you're in Mr. Miller's office, you must raid his drink cabinet and plunder what's left."

* * *

Louisa remained in Mr. Miller's office, suffering overwhelming curiosity around Miss Collier's will. It made no sense to her, and the fact Mr. Founts accepted the circumstances did not sit easily with her either. Being a trusted confidant, she assured him she was not precisely aware of what she was looking for but would know if it was necessary. Mr. Founts found this all too female and irritatingly intuitive method of working pointless. A haphazard approach to evidence he was unwilling to undertake but nonetheless did not challenge. It was for Louisa to follow her own path if it proved fruitful. Her involvement, to this point, assured him her research wasn't in vain.

There was a light knock on the door, and June Birch peered around the door of Mr. Miller's office, expecting to see her sitting there.

"How did you know I was here, Miss Birch?" Louisa asked,

"I called to Castle Farm, but Mr. Smith told me I'd find you here."

"And what may I help you with?"

"April wants you to come to Hangman's Cottage."

"I'm afraid I don't have the time right now, Miss Birch. What does April want me there for?"

"She has a theory."

"I see."

"Miss Taylor visited. And well, April accused her of murder."

Louisa knew a shade of meddling such as this would eventually surface. There were possibly two murders in a brief period, to which she must give her urgent attention. There must be more. She was sure of it.

"And how did Miss Taylor react to such an accusation?"

"Not very well. But April also accused her of having Mr. Miller persuade Miss Collier to change her will."

"How on earth would Miss Taylor manage that?"

"Miss Taylor was often seen here. At uncivilized hours."

"Yes, I believe this is the case. Was she seen in Mr. Miller's office in October when Miss Collier's will was drafted?" Louisa asked.

"I saw her going into Mr. Miller's office, Miss Alcott," June said.

Before realizing it, Louisa's face darkened.

"Someone might have had the decency to tell me?"

"It wasn't appropriate to accuse Miss Taylor of such behavior, and April liked Mr. Miller."

"But now it's perfectly appropriate to accuse her of murder? And him coercive will writing?"

"April is sure she's involved somehow with Miss Collier's death."

"Well, as it turns out, Miss Birch, I am searching for Miss Collier's will. I have no real understanding of why she would leave so much to Miss Taylor, and it makes no sense."

They both set about the task of finding the will, and Louisa found it among the smallest stack of papers set to one side on the window ledge by Mr. Founts. The most recent correspondence which required attending to, the most urgent of which, on top, was Miss Collier's file.

The will had been meticulously inked in Mr. Miller's steady hand. Louisa turned it towards June Birch.

"Would you know Miss Collier's signature?"

June's face lit up as though she'd discovered some long-lost treasure.

"That's not Miss Collier's handwriting."

"How can you be sure, Miss Birch? I must have some basis for your rationale."

"Miss Collier often wrote notes on the music scores I gave her for the choral society. This writing is much bigger, and she had such tiny writing."

"Have you a sample in Hangman's Cottage?"

"April certainly has."

"You must go back at once and find some samples. Please do not alert your sister."

"Why?"

"Why do you think, Miss Birch? Please do as I say." June stalled by the doorway.

"Hurry," Louisa said.

* * *

Miss Taylor pushed the gate into Rosebud Cottage. It took all her strength, and she wasn't in the mood for trivial tasks. When she became Rosebud Cottage's owner, she would create an elegant lawn and put some order on the wild layout Miss Collier favoured. No doubt, for the benefit of the bees.

The Misses Birch never failed to get entirely on her nerves, and the more she encountered them, the less she liked either of them despite their enthralling civility. June and April were infuriatingly different. June seemed capable of grace and hospitality, but April was hostile. Neither were naturally evil. Both were suspiciously independent. It was difficult for her to approach the door of the cottage, remembering the last time she'd been there on that fateful night, her quick departure, and subsequent queries about her motivation. All of which hit wide of the mark.

Mr. Miller had given her the keys in a moment of manly weakness. She'd assured him all would be well; all he had to do was hand them over. After all, it was only a stroke of ink separating her from the transaction that could finalize the matter, leaving her in complete control. It felt strange, taking control and possession of someone else's home as if she were trespassing. The best she could do in the circumstances was to picture it on a golden summer's day in July, bursting at the seams with pink and yellow roses, the divine aroma of lavender lingering in the still air. A fragrant smell of hay and the unique tinge of sweetness, that harbinger of autumn. This was the perfect time of year for Miss Taylor, the divine months of August and September. If only she could live in those months forever.

For now, the inside of the house was dreary and cold. Breathing in deeply, the icy atmosphere was reminiscent of the tragic end Miss Collier met. A type of homage to her memory, instilling the place with a ghostly presence she did not believe in but could not discount. It was exactly as it was when Miss Collier died, not touched in weeks. She ascended the stairs, something she never did when Miss Collier was alive. Miss Collier stipulated, that guests—even ladies—use her outside restroom facility. Miss Taylor could only assume it was to keep April Birch away. Miss Murdock embraced the austerity of it all with unnatural glee. As did Miss Nash, used to the disarray and the generally inconvenient company of children. How anyone could be so accepting of atrocious living standards bemused her.

Miss Collier's sleeping quarters were simple. An expensive rug in the middle of the floor was the only natural embellishment. Like most ladies, her bedroom dresser betrayed her beautifying assistants in detail, a mother-of-pearl mirror and matching brush, a rosewood jewellery box in which she kept her rings. A curious mix of conservative and heathen, two silver rings with crescent moons set in onyx with a tiny diamond stood out from the clearly inherited gold ones with simple diamonds and emeralds. A larger wooden box contained what she searched for: the wretched trinket she was obliged to pass to the Misses Birch. She held it up to the light, what little there was, and wondered if the significance of amethyst and diamond. Birthstones? April and February. Its meaning would be lost in historical memory, no doubt, and gone entirely with Miss Collier's death.

She wound the thick chain around it and put it in her purse. She thought better and found a tiny square of silk in the box, which she pulled out.

A thick gold wedding band fell out.

"Strange for you to have this, Miss Collier," she said to the empty room, amused by the sound of her own voice against the silence.

There was no inscription—perhaps Miss Collier's father's ring, as it was too heavy for a woman's hand. The task of delivering the pendant to the Misses Birch was on her mind, but her curiosity was temporarily aroused.

"What other secrets have you got?" She rummaged unsuccessfully for a while. And then she found a stack of unread letters tied with a navy ribbon. The handwriting was thick-set—a man, no doubt—and she took them hurriedly, placing them in her purse. A good deal of exciting reading awaited her. She fixed her hair in the stained mirror and heard the faintest sound of footsteps.

She turned around. "Who's there?"

The sounds moved to the front of the house and out the front door. She ran to the window and pulled the lace curtains apart but could see nothing. She didn't want to open the sash window. Suddenly, the room was both darker and colder. She gathered her purse—hoping this wasn't an unearthly apparition warning her from meddling with Miss Collier's private papers and made her way quickly down the stairs. When she closed the door, her trembling hands calmed enough to lock the door.

And see the note.

A yellow envelope was addressed to her. She looked about her. There was no noise except for slow dripping ice water off the roof and the low hum of the bees out back. She opened it and took out a short letter written in red ink.

Meet me in Hapgood Forest by the Fairyland Pond.

She turned it over, and there was nothing on the other side, so she put it back and sniffed derisorily. It certainly wasn't there when she'd arrived, so whoever did place it there saw her in Rosebud Cottage, no doubt. The only other persons who knew she was there, were the Birch women, both too lazy to write such a letter, never mind, come this way to drop off an anonymous note. Someone else must have seen her. It was too difficult to tell if it was written by a man or a woman. It had no specific features. She could only rule out those who were dead. Mr. Miller and Miss Collier. For a moment, she wanted to bury it in her purse and return to Hangman's Cottage. Leave whoever it was playing this silly game to the cold and filth of dripping Hapgood Forest. But her curiosity fired, and she resolved to follow the road up to Kame Bluff and the tiny entrance behind Captain Briers' yard, which gave way to a long trail into the forest. And where exactly should she go?

Fairyland pond?

Hapgood was riddled with trails that could lead her astray. Unlike her Concord compatriots who knew the *Fairyland*, Miss Taylor had little interest—or experience—with its maze-like innards. Forests were like that; treacherous miles of sameness sent one insane.

The track got narrower as she approached Kame Bluff and passed it, the ground firmer and less icy. She walked by the bright white fencing at the edge of the farm and onto a much narrower track covered in grass, the snow still visible in patches where the sun struggled to reach. The trees crowded in, first the majestic row of ancient oaks to her left, then the dense foliage above, blocking out what little winter light remained.

She stopped abruptly. Why was she doing this? She kept walking, her mind addled with competing thoughts, and a feeling of unease crept upon her. There was no sense putting herself into this isolated place for little reason—or profit. She heard a twig snap. She turned around, and a figure stood before her.

"Oh. It's *you*."

She was about to take the missive from her purse to enquire if this was its author when a sharp breathtaking sensation overtook her followed by a stunning dull pain.

In her final seconds, she glanced down at three rusty prongs dug into her body.

Before the blood flowed down her blue silk dress, Miss Taylor staggered and fell backward, a gurgling from her throat and finally silence.

Worm in the Bud

Hangman's Cottage blazed in the early morning sun. April Birch abandoned her early morning brandy in anticipation of Louisa's arrival, out of respect and from a general feverish feeling that overcame her. She knew something had happened but was unable to adequately voice her concerns. It was like a worm in the bud, a slow creeping sensation she could barely describe.

"Do you need Doctor Jennings," June said. Knowing the answer, she quickly retreated towards the kitchen, where freshly brewed tea awaited. The only beverage guaranteed to soothe a sober April was tea. Even if it was unpatriotic, April liked tea when the effects of alcohol wore off. She preferred it with her pipe—it tasted better, and she said it reminded everyone of their colonial roots, whether they liked it or not.

When June returned, April was blowing her nose noisily.

"Can Doctor Jennings protect me from murderers?" April said. "He's a useless hen-pecked charlatan who wouldn't know the difference between roast beef and a rotting cadaver."

"I hope you never tell him that, April," June said. "He's very well regarded."

"Well regarded," April muttered. "His wife bought the practice, and she's well regarded. Not him. He's an ignorant fool."

"If you need to consult him," June stated.

"Thankfully, I've no need for Doctor Jennings unless I'm dead. I'd rather that drunk vet Parsons prepare me for my grave. I've survived perfectly well until now."

"It could be influenza."

"Don't be so dramatic, little bird. It doesn't suit you when there's no audience to appreciate it." April sneezed theatrically and leaned back into her sofa. "I need tea, June. Please hurry up."

April lit her pipe.

"Is it wise to smoke, April?" June asked. "It might inflame your gut."

"Must you behave like such a nun, little bird?"

As June tended to April's needs, there was a knock on the door.

"See who that is immediately and send them away," April said.

June opened the door, and Louisa walked in without any ceremony.

"Who is it, little bird?"

June froze to the spot, but Louisa put a reassuring hand on June's shoulder, inviting her to go with what Louisa had in mind as if everything would be fine.

"Louisa? What a precious signal from the other world," April said, fanning herself with her handkerchief. "Times are so dangerous."

June sat beside Louisa and glanced intently at her.

"Why are you examining Miss Alcott, little bird?"

"She found me in Mr. Miller's office, Miss Birch," Louisa said.

"Yes, I sent her," April said, looking suspiciously at June. As though she'd betrayed some confidence or removed the wind from her sails.

"I found Miss Collier's will," Louisa began, noticing April perk up considerably. "I harbored a suspicion about the circumstances under which Miss Taylor inherited."

"Isn't that what I said, little bird," April said. "I told you there was something sinister going on."

"I asked June to obtain a sample of Miss Collier's writing," Louisa said, prompting June. She got up quickly and withdrew to April's composing room.

"I apologize for my laziness, Miss Alcott, but I'm ill," April said.

"Nothing serious, I hope?"

"Nothing to kill me, thankfully. A brief chill, nothing more."

"You have some theories about Miss Taylor?" Louisa asked.

"I believe she prevailed upon Mr. Miller to force Miss Collier to change her will."

"When did you realize this?"

"Miss Collier leaving us an insulting sum of money in her will, Miss Alcott. It was totally out of character."

"And why do you think she did this?"

"To keep myself and June quiet, I suspect," April said.

"As if that's possible," June said, suddenly reappearing with a stack of papers.

"It wasn't just that. I cannot see her adding the evil flourish of a pendant. To shut us up. Of course, it was all for show. I gave Miss Collier that pendant myself. It was a gift for assisting us with the Choral Society. I don't believe that will was Miss Collier's word."

"Except she doesn't realize our silence can't be bought," June chimed in.

"Silence about what?" Louisa asked.

"In case we figured out her game," June said.

"Which is?"

April appeared exasperated and fanned herself continuously. "Tell her, June."

"She obviously persuaded Mr. Miller to have Miss Collier change her will. Miss Taylor is a philanderer. So is Mr. Miller. The worst kind in collusion."

"And Miss Collier?"

April pushed herself closer to the front of her sofa. "Miss Collier was murdered simply to make it all happen," she said. "I mean, it was the only possible theory imaginable."

"And then she arranged, somehow, to have Mr. Miller stung to death," June said.

Louisa motioned to June Birch for the papers. She took her trusted magnifying glass out and examined the Choral Society score notes quietly, comparing them to the signature on the will. Indeed, they were so different that it was hard to imagine a better effort could not be made in the enterprise. It was shockingly bad, Louisa thought. June's description of her tiny handwriting was accurate. Teeth-like pedantic lettering with a neat appearance. It was as if it was a person forced to write with a different hand to their natural or preferred one. This practice is common, Louisa thought. The will contained no clue other than the signature, which Louisa surmised had to be Miss Taylor's. It would have been too dangerous for Mr. Miller to sign the document, where his writing could be compared, with such abundant evidence in his offices. Louisa took a sample of Mr. Miller's writing, which didn't match.

The other possibility, which would be ordered by Mr. Founts on her approval, was to obtain Miss Taylor's sample when available.

"It must be Miss Taylor's signature," April said. "Brazen succubus."

"Possibly."

"I agree, Miss Birch," Louisa said. "I must get a sample of her writing."

"You'll need nerves of steel for that adventure. Miss Taylor is a difficult customer, and I'm astonished somebody hasn't murdered her already."

The thought wasn't too far from Louisa's mind.

"I must say I am worried about Miss Taylor's welfare," Louisa said.

April sniffed at the thought, but Louisa had a very fated feeling in her gut.

"May I take the choral scores, Miss Birch. I will need to disclose their existence to support our theory, and Mr. Founts must review this information."

"If it outs that awful devil, take what you will."

* * *

Louisa folded the items very carefully, preparing to tell Mr. Founts the full range of suggestions made to her, for which she secretly commended the Birch sisters. She worried this theory was largely correct, and although she wished it were not the case, she feared two strands of malicious actions converged into one, both with very different consequences.

"One more query, Miss Birch," Louisa said to neither in particular. "Evie Briers discovered the blood-bathed pail in your shed."

April Birch sat upright and took a monstrous pull from her pipe.

"What blood-bathed pail?"

"The one, I believe, was used to transport the blood spilled on Miss

Murdock's desk at the school. The scene we investigated after Miss Collier's funeral."

"What do you know of this, little bird," April said, rounding on June. "If you know something, you must tell Miss Alcott."

"I found it when I was outside, Miss Alcott."

"Oh, be more precise, June," April said, assuming control of the situation. "We have no need to be wandering about the extremities of Hangman's Cottage, Miss Alcott. Except for when June resolves on some lunar incantations on the new part of the month, and she's quite heathen in that regard."

"I am not heathen," June replied. "I use the power of the new moon and full moon to consider situations in my life."

"Nonsense," April said. "June will provide the details?"

"I found it thrown in the grass. It might have been the evening Miss Nash had been here."

"Good little bird. We know Miss Nash is a nasty woman capable of anything when it comes to her own reputation."

"Can I have your word neither of you are aware of where this bloody pail originated?" Louisa asked.

"Yes, Louisa. For heaven's sake, neither of us would touch the thing unless our hands were forced. I knew nothing about it until now, but I'm assuming June hid the offending item?" Her comment directed at June gave rise to a rare sight: June's furious blushing.

"I tried to scrub it clean, but instead, I filled it with water and left it there."

"Why? You could have told Captain Briers or me?" Louisa said.

"She's scared of Captain Briers, Miss Alcott. Afraid of his manly presence."

"Be quiet, April," June said.

"Easy to see she's not been in a manly presence in quite some time."

"It is physical evidence, Miss Birch," Louisa said, considering this situation carefully. She must have Paul retrieve the pail and bring it to Mr. Founts.

"Are you a member of the Society of the Bronze Oak, Miss Birch?" Louisa asked.

April's eyes narrowed, and she blew her smoke away.

"Member might be a stretch, Miss Alcott," April said. "I have hosted some social gatherings. I am not predisposed to traipsing around in the wet and cold admiring trees."

"Were these social gatherings held here at the cottage?"

"Well, yes."

"I believe Mr. Miller was a member, too?"

"It's not a sinister cult, Miss Alcott. We discuss the conservation of trees, oak trees specifically."

"And what happened at these meetings?"

"Mr. Miller attended. Miss Collier attended. She was concerned about general matters relating to her bees. Sometimes, Miss Taylor, Miss Chandler, and her mother, Mrs. Chandler, would attend. But they thought it was fashionable, you see. Mrs. Miller came to find out what her husband was up to."

"What occurred at the meetings?" Louisa said, feeling irritation build.

"I liked the dining and imbibing aspect, Miss Alcott. I was in charge of drafting the menus on yellow paper written in red ink. I used that to impose the idea of death. Paper from the trees and red ink signifying death. Yes, that was it."

"Yellow paper and red ink?" Louisa asked.

"Yes. Cutting the trees down was like slitting our own throats and bloodletting. This is what Mr. Miller used to say. It was all symbolic nonsense."

"Did he now?"

"Oh yes, he was quite descriptive after a few brandies."

"Did Miss Murdock or Miss Nash ever attend?"

April's face contorted. "Absolutely not. For most residents of Concord, our endeavors were viewed as secretive and malign."

"Where did you get the yellow paper and red ink?" Louisa asked.

"At the school, of course. Miss Murdock charged me an exorbitant price, too," April said.

"Was she aware what the paper and ink were for?" Louisa asked.

"Why? Is it important?"

"It is Miss Birch. If you could answer the question, please?"

"Not that I'm aware, Miss Alcott. It is difficult to source such materials, so the school was the most convenient avenue. If there was gossip about its use, I could not control that."

Which was precisely what Louisa was thinking. Unless, indeed, the clever Birch sisters were responsible for two murders. But there was practically no motivation—that Louisa knew of, except one lurking undetected in the style of Mr. Founts' outlandish theories. Her wildest suspicion, if it proved correct, was utterly different in character.

"Thank you both so much," Louisa said and rose quickly.

"She's leaving, little bird. Something we've said has stirred her mind to the point she's about to reveal the murderer's plot."

"I assure you, Miss Birch, I'm nowhere near such a conclusion, but your assistance has been most helpful."

April laughed as much as permitted, given her current debilitated state.

"See Louisa on her way, little bird," April said. "Walk her to where she needs to go."

"I'm quite all right, Miss Birch. I shall manage."

* * *

Louisa left Hangman's Cottage with an unusual spring in her step. She imagined the Birch sisters were confused by her approach to matters, but in truth, she was spurred on by a solution forming in her mind that defied all possibilities, except for the fact it might be true.

She reached Mr. Miller's office as quickly as possible, where she found Captain Briers and Mr. Founts in a solemn state.

She rested herself for several moments.

"We have some strange, unfortunate news, Miss Alcott."

Louisa recovered quickly and put up her hand to stall the revelation.

"Miss Taylor has been murdered," Louisa said. "I know."

Mr. Founts drew back behind the desk and regarded her with astonishment.

"How did you receive this information, Miss Alcott?" Mr. Founts asked.

"I did not receive it, Mr. Founts. The finer threads of this mystery are weaving into a tapestry."

Captain Briers fidgeted beside her.

"What is it, Captain?" Louisa asked. "Tell me all the details."

"Evie discovered Miss Taylor by the track into Hapgood Forrest," he said. "She's distraught, naturally."

"Kindly see to her, Captain Briers. I must speak with Mr. Founts privately."

Captain Briers glanced from Louisa to Mr. Founts.

"But surely you can entrust me with your confidence?" the Captain said.

"It is not about confidence or trust, Captain. It's about reassurance. Your sister needs your help, and we cannot stand in the way of that."

Mr. Founts remained uncharacteristically silent, but his eagerness to hear Miss Alcott's theory overwhelmed him. Captain Briers remained defiantly still.

"Please leave us, Captain, and see to your sister," Mr. Founts said.

"As you wish, Sir."

As he left, the Captain gave Louisa a poisonous stare. She wondered silently if the Captain was aware that she did trust him, just not at this precise moment.

"Now, Miss Alcott, what exactly happens next?"

"What happened to Miss Taylor?"

"Startled on the track towards the Fairyland Pond by all accounts. Skewered with a pitchfork."

"Was her purse retrieved?"

Mr. Founts rested his hands on the table and sighed. "I'm not aware if it was. She was brutally attacked and fatally injured, and I fail to see how her purse is relevant, Louisa."

"It is of great relevance, Mr. Founts."

"Are we any closer to understanding this disaster, Louisa?"

"I believe I am Mr. Founts, but you must trust me in this respect."

Mr. Founts summoned the guard on duty. The hallway in Mr. Miller's office remained closed with a note on the door, sending visitors away due to his death. Louisa felt the atmosphere of doom as if it touched her hand, icy and unrelenting.

"Ensure we remain undisturbed," he said to the guard.

"I believe Mr. Founts; I've discovered some patterns. I don't plan on procrastinating in the matter," Louisa said.

"Well, you can tell me, surely?"

"No, I cannot tell you immediately. I do, however, have a plan I wish to execute."

"What kind of plan?"

"One which will draw our murderer out, Mr. Founts."

"I see, Louisa. And how are we going to do this?"

"As a legal man, can you obtain some yellow paper and red ink?"

"For what purpose, Louisa?"

"You must trust me, Jeremy. We must procure it without alerting anyone to the fact."

Louisa left Mr. Founts to the task and went to visit Mrs. Miller. Louisa hoped the woman wouldn't be too miserable, but Mrs Miller was in the epicentre of grief, and utterly so.

"Louisa, I have been waiting for you to call," she said. There was a gloomy atmosphere in the house, as if she'd begun the torment of mourning continuously without end in sight. She was whiter than paste and dressed head to toe in the blackest clothes Louisa had ever seen. In fact, she wanted to ask her where she purchased it but felt it most inappropriate.

"A most distressful time," Louisa said. "I do hope you are keeping well?"

"Do I look well, Louisa?"

She didn't, but Louisa decided to lift the woman's emotions.

"Under the circumstances, Mrs. Miller, you seem as well as can be. I am truly sorry for your loss. You must understand that."

Mrs. Miller couldn't resist sniffing the condolences away.

"Mr. Miller proved himself to be a consummate liar and completely untrustworthy. I have nothing more to say, but I must, however, observe the traditions of grief."

When the tumult of such emotion subsided, Louisa stated her request.

"Mrs. Miller, can I have sight of Mr. Miller's private papers? If he keeps such items here?"

"Most of his paperwork is in that office he was so fond of. You might be able to find some in his study. He barely used it, and now I know why."

Her voice quivered, and she composed herself by straightening up.

"Honestly, I would like to burn his body on Market Street," she said. "A public event attended by anyone wishing to see his foul remains in flames."

Louisa remained silent rather than make the situation worse than warranted. A very trying time for a woman who was only now discovering the true extent of her husband's betrayal and treachery, where there should have been no real surprise. Louisa again wondered why women would burden themselves with limiting circumstances when it was possible to live a more fulfilling existence, if more complicated, alone. But then the Mrs. Millers of this world didn't see the contradiction in their lives, and they lived it willingly until the bitter end, regretting the passing of unworthy men daily.

"Such sentiments are powerful, Mrs. Miller. When one has lost a loved one."

"Loved one? Mr. Miller was nothing until he secured my wealth, Louisa. I gave him the means to become Concord's foremost lawyer. And with the post office, we were the hosts of Concord society."

"I believe what you say. But surely Mr. Miller made some wise investments during his life?"

Lucy smirked. "Wise? Well, I'm sure if there is anything wise about his investments, you're sure to find them in his study in a locked drawer. He wasn't the sharing type. He has died without my forgiveness. Isn't that enough?"

"And the keys?"

"You're welcome to search."

Louisa rose to the invitation and followed the hallway to a door at the end. Mr. Miller's study was comfortable but clearly unused. Two large candelabras with dusty beeswax stumps. A small bookcase with a few books scattered across the shelves. The table was polished clean, the rosewood inset gleaming pinkish in tone. An inkwell and some loose sheets of paper.

On a table near the small window, she spotted a tree ornament. An oak carved from a single piece of wood. Louisa turned it upside down, and inside a small cavity, she found a key. It opened the second drawer to the right of the table.

The other drawers opened without the need for a key and contained nothing. The locked drawer held several documents. The first was a drafted will and testament, unsigned. A tingle of triumph ran through her veins. Underneath, she found a handwritten journal. One glance told her it was not Mr. Miller who signed Miss Collier's will. The writing was different and resembled what she'd seen in his office in front of him on a few occasions on other documents. The will read to the assembled crowd following Miss Collier's funeral was clearly not the one intended by Miss Collier.

She folded the papers as small as she could manage and put them in her purse. She must confess to Mrs. Miller she'd found the key but nothing else.

"Any luck, Miss Alcott."

Louisa handed Mrs. Miller the key. "Nothing of note, Mrs. Miller."

"I'm burying Mr. Miller in two days. Miss Taylor will undoubtedly humiliate me, showing up in all her finery gloating. One husband is clearly not enough for her."

"I doubt Miss Taylor will be there, Mrs. Miller. She has been murdered."

"*Murdered*," Mrs. Miller said, clasping her pearls, the only funereal frivolity she'd allowed herself. "When?"

"Recently."

"I assure you I'm not capable of such a thing."

"Why would I think you killed Miss Taylor, Mrs. Miller?"

"I obviously despised her," Mrs. Miller said, "but I didn't kill her." She got visibly upset, pulled a charcoal handkerchief from her sleeve, and dabbed her dry eyes.

"This entire situation is monstrous."

"It is Mrs. Miller. Now compose yourself; you have much to do over the next few days," Louisa said.

"I don't believe the chapel has been busier with death in the last year," Mrs. Miller said.

"Quite right," Louisa said. She was anxious to leave. With the funeral pressures mounting, Mrs. Miller certainly had a point, and she could waste no time with the duties she'd to perform over the next day.

* * *

Already exhausted, Louisa made her way to Kame Bluff. The atmosphere was stuffy and yet damp all at once. A large fire thundered in the hearth, and Captain Briers appeared downcast and mournful.

"Miss Alcott, we are not sure what your presence here will achieve."

"I came to enquire after Miss Briers, Captain," Louisa said. "May I speak with her?"

"If you imagine it will do any good."

Louisa climbed the stairs and found Evie in her bed, mumbling inaudibly. An almost spent candle burned at the bedside and the curtains were drawn. Louisa drew them immediately and opened a window, sending a rush of cold, fresh air into the room. Evie stirred and, on seeing her, sat up.

"What a shock you've had, Evie," Louisa said.

Evie said nothing. Louisa handed her some water and watched the combination of air and hydration revive her.

"It was terrible, Miss Alcott," she said. "A terrible sight."

"How did you come to find Miss Taylor?"

The question startled Evie. "She was on the path into Hapgood Forest. Right over there," she said, pointing to the open window.

"What were you doing on the path, Evie," Louisa asked.

"Our kitten Rusty had gone missing. I went out to find him, and I heard voices."

"You heard voices?"

"Yes. Nothing I could rightly make out."

"A man's or a woman's?"

"I can't be sure, Miss Alcott; they were right up the path."

Evie took some more water and nestled into her pillow. Her eyes closed, and Louisa decided Evie was probably in too much shock to answer any more of her questions.

Downstairs, she found Captain Briers by the fire.

"What do you make of Evie's account of events, Captain?"

"What is that supposed to mean, Miss Alcott?"

"It's not a trick question, Captain. I merely was wondering if you have any details I don't."

"Evie went after the cat, Miss Alcott. It wasn't anything strange. We got a stray that gave birth weeks ago, and they can't roam about on their own."

"I meant the voices she heard? Surely, she must know if it was a man or a woman?"

"She said she couldn't make anything out. It was windy and dark."

"And she didn't see anyone as she ran after the kitten?"

"No," he said.

"Can we go outside and see the path, Captain?"

Irritated, Captain Briers rose from his seat and pulled his coat on. "I don't see the point of this."

* * *

The path was a distance to the left of the house. The wooden fencing tapered off, and the trees took over. On one side were the great oaks that flanked the back and side of the house, and the other was crowded with trees creating a dark canopy.

Further up, she spotted two figures, one with a lantern, but as the Captain had said—and Evie—making them out with any precision seemed impossible.

"Evie's eyesight isn't so great, Miss Alcott."

"I take your point, Captain."

It was the duty guard and Mr. Founts at the scene. As they approached, it was as if the trees crowded so far in, it was night. Mr. Founts held the lantern up and squinted until he could make their shapes out.

"What are you doing here, Captain?" Mr. Founts said.

"I asked him to show me the path into the woods, Mr. Founts. I wanted to see the precise spot. It's a blessing indeed you're here," Louisa said.

Mr. Founts scowled at the Captain and led Louisa over to the side of the path.

"There's a clear way out of here," he said. "Whoever did this could escape without being seen from the front or the side."

"I agree with you, Mr. Founts." Louisa walked further into the woods and then turned back.

"Have you procured the paper and ink?"

"Yes, Louisa, I have," Mr. Founts said with an irritable tone to his voice. "What is that all about?"

"I'll arrange the details with you. I must see you at once in Mr. Miller's office."

"Right now?"

"It's imperative, Mr. Founts, we get this done right away. Two funerals are due in the next few days, and we cannot waste a moment."

"Very well."

"Did you locate Miss Taylor's purse?"

"What? Not that I know of, Louisa."

"I need you to exhume Miss Collier, Mr. Founts."

"*What?*"

"To prove something of my theories?"

Captain Briers appeared from the shadows. "What is going on, Miss Alcott?"

"All in good time, Captain," Louisa said.

"I must know," the Captain said.

"No, you must not know. I have some business with Mr. Founts, which is private."

"Does it involve my sister?"

Louisa stood back. "Why would it involve your sister, Captain?"

"She's vulnerable. She told you everything she saw?"

"I'm aware of that."

"I want to make myself useful."

"You can make yourself useful by seeing to your sister, Captain."

Louisa Summons the Devil

"Are you sure this will work, Louisa?" Mr. Founts asked.

They met in Mr. Miller's office that evening.

"It must work, Mr. Founts."

The scene in Hapgood Forest turned Louisa's strong stomach. She felt the imprint of horror, saw the blood leaching into the grass where Miss Taylor's body had rested. And in that moment, it occurred to her that Miss Taylor's murder existed within a different category.

There was the question of delivery of her missives, to which Louisa had the answer.

She walked across to the baker's store where John Davis prepared his premises for the next early morning rush. At this time of night, there was no welcoming smell of freshly baked bread or the sweet aroma of marzipan. The winter months weren't kind to the baker; his ingredients were limited, and the sweet delights of summer and early autumn fruits and berries would have to wait until the land burst open under the sun's late heat. The same went for honey to accompany the bread, with one having to wait well after the swarming season to harvest the honeycombs. Which reminded her of her own task: to take on the hives at Rosebud Cottage. She was not superstitious but wondered if she was the right person to take on the role of beekeeper, even if Paul would help her.

There seemed something forlorn and dangerous about the bees. As if they knew their mistress was dead and waited in quiet grief before attacking again.

The baker took pride in his work, something Louisa always felt one could taste in his product. Any leftovers were handed to local charitable stations or to help feed workmen clearing the rail tracks or digging up the quarry. She had practically no time in the last few weeks to enjoy a leisurely visit to his store where she could pick out some of what took her fancy. And this time was no different.

"What can I do for you, Miss Alcott," Mr. Davis said. He'd come out from his workshop covered in white flour dust, his hands smothered in caked-on bread dough. He worked alone, long days and early mornings with admirable dedication. A cat, the same coloring as Hierophant, lazed on the window ledge, and Louisa took a second glance to make sure it wasn't indeed Hierophant. He was used to good bread and anything else he could get his paws on; it wouldn't surprise her if he'd taken up residence here for the few hours she'd been out. Along with the heat from the ovens, it was quite the perfect spot for a spoiled feline.

"I was wondering if I could ask your delivery boy to do yet another small job for me?"

"I'll need him in the morning, Miss Alcott."

"This is, for now, Mr. Davis. I'll pay him separately for his services."

Mr. Davis nodded and returned, with the fresh-faced youth in his uniform of white coat and black peaked cap.

"You follow Miss Alcott's instructions and be here for six in the morning."

Timothy followed Louisa across to Mr. Founts' office, where they sat to prepare the surprise she had in store for some, not all, Concord residents. The first order of business was to change the lad's clothes into a dark ensemble of navy trousers and jacket. A peaked cap.

"Are you sure this will work, Louisa? Surely the guilty party will be suspicious?" Mr. Founts asked.

"That's the whole point, Mr. Founts. The element of suspicion will mean they will respond. Be curious, I hope."

* * *

Timothy set off, leaving Louisa looking forward to spending a well-deserved break in front of the fire with Hierophant and her father. As she returned to Castle Farm, she spotted a figure in the darkness, and it was Edward Lounsey waiting by the doorway, his cap in hand.

"Evening, Miss Alcott," he said. "I mean Louisa, of course."

"My deepest condolences, Mr. Lounsey, on the death of your wife. How may I help you?"

She remained on the doorstep, hoping Paul would hear the voices and make himself scarce. She refrained from asking Mr. Lounsey if he had knocked or rung the bell. Neither did she notice any obvious signs of grief in him on account of the death of his wife.

"I was hoping to have a word," he said.

"Well, just let me get things sorted inside. Perhaps you would like to look over Danny and Doodle to see they're thriving?"

He nodded and went around the back of the house where Louisa's sheltered pigsty contained the happy animals resting in clean hay. He didn't have the appearance of a man in deep mourning, but then Louisa wasn't sure what to expect from Mr. Lounsey at this time. She was glad Paul was there in the background, hidden from view, in case of any unpleasantness. She didn't believe Edward Lounsey was responsible for anything, but one never knew.

Once inside, the warmth of the house fell around her like cozy blankets. A pleasing odor of root vegetable stew filled the hallway, and Paul set the fire, as was his usual routine, greeting her from the kitchen.

"I have Mr. Lounsey for a visit. Would you kindly ask him to join us for supper? If there are adequate supplies for him?" Louisa said.

Paul nodded, added an extra table setting, and cut the fresh loaf Louisa got from the baker. Edward Lounsey filled the kitchen with his large frame. He sat at the table awkwardly, and Louisa served him stew and offered bread, which he took gratefully.

"I had nothing to do with Miss Collier's death, Louisa."

"I'm investigating the matter thoroughly. Not one single person I've spoken to is likely to own up to the murders, Mr. Lounsey."

"And I didn't kill my wife."

Louisa continued eating, ignoring the temptation to query this statement in full.

"How do you find the pigs, Mr. Lounsey?"

He was taken aback by the conversation change and nodded before taking a few mouthfuls of stew.

"Good."

He glanced at Paul Smith a few times, but there wasn't much by way of recognition.

"I just wanted you to know I didn't kill her."

"We shall see tomorrow, Mr. Lounsey."

Mr. Lounsey looked up from his food. "I see."

"Did you visit Miss Collier the night she died?" Louisa asked.

"After that ladies' party?" Mr. Lounsey asked. "No. I didn't."

"A witness has said you were at Miss Collier's cottage. That night."

"What witness?"

"Were you there, Mr. Lounsey?"

"I told you. I wasn't there."

* * *

The following morning, at half past ten, Louisa made her way to Concord Chapel. It was a fine morning, cold but pleasant, and she looked forward to what she hoped would be the end of this sad saga. Pastor Williams was present at the doorway when she arrived, giving her a broad smile.

"Everything is ready, Miss Alcott."

"I can't thank you enough for your assistance; I'm so grateful."

As the morning sun pierced the stained-glass windows, the Concord residents she'd invited appeared one by one. June and April Birch walked in, and both smiled at her. Mary Chandler and her mother followed, along with Captain and Evie Briers. After a few moments of silence, Miss Nash and Miss Murdock arrived and took their place. Edward Lounsey appeared with Paul Smith and, last to arrive, Mrs. Miller, adorned in mountains of black mourning clothes.

Mr. Founts arrived just at the right time as the bells rang out for eleven. The noise reverberated through the stone building, and Louisa waited until the final chimes died down, leaving the slightest ringing in her ears in their wake. Mr. Founts' instructions were, along with his duty guard, to secure the doors to the chapel.

She glanced at the assembled crowd and noticed the Birch sisters were the only ones in good spirits, and acknowledged her glance with a knowing smile as she passed by each face.

"How exciting," April boomed. Much to the annoyance of a few.

"Thank you all for responding to my invitation," Louisa said. "The chapel seemed the most appropriate place to be."

"What are we doing here?" Mrs. Miller asked.

"What do you think you're doing here," April said. "Louisa obviously knows the depth of the horrors taking place in Concord, and she will expose it all."

"Yes, and we are going to expose some truths," Louisa said.

She let that linger over her audience. Nobody moved, but then, the guilty parties needed to remain calm in the face of adversity, which, until now, had been admirable.

"Do tell us the gory details, Louisa," April said.

Louisa took her spot on the velvet upholstered chair reserved for visiting dignitaries. She would be unable to stand for the entire performance, and the ensuing saga would take some time to disclose.

"We start during the summer, August specifically. Emily Collier agrees to sell Rosebud Cottage to Edward Lounsey and then changes her mind. At the time, Miss Taylor was married to Mr. Lounsey, which appears to be common knowledge in Concord, except to myself," Louisa said.

There was a slight whispering.

"So, we have three murders," April said.

"Two murders, Miss Birch. Not three."

April sat back in her seat as though admonished.

"Miss Taylor also involved herself with Mr. Miller in an affair," Louisa continued. "There is no question Mr. Miller was enthralled by her."

Mrs. Miller stiffened and raised her head, glancing about proudly as though this was known to her all along.

"Miss Taylor was adamant she wanted Rosebud Cottage to allow her husband the much-needed right of way over Miss Collier's land. And so, she planned this with Mr. Miller, whose expertise and standing in Concord would go a long way to achieving this," Louisa said.

"So, they changed Emily's will?" April interrupted. "To make it happen."

"Please, Miss Birch," Louisa said and glanced at June, as if it were her role to curb April Birch's enthusiasm.

"Would you shush for once, April," June said.

"There was no will," Louisa said. "Mr. Miller and Miss Taylor forged a will, signed by Miss Taylor. I have seen Miss Taylor's writing and Miss Collier's, and there is no doubt. Miss Collier had never made a will."

Louisa held the document up for all to see: the document which sealed Miss Collier's fate.

"An entirely fictitious document, borne of an evil plan."

April glanced around the room before quietly saying: "Did she murder Emily?"

"Oh yes, she did, Miss Birch."

"At the party?"

"Yes, but not the way everyone thinks. She administered thallium, a slow-acting poison, to her tea. It has the effect of making the victim also lose their hair, and this was confirmed this morning."

"Was it put in the oat squares?" Miss Nash asked. "She must have put it in them."

"The oat squares," Louisa stated without any emotion.

"Miss Taylor knew Miss Collier was allergic to oats. Did you tell her, Miss Nash?"

Miss Nash blushed from her neck upwards. "No, of course not."

"But in any event, Miss Taylor couldn't take the risk of poisoning cakes at the party when any one of its attendees might have eaten them."

"I'm so grateful I never attended," April Birch said, fanning herself. "What a horrific thing to do."

"Then something else happened. Miss Taylor witnessed Evie Briers throwing the oat cakes out in her garden, and the Briers' dog Scout ate them. At that stage, a very convenient story began circulating in Concord, which I myself believed, that the oat squares served at Miss Collier's party contained poison."

"Miss Taylor killed Scout?" the Captain asked.

"Oh, there is no doubt, Captain."

"You can't be sure of any of this, Miss Alcott," April Birch said.

"Miss Taylor was seen placing a poison in Miss Collier's teacup," Louisa said, pausing to let the information sink in and ignoring April Birch. "Isn't that correct, Miss Briers?"

Evie startled upright.

"I didn't see anything," she said. She looked around at the rest of the audience. "I swear I didn't see her do it."

"But you did, Miss Briers. Miss Taylor paid you a visit, didn't she?"

Evie swallowed hard.

"It wasn't something she saw you do; it was something you saw *her* do."

Evie looked as if she would collapse.

"Have you any proof of this, Miss Alcott?" April asked.

Evie stood up straight and looked around. "Yes. I saw Miss Taylor put something in Miss Collier's cup. I didn't know what it was until Miss Taylor stared right at me. I thought it was the oat squares, and I did. I was confused with all the talk of it afterwards. I didn't know what I saw."

A low gasp went around the room, and Captain Briers took his sister by the shoulders and guided her back to her seat.

"I didn't know for sure," Evie continued to mumble.

"Around the same time," Louisa said, unperturbed, "Captain Briers sends his ill-timed telegram to Miss Chandler. *Miss Collier poisoned. We cannot marry.* This relationship between Captain Briers and Miss Chandler is well known, but why had Miss Collier refused to support their marriage?"

Louisa gave Miss Nash a long, hard look.

"The school records are disturbed during a break-in, and the roof money is stolen. Miss Taylor broke in with the help of Miss Nash, and I'm sure

Miss Taylor was offering a payment?"

Miss Nash was on her feet. "This is preposterous. I will not hear anymore."

"Miss Taylor acted on information known only to Doctor Jennings' secretary, information contained in the school records. Where Miss Nash also worked and had knowledge of their contents."

Captain Briers gripped his sister, who was about to leave, or pass out, Louisa wasn't sure which.

"Stay where you are, Miss Briers."

"Please, Miss Alcott, I beg of you," Evie said. "Please don't tell them."

"What is going on, Miss Alcott?" the Captain said. "What on earth is this about?"

"The records will show Mary Chandler is Evie Briers' daughter. Miss Collier had received this information from Miss Nash, concerned about the nature of Captain Briers' relationship no doubt. A concern which naturally worried her deeply."

There was a low hum of chatter, and Louisa put her hands up to urge some silence.

"Doctor Jennings would not be aware of this. He had no knowledge of his patient register, in fact the good doctor had files and information he'd no idea about. But I discovered Mr. Miller was well aware of this fact after I searched his private desk," Louisa continued.

"This is outrageous," the Captain said. "Simply ludicrous."

At this point, Miss Mary Chandler rose from her seat and proceeded to march into the chapel aisle, where Mr. Founts stood in her way at the doors.

"It's a lie," Mary Chandler roared from where she stood. "A damned evil lie."

"I wish it were Miss Chandler. But unfortunately, it's true, and you cannot marry your Uncle Captain Everett Briers."

She glanced at Captain Briers, who simply looked at the ground and then clasped his head in his hands.

"Mrs. Chandler, you didn't know this, did you?" Louisa said.

Mrs. Chandler shook her head, high color in her cheeks.

"Mary Chandler came from an orphanage in Boston. There was no connection to be made except in the school records and medical records, which recorded her real mother's name. And what better information could Miss Taylor have to blackmail the one person into silence who'd seen her put poison in Miss Collier's tea."

"Good Lord," April Birch said. "What is next?"

Louisa stood for a few moments, her legs aching terribly. It was easy to see the invited occupants assembled reeled with disgust at the revelations, and she only hoped it wouldn't precipitate some further violence.

"During this time, Mrs. Miller became sure of Mr. Miller's adulterous liaisons. So much so that she wrote herself a death note, isn't that right, Mrs. Miller? You were desperate for his confidence."

"Well, you know it all, obviously," Mrs. Miller said. "I don't care what you say now."

"Mrs. Miller's meddlesome antics began with writing notes on yellow paper with red ink, the sort used by Miss April Birch to write menus for Society of the Bronze Oak dinners. No doubt, this is calculated to instil fear and intimidation in Mr. Miller. Perhaps to garner some wifely sympathy."

"What a shameful thing to do," April Birch said.

"This part of the tragedy cost Mr. Founts and me a great deal of wasted time and ultimately another life," Louisa said.

"I'm not listening to any more of this," Miss Murdock announced.

"Yes, Miss Murdock, it is interesting you assisted Mrs. Miller in this enterprise, is it not? Supplied Mrs. Miller with the paper and red ink?"

Miss Murdock's mouth rested in its usual grimace. She raised an eyebrow, and her lip trembled.

"You see, I know Mrs. Miller and Miss Murdock detested Mr. Miller a great deal."

"There is no need to disclose this, Miss Alcott," Miss Murdock said. "It contributes nothing to the situation. I implore you."

"He fathered your child, didn't he, Miss Murdock? Paul Smith. The man who came to Concord with instructions to find his mother, Miss Collier. He had been told his mother was a teacher at the Concord School. You were in love with Mr. Miller for many years, but your bitterness at his refusal to

239

be your child's father festered a hatred you could not bear."

Mrs. Miller let out an unearthly gasp and howl.

"And as the fictitious will is read most theatrically in Mr. Miller's office, I noticed you sat alone. I saw the confusion on your face when Mr. Smith announced his presence, claiming Miss Collier's inheritance. It couldn't be the truth, could it, Miss Murdock? It couldn't be the truth that after all this time, your son would emerge from obscurity and announce his presence and that you knew it was your son, and his father was oblivious to it. Just like he'd always been."

A shimmer of tears swelled in Miss Murdock's eyes, which she dabbed with austerity in several efficient movements.

"You helped Mrs. Miller engage in the letter writing, of course, with your own motive for revenge. The blood and the sheep were all part of this desperate attempt to focus suspicion on Mr. Miller. Those silly little symbols and the letter with *most evil deeds are not the musings of one diabolical man but many.* Indeed, this Miss Murdock brought my attention firmly to Miss Taylor and Mr. Miller. But then you, Miss Murdock, received a different note, one claiming you cannot keep secrets forever. And it was then I knew the depths of the mystery and why you would help Mrs. Miller in her ridiculous rampage."

Miss Murdock's chin went aloft as though her revenge was reaped in some small way and she no longer must be vindicated.

"But what about Mr. Miller's murder?" April asked.

"No, Miss Birch," Louisa said. "Mr. Miller was a victim of the bees. Just that."

"But why was he there?" April persisted.

"Perhaps Mrs. Miller will tell us? She wrote both notes to Captain Briers and her husband. She knew the Captain would go if he thought Mary Chandler wrote the note, and she knew her husband would go out of malicious curiosity. She also knew—or hoped—her husband would not survive if the angry bees were to attack when their sanctuary might be disturbed by the noise of two men arguing and shouting together. It would only take the venom of one stray bee to put Mr. Miller in his grave. Isn't that true, Mrs. Miller?"

Mrs. Miller didn't contradict Louisa's version of events.

"And we know Mr. Miller was unlucky to be struck down, but for some, in this gathering, he simply got his just desserts. For others, it meant he was not available to manage Miss Collier's estate."

"And what about the villain of the day, Miss Taylor?" April persisted.

Louisa sat down again; the revelation was something she herself knew nothing about. She was nearing the end of the piece, but for sure, the final part brought her the most sorrow, for the person who killed Miss Taylor did so out of desperation. And she had an idea who that person was. But proof of such would require a different action.

"Miss Taylor's killer was already at Rosebud Cottage on that day. By now, the tiresome distraction of yellow paper and red ink was common knowledge. I found the note in Miss Taylor's purse along with letters from Miss Collier's dressing table."

"Well, who murdered Miss Taylor?" April repeated.

"They might have been at Rosebud Cottage to tend to the bees," Louisa said. A ripple of whispers reverberated at this point. Paul Smith looked around him, anxious to figure out what was about to come next, sure he would be accused.

"And it was easy to leave the note for Miss Taylor inviting her to Hapgood Forest because it was directly beside Kame Bluff."

"What?" Captain Briers said. "Please tell us you have some evidence for this?"

"Whoever saw Miss Taylor at Rosebud Cottage was not far from Kame Bluff, where they took a chance in writing the letter and luring Miss Taylor to the path into the woods. It was their only chance to murder Miss Taylor," Louisa said.

"Who was it, Miss Alcott? Evie is unwell," Captain Briers said. *"Evie?"*

"Fetch Doctor Jennings, Mr. Founts," Louisa said. In preparation for this event, Louisa took some water to Evie, who'd fainted and slumped into Captain Briers' arms. It didn't take Doctor Jennings too long to arrive amid a torrent of noise that echoed around the chapel. A confession from the actors

241

in the tragedy who were unwilling to endure another entire act would take some time. They sat there, revelations in hand, until Louisa felt it necessary to release them from their temporary prison.

One thing Louisa knew was that Concord wouldn't be the same again.

"Miss Alcott, you must come to Hangman's Cottage and give me the grimy details," April said, taking June by the arm. "What a splendid show. But we still must know who offed Miss Taylor."

At Hangman's Cottage, April allowed June to serve them brandy and coffee. Louisa felt utterly drained.

"How did Miss Taylor get away with it?" April asked.

"Misdirection, Miss Birch."

"I wasn't there. Such a shame."

"She had to do it quite quickly. I imagine her new coat caused quite a stir," Louisa said.

"Yes, I see what you mean. Take the attention away from slipping it to Miss Collier," April said.

"And, of course, she was careful to let me and everyone else know that she left early," Louisa said.

"The conniving vixen."

"And tell me she'd suffered from stomach pains," Louisa added.

"Quite. Perpetuate that ridiculous oat square drama. Let us think Miss Collier had been lightly gotten to."

But Louisa was preoccupied with her own thoughts.

"But who killed the manipulative snake, Miss Taylor?"

"I really must go home. I'm exhausted," Louisa said. She felt like a dray horse that had been plowing in a dry field from dawn till dusk.

When she returned, Paul Smith greeted her at the door to Castle Farm. He looked like a man battling mixed emotions, which was completely understandable. He'd discovered in a bittersweet way whose offspring he really was, and Louisa couldn't help thinking he was destroyed and disappointed by it.

"Captain Briers was looking for you," he said.

"I'm sorry you had to discover your mother's identity in such a public fashion," Louisa said.

"It can't be helped, Miss Alcott. At least I know."

"That's possibly the best way to look at it. Captain Briers is seeking me out, you say?"

"Yes, he was quite distressed."

"I'd imagine he was."

Despite her tiredness, Louisa left Castle Farm to walk to Kame Bluff. When she arrived, Evie Briers' plaintive cries reverberated throughout the house, and Captain Briers met Louisa in the hallway.

"Miss Alcott, please, you must speak to my sister," he said.

Louisa ascended the stairs, where she found Doctor Jennings tending to Evie, lost in a hysterical trance. Her arms flailed about as if fending off invisible creatures, and despite the Doctor's best efforts, it seemed as though Evie was possessed by a devil. She calmed somewhat when she saw Louisa and opened her arms towards her.

"I didn't kill Miss Taylor," she wailed. "I swear on my life I didn't kill her."

"Can you leave us, please, Doctor?"

Jennings hesitated but decided it was safe to leave. As he did, Evie's distress dissipated. Louisa was afraid the woman would suffer significantly if she didn't listen to what she had to say.

"What is it, Evie?"

"I was at Rosebud Cottage, tending the bees. But I didn't kill Miss Taylor."

"I know you didn't, Evie," Louisa said. "But you did see who killed her?"

Evie simpered, and the tears flowed down her cheeks. It seemed to assuage her fears now that she was believed.

"Why didn't you tell me the truth?"

The answer Evie gave provided her with the final truth as to who it was in the darkened woods that dreary evening. A murderer who took their chance when they got it, and she knew exactly why. An opportunist. With so much to lose.

"Captain, make sure your sister is well taken care of. She has been through quite a big ordeal."

"May I know what passed between you?"

243

"No, you may not," Louisa said, pulling her gloves on. "I must speak with the guilty party myself."

"But Evie has been through so much, Miss Alcott."

"I know. But I needed the truth, Captain. I was very sure about Miss Collier's murderer, and there's no doubt of that. But Miss Taylor drew out quite a bit of bad blood for many reasons. I just needed to figure out who it was. Please. Look after your sister, better Captain. She deserves this now."

"I see. Thank you."

"Good night."

* * *

A certain satisfaction overcame Louisa as she waited at her final doorway of the evening. Despite her horror and disappointment in the guilty party, the saga was now at an end.

When the door opened, she heard the familiar voice from within.

"Who is it, little bird?"

"It's nobody. It must have been an animal or something," June said.

"Ringing the doorbell? An animal?"

June stared at Louisa with large, sorrowful eyes.

"Can we speak outside?" June said.

They stood in the cold; April must assume June was doing one of her lunatic chants to the moon. It rose in the sky above them, illuminating them like pale statues in its opalescent light.

"It was you Miss Murdock saw at the school, wasn't it June?" Paul Smith had been there too, but Miss Murdock wasn't seeing apparitions with the female outline. It had occurred to Louisa that more than one candidate was possible.

"Yes, it was. April was accused, but it was me, and she knew it. I wore April's overcoat. Everyone knew it was hers."

"You stole the school roof money, didn't you?"

June looked at Louisa directly. "We have little money, Miss Alcott. We're quite poor, as it turns out. Hangman's Cottage is all we have; with April's expensive pastimes and drinking, we'll be destitute soon. I knew Miss Taylor would never give us any money from the will. Once I knew Miss Collier hadn't even written it. And with Mr. Miller dead."

Louisa took a sharp intake of breath and folded her arms. "What happened?"

"When you and I discovered the will wasn't Miss Collier's, I realized the sum of money in the will was a cruel joke, and as April already told you, we gave the pendant to Miss Collier. Miss Taylor didn't know we'd given it to Miss Collier. Miss Collier had always told us she would take care of us in her will, separately from the Choral Society. That's why I knew the will wasn't Miss Collier's even before you told me it wasn't."

"I see."

"And that day Miss Taylor came over here to tell us she'd get the pendant Miss Collier left us, which she had not, of course, it was so insulting. And when I knew she'd no intention of giving us any money, it was all a ruse. I knew she'd concocted the whole thing with Mr. Miller to make us look foolish. I hated her, Miss Alcott. I really hated her for what she did. For what she was trying to do to us."

"You took leave of your senses, Miss Birch."

"I followed her to Rosebud Cottage. I knew she was going there. She told us. I wrote the note before I left, and I was going to just threaten her, but…"

June paused. "How did you know I was going to kill her?"

"I didn't. I thought Mrs. Miller might have taken her campaign further, but it only left the most obvious motive. What happened?"

"She held the pendant up to me and asked me if I really thought she'd hand it back to us. "I suppose you think I'm going to give you some money out of the will, too," she said. She'd laughed in my face, and it was so humiliating."

June's large eyes turned glassy.

"There was a rusty old pitchfork in the grass, and it had probably been there since summer. I just picked it up and lunged at her. It was easier than I thought. I wasn't thinking. I just wanted her to stop."

June dissolved into tears.

Louisa put her arm around June's shoulder as she sobbed. Louisa felt the

245

sting of her indignation, and she could imagine the jeering face of Miss Taylor laughing at June the way she described. A moment of murderous passion and heat overcame June Birch. And although she also felt the wretched sting of Miss Taylor's last moments, she could not but feel the passion from Miss June Birch. And somewhere within that was the awful knowing Miss Taylor had so callously disposed of Miss Collier.

But still. Miss June Birch was indeed a murderer.

"Please don't tell April. I can't face her."

"Very well. But you must submit yourself to Mr. Founts' confinement and questioning."

Louisa and June walked to Doctor Jennings' surgery, where he'd retreated after seeing Miss Briers. There, they found Mr. Founts.

"What have we got here?" Mr. Founts said.

"June Birch. She has confessed to murdering Miss Taylor."

Mr. Founts looked from one to the other with shock on his face.

"I see," he said. "Do you need the Doctor, Miss Birch.?"

He nodded to Jennings to see to June and put a gently guiding hand on Louisa's shoulder.

"That was some performance, Louisa. How did you know it was June Birch?"

"I didn't," she said. "But I knew Evie Briers knew precisely who it was, and once again, she found herself compromised, this time by compassion for one of the few people in Concord who showed her respect. And Miss June Birch stole the school roof money. It was another crime of momentary passion, Mr. Founts. She took an opportunity when she saw it. Miss Taylor and Mr. Miller's little joke about money in the will pushed her to an act she most assuredly never imagined she would commit. Please see to it that the woman gets fair treatment."

Mr. Founts made to leave the room, then turned abruptly.

"Can I count on your assistance, Louisa, if we have another murder in Concord?"

"Another murder, Mr. Founts? I hope I have a vacation of at least five years before that occurs."

* * *

Louisa made her way to the doorway, and a carriage pulled up. For all his unusual theories, Mr. Founts was a decent man. And a kind one at that.

Paul answered the door at Castle Farm, and the warm air soothed her immediately. She had a good feeling about this; perhaps he would make his home in Concord. For the first time in weeks, Hierophant made his way to her lap as she sat by the fire and purred with satisfaction in almost the same way she did.

Acknowledgements

My Agent Cindy Bullard, Level Best Books and author Sam Blake.

About the Author

Elizabeth Dunne writes mystery and humorous fiction. Born in New York, she's lived most of her life in Ireland working as a privacy lawyer. She studied English Literature and Irish Folklore in University College Dublin providing her with a lifelong love for the written word and storytelling. When not writing, she enjoys investigating local history, reading, cooking and thinking of ways to do away with people.

SOCIAL MEDIA HANDLES:
  https://twitter.com/MedievalWisdom
  https://www.facebook.com/profile.php?id=100082254275604
  https://www.instagram.com/elizabethdunneauthor/

AUTHOR WEBSITE:
  https://www.elizabethdunneauthor.com/

www.ingramcontent.com/pod-product-compliance
Lightning Source LLC
Chambersburg PA
CBHW050158120726
47903CB00002B/676